D0503054

The Art of Murder

Also by Elaine Viets

Dead-End Job Mystery Series

Shop till You Drop
Murder Between the Covers
Dying to Call You
Just Murdered
Murder Unleashed
Murder with Reservations
Clubbed to Death
Killer Cuts
Half-Price Homicide
Pumped for Murder
Final Sail
Board Stiff
Catnapped!
Checked Out
Killer Blonde
(an e-book novella)

Josie Marcus, Mystery Shopper Series

Dying in Style
High Heels Are Murder
Accessory to Murder
Murder with All the Trimmings
The Fashion Hound Murders
An Uplifting Murder
Death on a Platter
Murder Is a Piece of Cake
Fixing to Die
A Dog Gone Murder

Francesca Vierling Mystery Series

Backstab
Rubout
The Pink Flamingo Murders
Doc in the Box

A DEAD-END JOB MYSTERY

Elaine Viets

AN OBSIDIAN MYSTERY

OBSIDIAN
Published by New American Library,
an imprint of Penguin Random House LLC
375 Hudson Street, New York, New York 10014

This book is an original publication of New American Library.

First Printing, May 2016

For more information about Penguin Random House, visit penguin.com.

LIBRARY OF CONGRESS CATALOGING-IN-PUBLICATION DATA:

Names: Viets, Elaine, 1950– author.
Title: The art of murder: a dead-end job mystery/Elaine Viets.
Description: New York City: New American Library, [2016] | Series: Dead-end job mystery; 14 | "An Obsidian book."
Identifiers: LCCN 2015047820 (print) | LCCN 2016001087 (ebook) | ISBN 9780451476135 (hardcover) | ISBN 9780698198449 (ebook)
Subjects: LCSH: Hawthorne, Helen (Fictitious character)—Fiction. | Women detectives—Florida—Fort Lauderdale—Fiction. | Murder—Investigation—Fiction. | BISAC: FICTION/Mystery & Detective/Women Sleuths. | GSAFD: Mystery fiction.
Classification: LCC PS3572.I325 A89 2016 (print) | LCC PS3572.I325 (ebook) | DDC 813/.54—dc23
LC record available at http:/lccn.loc.gov/2015047820

Printed in the United States of America
10 9 8 7 6 5 4 3 2 1

Penguin
Random
House

To Linda and the Cougars—
you're not a rock group, but you rock!

ACKNOWLEDGMENTS

The Bonnet House Museum and Gardens is one of Fort Lauderdale's undiscovered treasures, and I was lucky to be a volunteer at this lovely slice of Old Florida.

Evelyn and Frederic Bartlett mastered the art of living, and Evelyn worked hard to save Bonnet House, their mutual masterpiece, for future generations. She was a grand woman, and the museum has everything mentioned in this novel—lush gardens, cashew-eating squirrel monkeys, orchids, vivid art with impish touches, and inspiring classes, from painting to bird-watching.

Everything except murder.

There has never been a murder at Bonnet House, not even in a mythical vacant lot.

Treat yourself to a Bonnet House tour in Fort Lauderdale. Savor Evelyn's stylish living with the recipes in the museum cookbook: *Entirely Entertaining in the Bonnet House Style.* They're so easy, even Helen and I can make them.

After you visit Bonnet House, stop by some of the real Fort Lauderdale restaurants mentioned in *The Art of Murder*, including Brew Urban Café Next Door, Casa Frida Mexican Cuisine, Frida and

Sharo Cuban Cuisine, Kaluz, and the Warsaw Coffee Company. I've enjoyed them all.

FAT Village is a real place, and the free monthly art walks are fun. Check out the food trucks, including Mobstah Lobstah.

South Florida residents Jenny Carter and Robert Horton are friends in real life, just like Jenny and Robert in my novel. The real Jenny Carter loves to cook for friends and family and she volunteers at the Children's Diagnostic and Treatment Center in Fort Lauderdale.

The real Robert Horton loves the marine art of Robert Wyland, but he is the community business development manager of the Fort Lauderdale Barnes and Noble. A generous donation to a charity allowed these two friends to have their names in *The Art of Murder.*

Margery Flax is another real person who let me use her name. She's much younger than Helen's landlady, but both of them love purple.

Anne Watts, assistant director of the Boynton Beach City Library, lent me her six-toed cat, Thumbs, for this series.

A novel is a group project and I hope I've thanked all the people who have helped me with my fifteenth Dead-End Job Mystery. They include:

Detective R. C. White, Fort Lauderdale Police Department (retired) and licensed private eye. Houston private eye and mystery writer William Simon.

David Hendin, adjunct curator at the American Numismatic Society, for the information about coin collectors and hoarders.

Jinny Gender, my favorite anglophile. Poison expert Luci Zahray. Mystery writer Marcia Talley, author of *Daughter of Ashes*. Dorothy Simpson Krause, artist and professor emerita, Massachusetts College of Art, for background on the South Florida art scene.

Doris Ann Norris, Donna Mergenhagen, Molly Weston, Dick Richmond, Richard Goldman and Mary Alice Gorman. Supersaleswoman Carole Wantz, who can sell rain gear in the desert.

Femmes Fatales bloggers Charlaine Harris, Dana Cameron, Marcia Talley, Toni L. P. Kelner, Kris Neri, Mary Saums, Hank Phillippi Ryan, Donna Andrews, Catriona McPherson and Frere Dean James/Miranda James provided advice and encouragement. Read our blog at femmesfatales.typepad.com.

My fellow bloggers at The Kill Zone give award-winning writing advice. Read us at killzoneauthors.blogspot.com.

Thank you to the Penguin Random House team, including senior editors Michelle Vega and Sandra Harding for their deft editing and helpful suggestions, and their assistants, Diana Kirkland and Bethany Blair, for their endless patience. Publicist Danielle Dill for her enthusiastic promotion. Eileen G. Chetti is a first-rate copy editor.

But most of all, thank you to my hilarious husband, Don Crinklaw, who gave this novel its first read—and last line.

All mistakes are mine.

I love to hear from readers. Contact me at eviets@aol.com.

The Art of Murder

CHAPTER 1

Yep, his hand was on the blonde's bottom.

Helen Hawthorne looked again. She wasn't imagining it: The lad in the lederhosen was definitely lecherous. His hand disappeared behind her skirt, and the cute blonde in the dirndl was smiling.

This painting of rowdy rustics was next to Frederic Clay Bartlett's studio at the Bonnet House Museum. Bartlett was a respected artist who'd studied art in Munich and Paris, a man whose rapturous stained glass intimidated even Louis Comfort Tiffany. But he also painted playful hanky-panky.

"You saw it, too, huh?" Margery said, and grinned. "I told you this was no ordinary museum."

Bonnet House is on Fort Lauderdale Beach, a lighthearted oasis tucked next to trashy tourist shops and grim, gray hotels that Helen thought looked like pharaohs' tombs: expensive and dead.

The cheerful pale yellow Bonnet House was Frederic's idea of a Caribbean plantation house. Squirrel monkeys played in the trees, white swans preened in a pond and exotic orchids burst into bloom everywhere.

"I had no idea a historic house could be fun," Helen said. "I hate museum house tours. All those dark, gloomy rooms packed with dead people's things."

"Nothing dead about this place," Margery said. Helen's seventy-six-year-old landlady reigned over the L-shaped art moderne Coronado Tropic Apartments. Bonnet House was built around a courtyard alive with green plants and a splashing fountain. "Frederic and his wife, Evelyn, weren't your usual superrich—they both had brains and talent.

"Evelyn Bartlett is my role model," Margery said. "She appreciated good art, good booze, good living and good men. Made it to age a hundred and nine. After a scandalous divorce back in the twenties, she outlived her critics in style."

Margery had her own style and juicy scandals. She'd once been arrested for murder and wore a prison jumpsuit.

Today, her gauzy purple top looked cool in the heavy June heat. Margery wore her gray hair in a swingy chin-length bob. Time had marked her tanned face, but Margery made no effort to remove the lines and wrinkles that proved she'd lived and laughed.

Her silver bracelets jingled slightly, and Helen checked to see if her landlady's hands were twitching. Margery couldn't smoke her Marlboros on this tour.

"I could actually live here," Helen said, surveying Bonnet House as if she were going to buy it, "and I don't feel that way about most mansions."

Liz, their tour guide, gently herded them into Frederic's towering two-story art studio. Well-bred, well-spoken and gray haired, Liz could have been one of Evelyn's guests.

"Mr. Bartlett had an art studio at every one of his residences," Liz said, resuming her spiel as if turning on a recording. "He painted in this studio from 1921 until the early fifties. It has the clear north light that artists love."

The studio's faintly musty smell was mixed with the scents of oil paint and a sharp hint of turpentine. A fanciful white fireplace was flanked by two tall white-framed paintings: one of a stylish woman in a golden brown suit and the other an elegant man in a pinstripe suit.

"That's Evelyn on the left and Mr. Bartlett on the right," Liz said. The walls were covered with vivid paintings of the French Riviera. "All of this was painted by Mr. Bartlett. He collected the pottery and sculpture, too."

A striking painting of richly dressed dark-eyed men wearing jeweled crowns and turbans hung above all the art. "That big painting is Persian," Liz said. "Early nineteenth century. Those are courtiers and members of a royal family."

"All men," Margery said. "You know who counted in that bunch."

The studio's mix of paintings and sculpture was striking, sophisticated and energetic. Helen could almost see the boldly handsome Bartlett painting, a romantic figure with slicked-back hair and a mustache, holding his palette like a shield and wielding a brush. He looked like the sort of man who could get away with a poet shirt.

Liz led them through the butler's pantry, painted in Ragdale blue, a once-fashionable bluish turquoise. "This is where Evelyn staged her exquisite meals," Liz said. Next they peeked into the kitchen. "The Bartletts ate only the freshest food. They brought in meat and dairy products from their Massachusetts farm. Their cook, Marie Little, said Evelyn never went into the kitchen. She talked to the cook about the day's meals through the window."

"My kind of woman," Helen said.

Margery checked out the china and Helen admired the German beer steins in the dining room. "Mr. Bartlett collected those during his student days in Germany," Liz said.

"Did he empty them first?" Helen asked.

Liz laughed but didn't answer. Helen wondered if the tour guide had a crush on the long-gone Frederic Bartlett.

As Liz guided the two women from room to room, they admired the house's whimsical touches: the gilded baroque columns swirled around the drawing room doors, the brightly painted wooden giraffes on a courtyard walkway, the menagerie of carved monkeys, and the lacy wrought iron from New Orleans. They saw Frederic's murals and paintings. Evelyn's colorful, sensual art had its own white-walled gallery in a former guesthouse.

Helen and Margery lingered at the Shell Museum, a thirties bandbox housing Evelyn's shell collection, her Bamboo Bar and blooming orchids. "At the age of a hundred and one, Evelyn started a new hobby, collecting miniature orchids," Liz said.

"Wonder what I'll be doing at a hundred and one," Margery said.

"Whatever you want," Helen said, tempted by the Bamboo Bar off the Shell Museum. "I like the idea that her husband gave Evelyn her own bar."

"Most men won't even fetch their wives a drink," Margery said.

The bamboo-lined room had four padded barstools, a couch and cocktail table, and a well-stocked back bar.

"The clock is permanently set at five o'clock," Liz said. "This is where Evelyn served her famous Rangpur lime cocktail. She grew the limes herself."

Helen wrote down the recipe for Markos, the hunky young waiter who lived at the Coronado. "Maybe he can make it for our sunset salute by the pool," she said.

By the time they were back at the Bonnet House courtyard, Helen felt slightly dazed and dazzled, as if she'd watched Evelyn and Frederic's star-dusted lives on fast-forward.

The courtyard, sheltered by feathery palms and bright with flowers, was cool even at noon. "I like the giant birdcage," Helen said. The gazebo-sized hexagon cage was a gingerbread confection of pastel wood and screens.

"Mr. Bartlett built the aviary for his wife's pet birds and monkeys," Liz said. "She had macaws, lovely demoiselle cranes, cockatoos and more. The guests would feed the cranes bits of food at dinner."

Helen saw a flock of artists working on the loggia across the courtyard, seated at folding tables. "Is that a painting class?"

"We have lots of classes," Liz said. "That's our oils class. The teacher is Yulia Orel, a local artist who's quite good. Come on over."

Yulia looked artistic, even in jeans. Her exquisitely boned face was crowned by blond braids. Liz introduced Margery and Helen. Yulia nodded politely and went back to telling a slender brunette, "You must use more color, Jenny."

Helen found Yulia's Slavic accent charming. She wondered how Jenny managed to wear white Armani jeans and a navy striped top without getting paint on her pricy designer outfit.

"No, it's not working," Jenny told the teacher. "I'm going to put this away and forget about it for a week or so."

"I think it's pretty," a blonde with corkscrew curls said. She sat in front of Jenny. Her sturdy body was buried under hot pink, turquoise and yellow scarves, like a sale rack at a beach store.

"I don't want to paint pretty pictures, Cissy," Jenny said. "I want to paint art, like Annabel."

Annabel's nearly transparent skin turned as pink as one of Cissy's scarves, making her dark hair look black. She was about thirty-five, but so thin she looked like she might snap. A lime green cane was propped against her table like an exotic plant.

Annabel shared a table with the only man in the class—reluctantly. She held herself rigid to avoid contact with him but acted as if he didn't exist. Helen wondered why. He looked like a beefy businessman on casual Friday, in khakis and a navy polo that hugged his rolls of fat.

Helen could see the artwork from this angle, the students' and the teacher's. Annabel seemed better than they were—maybe even better than Yulia. She was painting the aviary with bluish gray cranes stalking across the courtyard. At first glance, the painting seemed slapdash, but Helen could feel the movement.

"I'm only a student," Annabel said. "I'm still perfecting my technique."

"Your technique is fine," Jenny said. "You've developed your own voice."

"To develop a voice, you need something to say," the beefy businessman said. Helen noticed his large nose was veined in red. A drinker?

Annabel paled.

"Hugo," Yulia said gently, "in this class, we are free to discuss one another's art, but we do not put down people."

"I don't *put down* anyone," Hugo said. "I tell it like it is."

The class seemed to close in on itself, fighting to ignore Hugo. Yulia examined Cissy's painting of a red hibiscus. Despite the vivid color, the flower was dull and lifeless.

"What am I doing wrong?" Cissy asked, corkscrew curls bobbing, multicolored scarves shaking in frustration.

"You keep flattening your flower," Yulia said. "It looks like a cutout. You're too careful. Be bold! What do you have to lose?"

"Time," Cissy said. "The class is over."

"All the more reason to act now," Yulia said. "I'll stay."

"Next time," Cissy said. "Next time I'll have more courage."

The class began packing up their easels and art supplies. Cissy helped the frail Annabel pack and said, "You really should drink your raspberry tea."

"Later," Annabel said.

Now Yulia took time to welcome Margery and Helen. "You should join our class," she said. "Painting is relaxing."

Margery shook her head. "No, thanks. I'm not creative."

"What about you, Helen?" Yulia asked.

"I wanted to be an artist when I was a kid," Helen said, "until I discovered I didn't have any talent."

"When you're a child, you have no idea if you have talent," the teacher said. "You can paint for enjoyment. It could help your work. What do you do for a living?"

"I'm a private eye," Helen said.

"Take up painting and you'll see the world differently."

"And it's so romantic here," Cissy said, eyes shining, scarves wafting in the breeze. "Can't you feel the atmosphere? Frederic Bartlett was amazingly handsome—you've seen his photographs. He had three wives and he loved them all. Each woman was an artist in her own way. His first wife was an artist and social activist, his second a musician and a poet, and Evelyn was a painter and a gardener. It's inspiring here."

Cissy and the others were packed and ready to leave. Annabel took her green cane and her tea thermos. "Don't forget to drink your tea," Cissy reminded her.

Liz said, "Helen, Margery, we have one more stop. The tour ends at the gift shop."

"Sorry," Margery said. "I'm dying for a cigarette." Helen was surprised her landlady had lasted more than an hour without a Marlboro.

"We'll walk them out, Liz," Jenny said. "Where are you ladies parked? In the Bonnet House lot?"

"No, across the way," Margery said, "on that vacant lot where those shops were razed. We're parked illegally."

"So are we," Jenny said. "I hope we don't get towed."

The women walked out together, Cissy carrying both her supplies and Annabel's. How she managed in that welter of scarves, Helen had no idea.

Once they passed through Bonnet House's wrought-iron gates, the otherworldly spell was broken. They were back in modern Florida, surrounded by condos, cars and construction. Jenny surveyed a half-built condo. "They should make the crane the state bird," she said.

Helen was relieved that no tickets flapped on their windshields. The sandy soil was littered with sparkling glass shards and construction debris, and Helen hoped Margery didn't get a flat tire.

"Who has that amazing red Tesla S?" Helen asked.

"Me," Jenny said, nimbly navigating the uneven ground in four-inch heels. "I love it."

"So do I," Helen said. "You're really sure-footed. I couldn't walk in this lot in heels."

"You don't need them," Jenny said. "You're how tall?"

"Six feet," Helen said.

"I have to wear heels. I'm only five feet tall."

Jenny and Yulia loaded their cars. Jenny drank the last of her bottled water, while Annabel gulped her tea. "Ick," she said. "I didn't put in enough honey. It's bitter."

Margery lit her cigarette with trembling hands and blew out a plume of smoke like a satisfied dragon.

"You should smoke e-cigarettes," Cissy said, firing up her own e-cigarette. "You won't be so addicted if you vape."

"I like my addictions," Margery said. "I've cultivated them carefully."

That should have stopped Cissy, but she had the fearless fervor of a new convert. "You'll save money," Cissy said.

"I enjoy burning cash," Margery said. Her look should have wilted Cissy's springy blond hair.

Cissy packed the art supplies into her blue Prius while Annabel finished the raspberry tea in her thermos.

"I wish you'd join our class," Jenny said to Helen.

"There's room," Yulia said.

"I'll think about it," Helen said. She was tempted.

"Are you working on a case right now?" Margery asked.

"No," Helen said.

"Perfect," Yulia said. She pulled out her cell phone and said, "Give me your name and address. We meet at ten every morning."

Before she knew it, Helen was signed up for class. Everyone waved good-bye to Yulia.

"That was quick," Margery said. "How do you feel?"

But it was Annabel who answered.

"Terrible," she said. Annabel was as white as milk and trembling. She dropped her cane, then collapsed in the sandy soil.

CHAPTER 2

"Nine-one-one. What's your emergency?" The operator sounded preternaturally calm.

"A woman passed out," Helen said, her voice shaking. She was leaning on the front fender of Margery's big white Town Car. "Annabel. She needs help."

Annabel had fallen in a makeshift aisle between two parked cars, Margery's white whale of a Lincoln and a big black BMW. Annabel's purse, thermos and cane were abandoned in the sandy dirt. The cane looked like a green shoot that had been cut down in the thin, rubble-strewn soil.

"Is she breathing, ma'am?" the operator asked. Her matter-of-fact tone gave Helen hope. The operator sounded in charge. She would get help there to save Annabel.

"Yes," Helen said.

"Are you with her, ma'am?"

"I'm standing right near Annabel. Her friends are with her."

Helen saw small, worried Jenny cradling Annabel's head in her lap. The artist's skin looked like old putty and her long dark hair was plastered to her head.

"Ma'am, what's the address?" the 911 operator asked.

"I'm not sure," Helen said. "There's no street sign. We're on the street behind the Bonnet House Museum."

"Is that the Birch Road entrance, ma'am?"

"No, we're in the little dead-end street off Birch. In a vacant lot, where they just tore down some shops," Helen said frantically.

She tried to calm down and give a better description. "There are six cars parked in the lot. It's dirt, not pavement." She looked around wildly. "There's a big yellow Caterpillar tractor behind a chain-link fence, a construction Dumpster full of debris, and a row of blue porta potties."

"I have the location now, ma'am," the operator said. "Stay with me. What's the nature of the injury?"

"Nature?" Helen said.

"How did she get hurt? Is she bleeding? Did she fall? Was she struck by a car?"

"I'm not sure she's injured," Helen said "There's no blood. I think she's sick. Annabel said she felt terrible and fainted. Landed in the dirt like someone cut her strings. Then she came to and started throwing up. Several times."

Helen saw Jenny brushing Annabel's limp, damp hair away from her pale, sweaty forehead. She was talking softly to her friend.

Suddenly Annabel went rigid. Her face looked like a skin-stretched skull and her sightless eyes were glazed. Her body bucked in jerky movements.

Jenny screamed.

"Cushion her head," Margery shouted. She and Jenny fought to keep the thrashing Annabel from injuring herself. Jenny knelt in the dirt, not caring that she wore five hundred dollars' worth of designer duds.

Helen's heart was pounding. "Hurry!" she shouted to the 911 operator. "I think she's having a seizure. Please, hurry!"

Helen saw the dark stain on Annabel's pants. She'd wet herself.

"Please remain on the line, ma'am," the operator said. "The paramedics have been dispatched. Did she eat or drink anything?"

"Just tea," Helen said. "But she's not in good health. She walks with a cane, but I don't know what's wrong with her."

Annabel appeared unconscious again, but her chest rose and fell.

"She's still breathing," Margery said to Jenny.

Helen could hear Jenny crooning to her friend. "Stay with us, baby," she said, patting Annabel's hand. "Help is on the way. You'll be better soon."

Margery had stubbed out her cigarette in the sandy soil and was fanning Annabel with her straw hat. A nicotine fiend like Margery would abandon a partly smoked cigarette only for a life-and-death emergency.

The blazing sun throbbed and turned the glass shards in the dusty lot into glittering fire, but Helen felt cold. She realized the operator was talking to her.

"How old is the person?" the operator asked.

"Early to mid-thirties, I think," Helen told the operator. "Her name is Annabel." The quaver was back in her own voice. "She's an artist. A good one."

"What's your relation to her? Is she a relative? A friend?" the operator asked.

She's trying to keep me calm until help arrives, Helen thought.

"Neither," Helen said. "I just met Annabel at an art class. She was with some friends and we walked out together to our cars."

Helen heard heavy feet crunching across the broken glass in the lot. Hugo was picking his way around giant tractor-tire ruts, dented soda cans and broken bricks. His face was rare-roast-beef red. Greasy sweat poured down his neck and soaked his polo shirt.

"Annabel collapsed," Jenny told him. "We're calling 911."

He grunted and ignored Margery and Jenny's efforts to revive Annabel. He stepped over Annabel's feet as if she were more construction debris, then stabbed the electronic key to unlock his car.

"Hey, jerk," Margery said, standing up and brushing off her purple clam diggers. "We've got a sick woman here."

Helen noticed her landlady held her keys. Was she going to stab him in the eye?

"Are you speaking to me?" Hugo said, glaring at her with small, mean eyes. His voice was a challenge.

"You answered to the name," Margery said. "You've just stepped over a seriously sick woman and didn't offer to help."

"Not my problem," Hugo said. "We're divorced. It stinks here."

He tossed his art supplies in the car trunk, then stepped around Margery and opened the driver's door.

The Beemer made a rude *whump!* when he plopped into the leather seat. He fired up the engine and floored the car, spewing dust and gravel as he screeched straight out of the spot and crossed the curb with a *thunk.*

Helen winced at the sound and wondered if he'd scraped the undercarriage. She hoped so.

Jenny was choking on the dust, but Margery was grinning. She held up her keys and said, "Oops, I guess Hugo didn't realize how close he was to my car keys."

"You keyed his car?" Jenny said.

"It was an accident," Margery said. She tried to look innocent, but it didn't work.

Jenny poured the rest of her bottled water onto a wad of tissues and wiped Annabel's sweating, dusty face. Annabel didn't react, and Helen thought that was a bad sign.

"I can't believe Annabel was married to that creep," Margery said. "Why does he hate her?"

"He says she ruined his career," Jenny said. "I'm glad she dumped him."

"Her husband, Clay, is wonderful," Cissy said. Helen had seen her hovering uselessly at the edges of the scene, wringing her hands and smoking her e-cigarette.

Now she powered up her cell phone. "I'm calling Clay," she said as she speed-dialed a number, then paused and listened. "In case Annabel gets sick, he's on my speed dial.

"No answer," she said. "His cell phone went into voice mail. I'll try to reach him at the college art department.

"Hello?" Cissy said into her phone. "Joanne, is that you? It's Cissy. I'm trying to reach Clay. Is he in his office? Not there? I need to reach him—is he teaching a class now? No? Look, this is a family emergency. Annabel's sick. Do you know where I can find him? Okay, I'll try his cell phone."

She hung up and speed-dialed a third number, then waited about thirty seconds. Helen guessed she was listening to the recording again.

"Clay, it's Cissy," she said, her words quick and urgent. "I'm sorry to leave this news as a message, but it's important. Annabel collapsed coming out of her art class and the paramedics are on their way. They'll probably take her to the closest hospital, Palmetto Hills.

"I'll meet you in the ER. I wish I could tell you more, but that's all I know. You know my number." She hung up.

"Annabel's husband is an artist, too?" Margery said.

"Oh, yes," Cissy said. Her voice softened. "An important one. He paints the most divine seascapes. Clay was a famous painter in New York before he moved to Fort Lauderdale. Now his work is carried by RH Gallery Ltd. That's a major gallery on Las Olas. If your art is shown in downtown Fort Lauderdale, you're a very big deal."

"I'll have to check him out," Margery said. "Why does Annabel use a cane?"

Jenny, who was still patting and soothing Annabel, said, "I'm not sure. She doesn't like to talk about what's wrong. She's a very private person, so—"

"I know," Cissy interrupted. "She has chronic fatigue syndrome. Some days she can't get out of bed, she's so tired. Clay is a saint—a saint—to take care of her. He's sacrificed his career for his wife, but that's the kind of man he is."

"Ma'am," the 911 operator said to Helen, "I asked if there were any changes in her condition."

"She's not moving," Helen said, "and her eyes are closed, but I can see her chest rising and falling."

"The paramedics will be there momentarily," the operator said.

"Excuse me." An older woman walking a spindly, bug-eyed Chihuahua marched briskly toward them, picking her way around the treacherous lot with surprising agility. She wore a flowered pantsuit and red Crocs. Her face was shaded with an enormous red visor. She had a photo of her dog on her huge purse, and Helen wondered if the little Chihuahua rode in the bag when it was tired.

"What happened to the lady? Can I help? My name's Gretchen." Helen thought the woman might be about Margery's age—mid-seventies.

"Thank you, Gretchen," Margery said, "but the paramedics are on the way."

That's when Helen heard the wailing sirens and nearly collapsed in relief.

"Help is here now," Helen told the 911 operator. "Thanks for staying with me. I'm going to hang up now. Thank you."

Annabel didn't react to the shrieking siren or the sudden silence when it was switched off. The red ambulance, lights dancing, crunched across the lot. Four paramedics who looked like bodybuilders poured out, carrying a portable stretcher and other equipment.

Brisk and businesslike, they took Annabel's vital signs and then lifted her onto the stretcher. Jenny and Cissy told them about Annabel's mysterious attack, and gave them her full name: Annabel Lee Griffin. Gretchen, the older woman, gathered up her little brown dog and stood off to the side, watching the show.

Jenny picked up Annabel's purse and cane and ran over to Helen and Margery. "Cissy and I are going to Palmetto Hills Hospital," she said. "Thank you both for your help."

Helen gave Jenny her Coronado Investigations card and said, "You'll call and tell me how Annabel is?"

"I promise," Jenny said. "As soon as I know something."

Helen watched the paramedics load the unconscious Annabel into the ambulance. Her color had gone from ghost white to gray. She looked like a stone figure on a tomb.

CHAPTER 3

"Do you think Annabel is going to make it?" Helen asked, grabbing the dashboard as Margery's big old Lincoln bumped and rocked across the vacant lot.

The ambulance had roared off, siren screaming, carrying the unconscious Annabel. Her friends Cissy and Jenny followed it to the hospital in their own cars.

Margery's strong, veined hands expertly steered her white tank around the ruts and debris, but it took all her concentration to get out of the lot.

Frigid air blasted from the air-conditioning vents, mixing with the acrid odor of old nicotine. Even the seats and dashboard were fumed with sticky yellow tobacco tar. Helen was grateful for the cool air but hated the cigarette stink.

When the Lincoln landed on the street with a resentful *clunk*, Margery put it in Park and lit a cigarette. She kept the air-conditioning running but powered down her window and blew a long, satisfied plume of smoke into the air. She closed her eyes and leaned against the headrest.

Helen let her savor her cigarette awhile, then said, "I was on the phone with 911 and couldn't really see what was going on. Was Annabel as bad as she looked?"

"Worse," Margery said, rolling up her window and pointing the faithful Lincoln toward the Coronado Tropic Apartments near downtown Fort Lauderdale. "Annabel had at least one seizure, a bad one, while we were waiting. Her head really jerked around."

They stopped at a red light, waiting to turn onto US 1, a main artery for Florida beach towns.

"I saw some of that," Helen said. "The way her body went rigid and then started flailing looked frightening."

"It was," Margery said. "Jenny and I kept Annabel from banging her head around, but that's all we could do. I hope that seizure wasn't a stroke and there's no brain damage. When the seizure was finally over, Annabel was breathing, but that's about it. By the time the ambulance showed up, she wasn't reacting to anything. She didn't move when Jenny wiped her face with cool water.

"I'm no doctor, but when the paramedics hauled Annabel away, she didn't look unconscious—she looked like she was in a coma."

Coma. Stroke. Brain damage. Helen didn't want to hear those words. She barely knew Annabel—they'd never even had a conversation. But Helen remembered what the artist had said when Jenny had admired her work: *I'm only a student. I'm still perfecting my technique.*

Helen had seen only one unfinished painting by Annabel, and she was no judge of art. But she liked Annabel's crisp, offbeat style and her humble response to Jenny's extravagant praise. Annabel had lots of talent, without the artist's big ego. It would be a shame to lose someone so gifted.

Margery interrupted Helen's gloomy thoughts. "Could you hear what the paramedics were saying?" the landlady asked. "They shooed us away and went to work."

"Not a word," Helen said. "They talked softly and looked serious."

"The ambulance put the siren on when they took her to the hospital," Margery said. "Another bad sign. They only use sirens for real emergencies."

"At least we know she was still alive," Helen said. "What was with her ex-husband, Hugo? He stepped over her like she was a hunk of wood."

"He's a real prize," Margery said. "I wonder why he's so bitter. He looks like a man who makes trouble for himself."

"I'm glad you keyed his car," Helen said.

"I didn't," Margery said, and grinned. "His car got in the way of my key. Wouldn't have happened if he'd used better judgment."

"About his wife?" Helen said.

"Ex-wife," Margery corrected. "Now he'll have a whopping repair bill to remind him of his bad behavior."

The two women were quiet the rest of the way to the Coronado Tropic Apartments. Margery smoked and Helen thought about Annabel and her vivid paintings. The art world would be a less colorful place without her.

Margery turned off US 1 onto the Coronado's street, a small slice of Old Florida lined with two-story midcentury modern apartments. At three in the afternoon, the street was cool and shaded by rustling palms, nine-foot scheffleras with thick, waxy green leaves, and Helen's favorite, graceful royal poinciana trees with flame red flowers. Cerise and purple bougainvillea spilled over the fences.

The idyllic scene called for birdsong, but instead Helen and Margery heard the screech and roar of heavy machinery.

"What are the developers tearing down now?" Helen asked.

"Sunny Vista Apartments, two streets over," Margery said. "Built the same time as the Coronado—1949. The late owner's kids sold it."

"More condos?" Helen asked.

"Town houses," Margery said. "The developers are tearing out the city's heart. Places like the Coronado are a dying breed."

"I hope not," Helen said. But the Coronado had had a close brush with destruction, until Margery found enough money to restore the place. Greed was wrecking the city.

"Phil's Jeep isn't in the lot," Helen said. "I hope he gets another job soon. He's bored and restless."

"And you're not?" Margery asked.

"I've been improving my mind," Helen said. "It will be fun to take art classes and play lady."

"Right. One look at you, and the word 'lady' immediately comes to mind," Margery said.

Helen tossed back her long dark hair. "Art classes will give me a whole new perspective on my profession," she said. "The art teacher said so."

"She was working her own angle," Margery said, and gave an unladylike snort.

But Helen thought their jokes sounded flat. She and Margery were both shaken.

Margery parked the car in the Coronado lot and Helen followed her through the gate into the sun-splashed courtyard.

She loved the building's sleek white curves and fresh turquoise trim. The two-story art moderne apartments were set around the aquamarine pool, shaded by palms and broad green-leaved elephant ears. Waterfalls of ruffled purple bougainvillea surrounded the pool, and the sidewalks were an imperial march of purple impatiens and spiky salvia.

"What do you want for lunch?" Margery asked.

"I'm not really hungry," Helen said. "How about a cold glass of wine by the pool? We can start the sunset salute early."

"Only if you eat a chicken and avocado salad to lay down a base," Margery said. "Then you can drink."

"Deal," Helen said.

Helen set one of the poolside tables with the purple umbrellas, uncorked the wine and poured two generous glasses, while Margery served the salads. Helen kept her cell phone on the table, hoping to hear from Jenny about Annabel. She and Margery didn't mention Annabel, but Helen knew they were both thinking about the young artist.

They were finishing their salads when Margery said, "Well, look who's here. Afternoon, Markos!" She waved him over to their table.

Markos Martinez, the youngest Coronado resident, was dressed for a late-afternoon swim. Helen thought the Cuban American hunk was dazzling, but today he was especially eye-catching with his smooth tanned skin and thick black hair with a slight curl. Helen tried not to stare at his tight white bathing suit. Instead, she focused on his brown eyes and told herself she was a happily married woman.

He flashed a smile and strode over to their table. "How was Bonnet House?" he asked. Now Helen could smell his coconut suntan lotion. His six-pack was right at her eye level. She fought to look him in the eye.

"Fabulous," Helen said. "After the tour wasn't so good. A woman we met in the art class collapsed and had to go to the hospital. We're waiting to hear if she's okay. She was very sick."

"I'm sorry," he said, and he really did seem regretful. "I hope she'll be okay. After my swim, I'll make you some mojitos, and I have a new snack I want you to try—roasted chickpeas. Spicy and healthy."

"Did you learn that recipe in a food and beverage class at Reynolds-White College?" Margery asked. "Or pick it up at your restaurant job?"

Markos was working on his degree at the Fort Lauderdale college and working at Fresh and Cool, an upscale restaurant specializing in healthy, low-calorie food.

"Neither one," he said. "Found the recipe on the Internet."

"Sounds like something Fresh and Cool would serve," Helen said.

"I'm going to suggest it as a happy-hour snack," he said. "Only a hundred forty-four calories in a third of a cup. Maybe they'll let me make a test batch. I want to cook there."

"We've brought you a drink recipe from Bonnet House," Helen said, "and hope you'll make us a test batch of that."

"Maybe it's one I learned at bartending school," he said.

"I doubt it," Helen said. "It was the favorite cocktail of Evelyn Bartlett, the grand lady of Bonnet House." She handed Markos her recipe notes.

"For me? That's so sweet." He read, "'The Rangpur lime cocktail is four parts Mount Gay Barbados Eclipse dark rum, one part fresh Rangpur lime juice, and maple syrup to taste.'

"Love the ingredients. Mount Gay is the world's oldest rum, and it's still popular. The first drink James Bond orders in the movie *Casino Royale* is Mount Gay rum with soda, instead of his usual vodka martini. I make a mean vodka martini, too."

"I'm sure you do," Helen said. "But your mojitos are amazing."

"I'd like to make this Rangpur cocktail," he said.

"I've got a bottle of dark rum and it's the right brand," Margery said.

"I have some Mrs. Butterworth's syrup," Helen said.

"Sorry, but that's pancake syrup," Markos said. "We need real maple syrup for this recipe. I know where to get some. I'll also have to score some Rangpur limes."

"I can get you regular limes," Margery said.

"Not the same," he said. "Rangpurs look more like mandarin oranges than Persian limes—those are the green ones you get at the grocery store—or Key limes."

"So you've tasted Rangpurs?" Helen asked.

"Oh, yes. They're a hybrid of a lemon and a mandarin orange. Their flavor is unique, but it's more like a lime. I've used them in gimlets and Tom Collinses. I could make those, too. But I'd rather try this cocktail."

"You should get some swimming in," Margery said. "We'll watch the recipe for you."

Markos left his towel on the chair and made a low, flat dive into the deep end of the pool.

"You can relax now," Margery said. "I thought your eyes were going to cross while you struggled not to look at his skimpy bathing suit."

"Margery!" Helen said. "I'm happily married."

"Of course you are. And you like sex. That young man is sex on a stick."

Before Helen could say anything, their neighbor Peggy stumbled down the walkway, looking tired after a day at work. Her green sundress set off her dark red hair, but her pale skin was oily. She plunked her orange straw purse on the umbrella table but didn't say hello. Instead, she stared at Markos as if she'd never seen anyone doing the backstroke. She couldn't seem to take her eyes off his muscular brown arms.

"Studying his form?" Margery said.

"Huh?" Peggy said. "Yes, of course. He's a good swimmer."

"Right," Margery said. "Swimming was the first thing that came to my mind, too."

Peggy ignored her wicked grin. She was digging in her big purse. "Did you see the condo burglary in today's paper?" she asked. "Someone's stealing gold from the units on the upper floors. Third burglary in two weeks in Blue Heron Crescent."

"There's a burglar in Little New York?" Helen said.

"How did the crescent get that nickname?" Peggy said.

"Because so many New Yorkers live there," Helen said.

"And those towering condos look like Manhattan skyscrapers—with palm trees," Margery said, punctuating her comment with a blast of smoke. "Ugliest condos in Fort Lauderdale, and you have to work hard to win that title."

"The burglar made off with more gold coins," Peggy said. "The police suspect the thefts are inside jobs, but they can't figure out how he's getting into the buildings. He's bypassing the security guards and the cameras. He only hits condos on the upper floors—and only condos whose owners have gold coins."

"Definitely an inside job," Helen said.

"Think they'll hire Phil to find the thief?" Peggy said. "Coronado Investigations has had some high-profile news stories."

"I sure hope so," Helen said. "We need someone to unload the gold—on us."

CHAPTER 4

Three twenty-six in the morning.

The glowing green letters on Helen's bedside clock mocked her attempts to sleep. She checked her cell phone for a call or text message for the third time since three o'clock. Nothing. No calls or texts from Jenny.

That means Annabel is alive, Helen thought.

I hope.

Annabel's medical crisis ran on an endless loop in Helen's mind. She saw the artist's plaster white face and her seizure-contorted body. Then she saw Annabel lying still in the rubble-strewn dirt. Dead still.

Margery's words haunted Helen: *I'm no doctor, but when the paramedics hauled Annabel away, she didn't look unconscious—she looked like she was in a coma.*

Was Annabel in a coma? People came out of comas, didn't they?

Helen wished she could talk to Phil about Annabel, but her husband slept like he was in a coma. She thought he looked adorable when he was asleep. Tonight, his long hair was spread out on the pillow, giving Phil an undeserved silver-white halo. He was forty-five but looked younger.

Phil was slim and muscular, with just enough chest hair to look manly. Helen thought his slightly beaky nose gave his long, elegant face distinction. He looked like an English nobleman. He'd look sexy as a Regency dandy in knee breeches and blue brocade the color of his eyes.

It's too bad men don't wear knee breeches, she thought. My man has great legs. He should be able to show them off in something sexier than baggy board shorts.

Last night when he came home, Phil had been tired and discouraged, his crisp summer shirt wilted and sweat stained.

"It's harder to look for a job than actually work," he'd said.

"Looking for a job is hard labor," she'd said. "Neither prospect panned out?"

He shook his head.

"I thought you'd get the bar gig for sure," she'd said. "The owner told us his cook was stealing thousands of dollars' worth of prime meat."

"He was," Phil had said. "The owner wanted me to work undercover as a bartender to catch the dude. Instead, he caught the cook leaving work with twenty pounds of prime rib stashed in his gym bag under his smelly workout clothes. That's how he's been smuggling meat."

"Ew," Helen had said. "The cook actually eats that?"

"No, he sold it to his neighbors," Phil had said.

"I'd love to hear their court testimony when they find out how he smuggled that meat out of the bar," she'd said.

"Won't happen, Helen. The cook confessed and agreed to make restitution."

"How's he going to pay if he's fired?"

"He'll be cooking for free for at least six months, and the owner will be watching him. Then I'm guessing he'll be fired without references."

"DIY detectives are bad for business," Helen had said. "What about the runaway teen?"

"He called his mom at six thirty this morning. A night of dodging the chicken hawks who prey on pretty boys at the bus station convinced him that living by his parents' rules wasn't such a bad idea. He's at home, cleaning his room."

"We've got enough money to tide us over for a while," Helen said, "but I'd rather work."

"Tell me about it," Phil had said. "I am a man of action."

"So I've heard," Helen had said. "Why don't you demonstrate?"

She'd kissed him hard on the lips, and his kiss was equally passionate. They shed their clothes across the living room and ended up on the couch. After a quick, steamy session, they'd moved to the bedroom to make leisurely love.

Afterward, Helen had opened a bottle of chilled wine while Phil whipped up cheese omelets. They ate their meal in Helen's small kitchen and went back to bed. Phil was softly snoring in seconds, while Helen stared at the clock, waiting for news about Annabel. She'd hoped that third glass of wine at dinner would help her sleep, but here she was at—she glanced at the clock—three forty-two in the morning, wide-awake and worrying about Annabel.

As Helen listened for a text message alert, she thought, I'm sure Annabel is fine. Jenny will tell me that at tomorrow's art class. I wonder if . . .

Then Helen woke up, sunlight streaming through the bedroom window. Phil was whistling in the shower, and their six-toed cat, Thumbs, yowled for his breakfast and prodded her chest with his huge, polydactyl paws. She caught the lifesaving scent of fresh coffee drifting from the kitchen.

"Hang on, bud," she said to the cat. "I'll feed you as soon as I find my head."

Helen stumbled out of bed, wondering how her husband could be so chipper in the morning. She carefully carried the empty wine bottle into the kitchen. Her head ached.

Must be worry over Annabel, she thought. I feel flu-y, too. Oh, cut it out. You had three glasses of wine last night. You're hungover.

She checked the kitchen clock: nine oh nine. She'd have to hustle to make the art class. She didn't even have any painting supplies. Well, she'd worry about that later.

Thumbs' insistent breakfast howls raked her throbbing brain like wicked cat claws. She poured dry food into his bowl, then poured herself a cup of coffee and winced at the bitter taste. Phil liked his brew strong.

She was dressed when he emerged from the tiny bathroom in clouds of steam, wearing only a towel. "You've got that glow," he said, kissing her good morning. "How about if we work on improving it?" He kissed her neck and was working on her shoulder, but Helen's thoughts were elsewhere. All she could think about was Annabel.

"Later," she said, kissing him back. "I have to get to art class at Bonnet House. I want to find out about Annabel."

Outside, the hot, muggy Florida morning felt like a slap in the face with a warm, damp towel. Helen was glad her sunglasses hid her red eyes.

By the time she got to Bonnet House, she felt better. She was glad there was parking in the museum's lot today. She couldn't bring herself to park in that vacant lot again. Not after Annabel's collapse.

She parked as far away from Hugo's BMW as she could, and she smiled at the deep scrape along the driver's side. The shining paint was slashed from the driver's door to the taillight. Margery had left her mark.

"Helen!" A woman's voice. She sounded like she was in tears.

Helen stopped admiring the damage to Hugo's Beemer and saw Jenny tottering down the gravel path from the museum in her sky-high heels, nearly blinded by tears. Jenny still wore the same white jeans and navy striped top she'd had on yesterday, but her expensive clothes were creased and stained. Helen could see where she'd kneeled in the dirt to help Annabel.

"Class has been canceled," Jenny said, her voice wobbly.

"Oh, no," Helen said.

"Annabel is dead," Jenny said, and the tear storm broke. Helen gathered Jenny into her arms. She felt fragile and slightly sweaty.

"She was so talented," Jenny said. "She was going places. It's such a loss."

"It is," Helen said, rocking her. "I was impressed by her work and I only saw one painting. When did she die?"

"About three this morning," Jenny said. "I stayed at the hospital all night. She never came out of the coma, but I was with her at the very end."

She started crying again, sobs that made Helen's heart twist. She wished there was something she could do to ease Jenny's pain. Helen felt something sting her neck and realized they were in a cloud of mosquitoes. She caught a faint rotten egg stink. They were at the edge of the mangrove swamp that bordered the Bonnet House parking lot. They'd be eaten by mosquitos if they didn't move.

"Have you had any food, Jenny?" she asked.

"Nothing except vending machine coffee at the hospital," Jenny said.

"Let's get you something," Helen said. "We can go to a cute place near here on the beach."

"No," Jenny said. "Get me away from here, please."

"Then follow me to the Warsaw Coffee Company on Thirteenth Street," Helen said.

It was easy to spot Jenny's fire-engine red Tesla S in Helen's rear-view mirror as they threaded their way through the late-morning traffic.

Thanks to hard work by the neighborhood, Thirteenth Street was now landscaped with plants and palms and lined with offbeat shops and pretty, painted bungalows. The locals were especially proud of the Warsaw Coffee Company. More than a hipster hangout, the Warsaw was solid proof the area was on the way up.

The sleek white building with the big windows was decorated in industrial chic: cool gray and black colors, deceptively plain lights, steel chairs and copper-topped tables.

Jenny parked her car and joined Helen inside.

"This place is so cool," she said.

Twentysomethings sprawled on leather couches, working on their laptops and iPads. At a long shared table near the door, a young brunette frowned at her laptop and sipped a latte. Three seats down, two Asian women chatted in a language Helen didn't recognize, wolfing down the restaurant's homemade version of Pop-Tarts.

Helen snagged a copper-topped table for her and Jenny. "Hold the table," Helen said. "What do you want?"

"The sausage burrito with avocado and roasted tomatoes," Jenny said. "And a cinnamon brown-sugar latte. I'll worry about calories tomorrow."

"You missed two meals yesterday," Helen said. "I'm getting myself a blueberry muffin as big as a softball and an Ethiopian coffee."

Jenny checked her iPhone while Helen placed their orders, then returned with their drinks.

The sugary latte seemed to revive Jenny. By the time a bearded server brought their food, she'd lost that shocky white look. While Helen wolfed down her warm muffin and Jenny ate her enormous burrito with small, methodical bites, they made appreciative noises.

After Jenny had a good start on her breakfast, she was ready to talk.

"I'm sorry I didn't call you last night," she said. "I came to art class to tell our teacher, Yulia. I should have called you when Annabel died, but by the time I thought about it I was already at Bonnet House. I figured I'd meet you in the parking lot."

"What happened after you got to the hospital yesterday?" Helen asked.

"It was chaos in the ER. There was a bad accident on I-95—a carful of teens crashed into a light pole and one didn't make it. The waiting room was full of worried, weeping parents. Cissy couldn't track down Annabel's husband, Clay, for nearly an hour."

"Did Annabel's death have anything to do with her chronic fatigue syndrome?" Helen asked.

"I don't think so," Jenny said. "The doctor said she'd been poisoned.

"The hospital gave her activated charcoal, whatever that is, and something to try to stop the seizures—she had more." She shuddered and Helen saw her eyes cloud with tears. "The seizures were terrible to watch. When Cissy started screaming, the ER staff said we were in the way and made us sit in the waiting room.

"By that time, Annabel was having trouble breathing. She was gasping for air, and her lips and nails were this weird blue. They put her on a ventilator. Clay, her husband, finally arrived and got to stay with her.

"The doctors stopped the seizures, but she never came out of the coma. About two in the morning, she took a turn for the worse. Cissy and I were allowed to come in and stay with her. She died—" Jenny stopped, gulped, then forced herself to finish the sentence. "She died—at three oh two."

Now that she'd said the words, Annabel's death seemed to be real. Jenny couldn't hold back her tears. Helen patted her hand, and Jenny wiped her eyes and said, "I'm sorry. I don't mean to be so emotional."

"You should be," Helen said. "Annabel's death was horrible. How is her husband?"

"Clay's in a trance. He was a zombie."

"What was Annabel poisoned with?" Helen said. "And how? Did she commit suicide?"

"No!" Jenny shouted the word as if that would erase the ugly possibility. "The police are investigating her death as suspicious."

"Suspicious how?" Helen asked.

"Maybe suicide—though I don't think so—or murder," Jenny said. "Maybe she took the poison accidentally. I have a friend in the medical examiner's office who's promised to tell me more when she finds out. That's why I keep checking my phone, hoping I'll hear from her.

"The hospital thinks Annabel was poisoned with nicotine, based on her blood and urine tests."

"Where would Annabel get nicotine?" Helen asked. "I've heard of nicotine tea, made from cigarettes soaked in water, but why would she have that?"

"It's also in e-cigarettes," Jenny said. "And those nicotine patches to help people stop smoking. Nicotine is used in some pesticides and I think it has some medical uses. But nicotine poisoning doesn't make sense.

"The police asked me a bunch of questions, but I was too dazed and tired to talk. They finally let me go about nine thirty, but I'll have to give a statement later. Cissy drove Clay home and I came to art class to tell everyone."

"But how did Annabel get poisoned with nicotine?" Helen asked.

"The best guess—and it's a guess—is that the poison may have been in the thermos of raspberry iced tea she brought to our class," Jenny said.

"She complained it was bitter," Helen said. "After she drank it all."

"We couldn't find the thermos, so we can't prove the poison was in there," Jenny said. "The last time I saw Annabel's thermos was when we were in the parking lot. I went over to the lot this morning before class, but I didn't see any sign of it. I asked the construction workers if they'd seen it, but they said no."

"Maybe one of them wanted a nice thermos," Helen said.

"I don't think so," Jenny said. "I told them it was full of deadly poison."

"Maybe Cissy has it," Helen said. "She put Annabel's things in her car."

"Cissy checked her car trunk, but the thermos wasn't there."

Helen heard a chime.

"That's my cell phone," Jenny said, and checked it. Helen watched the color drain from her face as she read the message.

"Oh, no," she said. "My friend at the coroner's office texted me. Annabel was murdered."

CHAPTER 5

"Helen, I want to hire you to find Annabel's killer," Jenny said. "I saw the news stories about the cases you've solved. I know you're good."

"Uh." Helen stalled for time. The rumble of conversation at the Warsaw Coffee Company faded into the background while she considered Jenny's request.

Jenny sat quietly, but her tired, hope-filled eyes pleaded with Helen. "I can afford your fee."

If the red Tesla in the parking lot and Jenny's Armani outfit were any indication, she was loaded—or deeply in debt.

Helen carefully chose her words. "I could investigate Annabel's murder," she said. "But I'd be duplicating the current investigation. The police are already on the case."

"And going in the wrong direction," Jenny said.

"You don't know that," Helen said. "You haven't given the cops your statement yet."

"I can tell by the questions they asked me," Jenny said. "The detective in charge wanted to know if Annabel had any enemies.

Of course I told him about Hugo, her ex-husband. You saw how he acted. The man's a pig."

"I'll say. That prize porker stepped over her in the parking lot," Helen said. "She was passed out and he didn't offer to help."

"Exactly," Jenny said. "And he's always sniping at her in class, putting her down. But the cop brushed off my suggestion. He said Hugo was a well-known businessman and poison was a woman's weapon."

"What!" Helen said. "Where'd the detective get that stupid idea?"

"From watching *Game of Thrones*?" Jenny said. "On that show, poison is the favorite weapon of cowards and women."

"That detective needs to see the stats," Helen said. "Men kill more than women—a lot more. Men commit seven times more murders than women—and that stat is straight from the Justice Department. Here's another he won't like: Sixty percent of poisoners are men."

"Really?" Jenny said. She pushed her half-finished breakfast burrito aside. Helen wondered if talking about poison had affected her appetite, or if she'd had enough of the huge entree.

"That detective doesn't know his crime history," Helen said. "History has tagged Lucretia Borgia as a poisoner, but men are the real killers. What about Dr. Thomas Neill Cream?"

"Who's he?" Jenny asked.

"A dashing Victorian doctor who poisoned at least eight prostitutes about the time Jack the Ripper was slicing and dicing them."

"That was a long time ago," Jenny said.

"There are plenty of modern cases," Helen said. "Another Brit, Graham Frederick Young, the Teacup Poisoner, killed his stepmother and at least four other people. That little twerp started poisoning people when he was fourteen.

"And we've got homegrown poisoners, too. Remember George Trepal, the Mensa Murderer?"

"No," Jenny said.

"George lived right here in Florida. He poisoned his neighbors for making too much noise. Then this so-called genius opened his big mouth and talked his way into a murder conviction."

"How do you know all this?" Jenny asked.

Helen was ashamed to admit she'd been surfing crime stats and stories on the Net.

She put a noble spin on her boredom. "I keep up with the research," she said. "And I'm sick of stereotypes. I've heard other cops say that guns are a man's weapon, but that's not true, either. We've achieved equality when it comes to killing. Most women use guns, same as men. A woman is more likely to knife you than poison you."

"They sure are at my office," Jenny said. "I work with a real bunch of backstabbers."

Suddenly Helen realized she was at the Warsaw Coffee Company, lecturing a woman she'd met yesterday. "Sorry," Helen said. "I didn't mean to rant."

"Don't say sorry," Jenny said. "Amy Poehler says women apologize too much. She's a comedian, but it's true. That wasn't a rant. Everything you've told me says you're the right person to take this case.

"Please, Helen. You know statistics don't lie. Someone killed my talented friend. Annabel had so much to live for. I want her killer to pay for what he did. I know it was Hugo and the clue to her murder is in our art class."

"Well," Helen said. She had been bored and she did want this case. Besides, she'd get paid to attend art class.

"You don't know anything about me," Jenny said. "I sell waterfront real estate, and I'm good at it."

"I'd say so, judging by that Tesla," Helen said.

"It gets me the kind of clientele I want," Jenny said. "So does taking painting lessons at Bonnet House. The volunteers and patrons are rich and connected. Those art lessons are good for my business. Please, Helen, take Annabel's case."

"Let me get you another latte," Helen said, "and you can tell me why you think Hugo killed Annabel. Then I'll decide."

She gathered up their plates and carried them to the steel dish cart, then ordered more drinks.

When Helen returned to the table with their coffees, Jenny had spruced herself up. She'd combed her dark hair, washed her face, and put on lipstick. She couldn't do anything about her wrinkled clothes or the dark fatigue circles bruising her eyes, but Jenny seemed more alert and energetic.

"Now, start at the beginning," Helen said. "How long have you known Annabel?"

"About five years," Jenny said. "I sold Annabel and her husband, Clay, their house. Annabel and I are both the same age—thirty-five. Like most artists, Annabel was a free spirit."

"What's that mean?" Helen asked.

"She liked to experiment. Not just with art. With life, too. I gather she had at least one affair with a woman."

"She was gay?" Helen asked.

"I don't think so," Jenny said. "But I'm not sure. I think Annabel felt guilty about the affair and I didn't push her. I know she went from living with her lesbian lover to marrying Hugo."

"Why would she marry him?" Helen asked.

"I've seen the photos when he was younger," Jenny said. "He had a certain charm. He was up for a big CEO job and hired a publicist to get puff pieces in the newspapers. And maybe he wasn't such a big jerk before their divorce. I know the split was bitter."

"Do you know the details?"

"Sure, but I'm too tired to go into them now," Jenny said. "I'll tell you more tomorrow, when I can think straight. We can go somewhere after class. The newspapers covered some of their divorce. When I met Annabel, she'd just married Clay. She seemed madly in love with her new husband. I sold the couple a fabulous five-bedroom house in Coral Ridge Country Club Estates."

"Where's that?" Helen asked.

"Fort Lauderdale," she said. "Near Oakland Park Boulevard. Built in 1975. Their home has ninety feet of deepwater dock."

"Do they have a boat?" Helen asked.

"Never got one," Jenny said, "but they liked the water view. The house was a good deal at a million nine: twenty-five hundred square feet, a covered patio, dome-screened pool, Turkish sandstone paver circular drive and a—"

Helen felt her eyes glaze over. Jenny sounded like a real estate brochure.

She stopped and said, "Sorry. It's easy for me to slide into real estate–ese.

"Clay and Annabel's home has a beautifully landscaped yard. Annabel loved to paint the flowers and birds there. Clay has a studio by the ocean. He's an artist, too. He paints seascapes."

"What's Clay like?" Helen asked.

"I don't know him that well," Jenny said. "Annabel was proud of the fact that Clay was a big-deal painter in New York. Now he's repped by RH Gallery in downtown Fort Lauderdale. RH is run by my friend Robert Horton. I don't understand the local art scene, but Robert does. He can fill you in."

"You seemed surprised yesterday when Cissy said that Annabel had chronic fatigue syndrome," Helen said.

"I was," Jenny said. "I don't want to sound like I'm in high school, but I thought Annabel and I were best buds. I don't know how Cissy knew about her health situation. Cissy can be pushy and pry information out of people. Annabel never talked about what was wrong with her. Never. All I knew was that she sometimes uses a cane and complains that she is tired."

Jenny stopped, and a fresh stream of tears trickled down her face. "I mean she sometimes *used* a cane and *complained* that she *was* tired. She's dead, dammit, and I don't think I'll ever get used to that."

She stood up, rocking slightly on her high heels. "Can we go, please? Don't I have to sign some papers or write you a check if you're going to take my case?"

"Yes, you do," Helen said. "Follow me to the Coronado Investigations office."

Jenny's bright red Tesla tagged behind the Igloo, Helen's white PT Cruiser, all the way to the Coronado Tropic Apartments. Jenny parked next to Helen and surveyed the Coronado with a real estate agent's shrewd eye.

"This place is beautifully restored," she said. "It's a prime piece of Old Florida. Bet the developers are licking their chops when they see this much land so close to downtown."

"So far, they haven't swallowed it up," Helen said. "Why do developers want to tear down these charming old places? You'd think the buildings would be worth more restored."

"Bathrooms," Jenny said.

"We have plumbing," Helen said.

"But not modern bathrooms," Jenny said. "The johns in these places are the size of phone booths."

"Young hipsters will put up with small baths for a lot of charm."

"You'd be surprised," Jenny said, following Helen past the plant-fringed pool and upstairs to the Coronado Investigations office.

Helen had the uneasy feeling Jenny was sizing up the property for a bigger building. The private eye unlocked the glass-slatted jalousie door and Jenny followed her inside.

"This is exactly what a PI's office should look like," Jenny said. "Love the terrazzo floors."

She checked out Helen and Phil's chrome-and-black club chairs and the yellow client chair, nodded her approval of the tanklike gun-metal desks and the beat-up gray file cabinets.

"That poster of Sam Spade from *The Maltese Falcon* is the perfect touch," Jenny said, and dropped into the yellow client chair.

Helen saw that Jenny's face was gray with exhaustion. "You

look so tired," she said. "Let me drive you home. It's okay to leave your car here overnight."

"I only live a few blocks away," Jenny said. "Show me where to sign and I'll write you a check and head for home."

Jenny efficiently completed their business and Helen walked her downstairs to her car.

"I'll see you at class tomorrow," Jenny said. "How long will it take you to prove that Hugo is the killer?"

"I'm not sure he is," Helen said.

"But you saw how badly he treated Annabel," Jenny said. "He hates her."

"Jenny, if every man who hated his ex was a killer, there would be no room in the prisons," Helen said.

"I'll find out who killed Annabel. But I'm going to catch the real killer—not the man you want it to be."

CHAPTER 6

"Executive Decision: Fort Lauderdale Executive Hugo Hythe Tapped to Head Fortune 500 Company," the newspaper headline trumpeted in May 2009. Helen looked down the telescope of time at a younger, thinner Hugo. He was grinning triumphantly in the blurry newspaper photographs, a man who'd climbed to the top of the financial world.

Business writers heralded him as the salvation of the scandal-wracked WDQ Financial Services Corp. Hugo was the white knight who'd rescue the corporation and its soiled reputation.

Then the news stories rehashed an older, embarrassing story: WDQ's previous CEO had been fired for telling the new CFO—the company's first female financial officer—that he'd promoted her because she had a great ass. Worse, he said that in a meeting, in front of six shocked witnesses.

The outraged CFO sued, and truth was no defense in this lawsuit. A graduate of Wharton with a sharp mind as well as a shapely derriere, the CFO was awarded a multimillion-dollar judgment.

WDQ's punishment had just started. Women's groups and sympathetic companies no longer wanted WDQ Financial Services.

The stock had dropped like an anvil out a twenty-story window and the former CEO's fortunes plummeted along with it.

After a nationwide search, clean-cut Hugo had looked like the ideal candidate. He'd quietly hired a press agent who'd helped Hugo get his name in the media in dozens of positive stories, from hospital fund-raisers to Humane Society benefits.

One photo spread showed a grinning Hugo and two women on the roof of a thirty-story building in July. Wearing climbing gear and carrying their helmets, they were about to rappel down the skyscraper for a breast cancer charity. Hugo had paid their thousand-dollar fees, the article said.

Helen's stomach twisted when she saw the thirty-story drop behind the three rappellers. The reporter asked the three: "Aren't you afraid?"

A hatchet-faced brunette called Xenia Mathews said, "I thrive on challenge. I work with Hugo Hythe and have the greatest respect for him."

A small, muscular woman named Cady Gummage had a determined look on her heart-shaped face and a blond buzz cut. "I'm a cancer survivor," she said. "Nothing scares me anymore, not after chemo and radiation. I came back stronger than ever. Rock climbing is my hobby, and I've been everywhere from Austria to Australia. Rappelling off a thirty-story building is a piece of cake."

"I wanted to give back to the community," Hugo said. "You can't be afraid of heights if you're going to make it to the top."

Hugo had leaked the news that he was the next CEO, hoping once the information was in print his position was secure. But WDQ had been badly burned by their last top executive. They looked past the puff pieces in the press and hired a detective agency to investigate Hugo. A private eye interviewed Annabel, Hugo's ex-wife.

Annabel told the PI that Hugo was a hopeless hound who'd had a fling with his office manager. After the woman had a baby boy, she sued Hugo for child support. Hugo refused to pay. He told the court,

"Yes, she slept with me, but she's had sex with every man at the office." DNA proved Hugo was definitely the baby daddy.

WDQ no longer saw Hugo as their salvation. He'd barely managed to hang on to his old job. Now Hugo was fast-tracked to nowhere.

As Helen read the sorry saga of Hugo's decline and fall, she saw many unanswered questions: Why did Annabel rat out her ex? Was she a vindictive woman? Or did Hugo wound her so badly she had to fight back?

Maybe Jenny would know the answers. She certainly thought Hugo was angry enough to kill his ex-wife as her own star was rising.

Helen worked at her laptop until her eyes ached. She rubbed her forehead, looked up and saw Phil, relaxed and smiling, strolling into their office. "It's time for the sunset salute," he said. "You look like you could use a drink."

"And you look cheerful for the first time in weeks," Helen said. "Did you find a job?"

"I think so," Phil said. "I've been talking to some board members at the Silver Glade Condominiums in Little New York. They're scared spitless they're going to be the Gold Ghost's next target."

"The who?" Helen said.

"The gold thief." Phil looked embarrassed. "The burglar who's stealing gold coins from Little New York condos. TV stations are calling him the Gold Ghost because he slips in and out of the buildings like a phantom. The thief is never caught on the security cameras and leaves no traces."

"Do you think he's that clever?" Helen asked.

"Hell, no," Phil said. "Most condo security guards are retirees. They sit in plush, air-conditioned lobbies, dealing with loud neighbors and chasing visitors out of residents' parking spots. Condo security isn't trained to handle serious crime. They're supposed to call the police if there's a real problem.

"That's why Silver Glade needs me. The board is taking major heat from the condo residents. They're holding a special board meeting this afternoon. If they vote yes as expected, then they'll meet with the condo manager, and I'll have a job before dark."

"Wonderful!" Helen said, kissing her husband. "I have a job, too." She told him about Annabel's sudden death and why Jenny had hired her.

"I'm sorry about Annabel," Phil said.

"Me, too," Helen said. "I barely knew her, but she seemed so talented. Jenny wants her killer caught."

"At least our job dry spell is over," Phil said. "Let's go down for the sunset salute."

"I think Markos is working tonight," Helen said. "We'll have to do without his mojitos and homemade appetizers."

"I like Markos," Phil said, "but I'm relieved he's not making his healthy snacks tonight. Those roasted carrots the other night were awful." He made a face.

"I liked them," Helen said. "Roasted carrots have a sweet, nutty flavor. I loved the fresh thyme."

"It was a carrot, no matter how he dressed it up," Phil said.

"If you don't like something, you could just say 'no, thank you,'" Helen said. "You carried on like Markos had served you a dead mouse."

"At least a mouse has meat," Phil said. "I'll make the popcorn at my place and bring it over."

Helen and Phil had an unusual housing arrangement. Before their marriage, they'd both lived at the Coronado in one-bedroom apartments. They'd kept their small apartments after the wedding. Thumbs, Helen's cat, didn't mind switching homes as long as he was fed, but the two independent PIs needed their separate retreats when Phil blasted his Eric Clapton CDs or Helen wanted to read in peace.

But they always slept together. Helen thought the arrangement gave their love life a slightly illicit thrill.

"Good," Helen said, kissing him again. "Make the popcorn in your kitchen, so you can clean it up."

"You love my popcorn," Phil said. "I use my mom's old corn-popping pot. Makes the best popcorn on the planet."

"You use a gallon of oil and don't put the pot lid on until the last minute, so the stove, walls and floor are spattered with hot oil and popcorn flies everywhere. Last time you made popcorn at my place, I crunched it underfoot for days."

"A chef needs freedom," he said, and grinned. "I'm having a beer. You want some white wine?"

"Not if Margery is making screwdrivers," Helen said. "I'll get my own drink. Will you feed Thumbs? I think he's at your place."

By six o'clock, there was a cool breeze. Helen found Margery relaxing in a chaise by the pool in a cool cotton tie-dyed purple caftan and purple sandals that showed off her tangerine manicure. A pitcher of screwdrivers sweated on the umbrella table. "Helen," she said, waving her over. "Have a cold one."

"I was hoping you'd make screwdrivers," Helen said. "Phil is on his way with popcorn."

Margery handed her a frosty glass filled with pale orange liquid that could knock a strong woman sideways. Helen knew her landlady had her own recipe—a jigger of orange juice in a tall glass of vodka.

Phil arrived with a mixing bowl of warm, buttery popcorn and kissed Margery on the cheek.

"As useful as you are handsome," she said, batting her eyes at Phil. "You make real popcorn, not that microwaved Styrofoam. I love a man who cooks."

They clinked glasses, but Helen took only a polite sip of her screwdriver until she'd had a few handfuls of popcorn. Then the three crunched in silence, watching the setting sun gild the windows and turn the old white building a soft pink. Helen caught the sharp smell of pool chemicals and hot popcorn. It was so peaceful, she nearly drifted off to sleep.

Awk! Helen heard a rumble on the pool deck as Peggy, their downstairs neighbor, rolled out the big cage that had her two Quaker parrots, Pete and his mate, Patience.

Pete's got a girlfriend. Pete's got a girlfriend, the little parrot chanted as he perched on the double swing next to Patience.

Pretty boy, the parrot replied. Patience was learning to talk.

"I brought my lovebirds out for some air," Peggy said. "This is their favorite time of day."

"Mine, too," Helen said. "Glad to see that Pete has resolved his relationship problem."

"At least I have one man in my life who isn't afraid to commit."

Uh-oh, Helen thought. Peggy must be ticked at her boyfriend, Daniel. An uncomfortable silence descended until Margery said, "I heard on the news there was another gold heist last night in Little New York." Only Margery could get away with using "heist." "The burglar got away with thirty thou in gold coins."

"No wonder Channel Seventy-seven calls him the Gold Ghost," Peggy said. "Valerie Cannata is breaking in on TV every thirty seconds with news updates—and there isn't any news. The cops don't know a thing."

Helen opened her mouth to say the Gold Ghost name was stupid, then swallowed her words along with another gulp of her screwdriver. Valerie was a friend whose news stories helped build Coronado Investigations' reputation. Helen didn't want to attack the person who'd helped their business.

"Like I said before, you and Phil should take that case," Peggy said. "Have you talked with any of the condos in Little New York?"

"There's a possibility one might be interested in hiring us," Phil said. "I'm hoping to get a call soon." He patted his cell phone on the table between his beer and popcorn bowl.

"If we do get this job, Phil's going to have to take it without me," Helen said. "I'm investigating a murder." She gave Peggy a stripped-down version of her new case, without revealing any names or places.

When she finished, Peggy said, "I had no idea that nicotine could kill you."

"It doesn't take much, either," Helen said. "Only—"

She was interrupted by Phil's ringtone, Clapton's "Layla."

Phil didn't put the phone on speaker—to protect client confidentiality—but from the way he was smiling after he answered, Helen guessed it was probably the Silver Glade Condo manager.

"Certainly I can discuss the matter with you," Phil said. "Would you like my partner and me to come to your building?"

After a pause, he said, "You'd rather come here? Smart. Yes, I agree there's a possibility these could be inside jobs. When would you like to meet? As soon as possible?"

He looked over at Helen and raised an eyebrow. She nodded yes.

"Why don't you meet us here in half an hour?" Phil said. "Let me give you our address."

After Phil hung up, Helen said, "Yes! The Gold Ghost is ours." Now that name didn't seem stupid at all.

CHAPTER 7

Victor Trelford, general manager of the Silver Glade Condominiums and licensed community association manager, wore Florida formal wear to meet with Helen and Phil.

He braved the humid June evening dressed in dark pants, white shirt, navy blazer and red tie. Victor had a slightly wilted, end-of-the-day look, as if his round face had been lightly misted with cooking oil, but he put on a brave smile.

"Thank you for meeting with me after business hours," he said. "This is an emergency. You know the buildings in Blue Heron Crescent have been hit by a series of burglaries."

"The Gold Ghost," Helen said.

Victor winced. "I don't like it when the media romanticizes criminals, but yes."

"We've been following the story," Phil said.

His worried brown eyes peered out at the PI pair from heavy black spectacles. "The burglar seems to be hitting a different condo every night," Victor said. "It's only a matter of time before he goes after Silver Glade, the most prestigious building on the Crescent." He pulled on his tie, as if it were strangling him.

"It would help if we had more details," Helen said. "Can you give us any information that hasn't been released to the media?"

Victor paused and ran his fingers through his fashionably spiked dark hair, as if he could pull the information out of his head. "I met with the managers of two condo buildings that were burglarized. The thief helped himself to a substantial number of gold coins. Naturally, we want this man caught."

"What time did the burglaries occur?" Phil asked.

"The first time, he robbed three condos in one building around one a.m.," Victor said. "The second time, he struck three more condos about three a.m. So six in all."

"Was security on duty in both buildings during the burglaries?" Phil asked.

"Yes. All Blue Heron Crescent buildings have twenty-four-seven security," Victor said.

"Any other patterns, besides the after-midnight hits?" Helen asked.

"Both buildings are the same height: twenty stories tall," Victor said. "Only condos on the top two floors—the nineteenth and the penthouse floors—were burglarized. Both buildings have balconies overlooking the ocean, and the thief appeared to have entered through the balconies' sliding doors."

"Were the sliders locked?" Phil said.

"No," Victor said. "The condo owners never expected anyone to come in from the outside when they lived so high up."

"Did the condo residents hear anything during the burglaries?" Phil asked. "Did the thief stumble over anything on the balconies?"

"No," Victor said. "If you live near the water, you know sound has odd properties—it carries farther, but the ocean is noisy. There's the constant clamor of the surf and the wind. Plus, at least two owners are, uh. . . mature, and I think they're slightly deaf."

"What about the second building?" Helen said.

"Same situation: Those condos were also unlocked. The owners thought the first burglary was a onetime thing, not a crime wave."

"How many people live in the condos that were hit?" Phil asked.

"A total of eight," Victor said.

"How old are they?" Phil asked. The condos in Little New York catered to wealthy older people.

"Three are men, ages seventy to eighty-five, who live alone," Victor said.

"Two are widowers and one is divorced. There's also a couple who've been married forty-six years. The other couple is also married. He's eighty and she's twenty-eight."

"How long has that couple been married?" Phil asked.

"Two years," Victor said. "She's from Belarus."

"An older man married to a much younger wife," Phil said. "Does she have any boyfriends? She might be the insider."

"I don't know Marina personally," Victor said. "I've heard she's very attractive. But her husband is supposed to be quite . . . ah, vigorous."

Helen glanced at Phil and raised an eyebrow. They both knew a randy eighty-year-old man was not the same as a hunky thirty-something.

"Can you get us contact information for the people who've been robbed?" Phil asked.

"I can try," Victor said, wiping his damp face with a pocket handkerchief. "I know some may be reluctant to talk, but I'll do the best I can."

"Any evidence left behind? Hairs, fibers, shoe prints, fingerprints?"

"Nothing," Victor said. "This hasn't been released to the public, but the police did find some smudges on a glass door. They think the burglar doesn't have fingerprints."

"No fingerprints?" Helen said. "I thought everyone has fingerprints."

"*Most* people have them," Victor said. "But some people are born without fingerprints. It's rare, but it happens. They don't have fingerprints or sweat glands, so they can't sweat."

"That would come in handy here in Florida," Helen said.

"Not really," Victor said. "If you can't sweat, you can die of heat-stroke."

Poor Victor looked so hot and miserable, even in the office air-conditioning, that Helen let that subject drop.

"People can lose their fingerprints, too," Victor said, "especially if they've had certain types of chemotherapy. Some jobs can even wear down fingerprints. Bricklayers, for instance, lose the ridges on their fingerprints by handling bricks and heavy materials. People can also lose their fingerprints as they age."

"You don't think an old person is committing these burglaries, do you?" Phil asked.

"Of course not," Victor said. "It's obviously someone very athletic. But because he doesn't have fingerprints, he got the name the Gold Ghost. He's not in any fingerprint database."

"What about photographs? Do the buildings have security cameras?" Helen asked.

"Of course," Victor said, as if Helen had asked, *Do the buildings have windows?* "Both condos handled the thefts the same way. After the break-ins, the managers, the police and the security staff all went over the security footage.

"Both buildings recently updated their security. The residents need computerized key cards to access the buildings and their apartments. There are no old-fashioned locks that require physical keys.

"Visitors have to park in a special section near the door. They need a parking pass and must sign in at the front desk. Then the security guard calls the condo owner. If no one answers, the visitor must leave or wait in the lobby until the owner comes home. All delivery and repair people must park in another designated area and sign in. These routines are standard for all Blue Heron Crescent buildings."

Helen and Phil nodded. "Most of the condos were built in the mid-sixties," Victor said.

"What prompted the recent security change?" Phil asked.

"I can tell you what happened at Silver Glade," Victor said. "We changed our routine about the same time as the others. Like most Blue Heron condos, we used to have a system where the condo owners had ASSA keys—big square, metal things—for the elevators and building doors. The keys cost a hundred dollars to replace, but our condo didn't collect them when people moved out. Owners handed out keys to their house cleaners, visitors, relatives and repair people. We had no idea how many keys were floating around.

"One night, four men unlocked our common room with an ASSA key and carried off the new seventy-five-inch television."

"You caught them on-camera?" Phil said.

"Yes, but it was dark and the burglars never turned on the room lights. They used the light from the parking lot. We couldn't see their faces. All we had was a rough idea of their height and build and the impression they might be younger than most of our residents. We didn't know if they were professionals who'd gotten a key from a careless resident or someone's dishonest grandchildren.

"After that, we upgraded the CCTV system and got the computerized keys."

"So the footage the condos looked at after the Gold Ghost thefts was on the upgraded systems," Helen said.

"Exactly," Victor said. "The staff could see the faces much better. When they examined the security footage, they were able to identify everyone in the hallways or the elevators."

"How long before and after the thefts did the condos check the security system?" Phil asked.

"Twelve hours each side," Victor said, "in case the burglar was hiding in an empty condo or a janitor's closet. They even checked the trash chute rooms.

"All the service personnel were accounted for. They'd registered with the desk guards on entering the buildings and signed out when they left. Everyone else was either a resident or a legitimate guest of a condo owner."

"Do the condos have cameras in the stairs and the elevators?" Phil asked.

"Yes, that's standard for Blue Heron Crescent buildings," Victor said, "including ours. Silver Glade needs a new lobby elevator, but the condo association put off getting one. They've finally voted for it. Meanwhile, we're using a backup generator to restart the lobby elevator when it goes out. That will be one of your duties, Phil—turning on the generator when the elevator goes."

"So if all the buildings have security cameras in the stairs, entrances and elevators," Helen said, "the Gold Ghost burglaries are probably inside jobs."

Victor sighed and looked very tired. "I know. I feel terrible, but I don't trust my own people anymore. I've known some of them for years, but I can't risk it. That's why I wanted to meet you here at your office. Everyone at Silver Glade thinks I went home after work.

"Our condo staff is carefully vetted by a detective agency. Unfortunately, I have no choice but to consider that someone on the staff is betraying the residents."

"How many guards do you have?" Phil asked. "How old are they?"

"We have two guards on each shift, and we have three shifts for round-the-clock protection. The day guards are Billy and Edwin. Billy is forty-seven, a former police officer for a small force in upstate New York. Edwin is fifty. They come on duty at six thirty in the morning and leave at five.

"The evening shift is five to midnight. That's Patrick and Janice. Patrick is fifty-five and has worked for us for ten years. Janice is forty and has only worked for us for five years. She was downsized from an office job. The graveyard shift, from twelve to six thirty, is very quiet. Kevin is an active seventy but looks ten years younger. He's retired from the Boston PD. Jimmy is seventy-two, a former firefighter. Some of our security is retired, but none are what I'd call old.

"I want to hire you for the graveyard shift, Phil," Victor said.

"Me?"

"Yes. Jimmy wants to take a long weekend. I'd like you to start tomorrow night. That will give you a chance to work with Jimmy for a night. He'll show you the ropes, then leave for his vacation. The next night, Kevin can walk you through the routine. After that, you'll be on your own, and I hope you catch the crook before Jimmy comes back.

"What do you say, Phil? Will you help me?

"You'll have to wear a uniform, but it's a nice one. You'll look like a police officer, except for the patch on your arm."

"Well," he said.

"I'll pay for the uniform," Victor said.

Phil looked at Helen. She could almost read his mind. He wanted the job, but the late hours would cut into his evening beer drinking. She decided to give him a slight nudge.

"I love a man in uniform," she said, and winked at Phil.

"I'll take it," he said.

CHAPTER 8

Helen and Phil watched Victor Trelford climb into his black Cadillac Escalade. The condo manager's responsibilities weighed heavily on his bowed shoulders. Victor was wrapped in a thick gray cloud of worry.

Helen and Phil were ready to celebrate. Victor had signed a contract and a hefty deposit check, so he left Coronado Investigations as a client. Out of respect for his feelings, the PI pair waited until his SUV turned the corner. Then they high-fived.

"Yes!" Phil said. "The dry spell is over, though I'm not thrilled about working the graveyard shift as a security guard."

"I noticed your lack of enthusiasm," Helen said.

"Hey, I sucked it up and took the job," he said.

"And got Victor to shell out money for your uniform," Helen said, rubbing his broad chest. "Nice negotiating. I'll feel so much safer sleeping with a security guard."

"You will?" Phil said.

"Absolutely," Helen said. "That uniform will be fun to remove."

"How about if I help you out of that sweaty outfit you're wearing tonight?" Phil said. He cupped her face in his hands and kissed her hard.

"Your place or mine?" she said. She liked asking that question now that she was married.

"Yours," he said. "Mine has popcorn all over the floor."

Helen and Phil were no longer newlyweds, but they still enjoyed steamy sex. They raced up the purple-flowered path to Helen's apartment, opened the door, and shed their clothes all the way to the bedroom.

Phil was kissing her neck and working his way down when they fell onto Helen's bed, giggling.

Afterward, she lay content in his arms.

"Hungry?" he asked, brushing her hair off her forehead.

"Not anymore," she said.

"I mean for dinner," he said.

"There are chicken breasts and mushrooms in my fridge," she said. "You could make a stir-fry."

"Deal," he said. "If you'll feed the cat. He's at my place, howling for dinner."

Helen stretched luxuriously. "I'll get dressed and get the cat," she said.

Half an hour later, Thumbs was crunching his dinner in Helen's kitchen and Helen and Phil were eating their stir-fry in bed.

"What do you know about gold coins?" she asked.

"Not a thing," Phil said. "I kept hoping our client wouldn't ask me about them. We need to find an expert. I don't even know where to buy them. Who wants gold coins?"

"Pirates?" Helen said.

"That's it!" Phil said.

"You know a pirate?" Helen said.

"The next best thing—Max."

"Right. Max. The treasure hunter. He's found real pirate treasure. And he helped us on that emerald-smuggling case."

Phil put his cell phone on speaker so Helen could hear, and called Max.

"Max Rupert Crutchley Enterprises. Max speaking. Hey there, Phil," he said, and Helen figured he had caller ID. "How's your beautiful wife?"

"Still beautiful," Phil said, putting his arm around Helen as if Max could reach through the phone and steal her.

"If I were twenty years younger, I'd ask her to run away with me," Max said.

"Fat chance," Phil said.

"Overconfidence," Max said. "Not a good idea when you're married to a looker who's smarter than you. What can I do for you?"

"I need to know about gold coins," Phil said.

"You buying?" Max said. "I could get you a good deal."

"No, I'm working a case involving stolen gold coins," Phil said.

"So you're working the Little New York break-ins."

Phil didn't confirm or deny that. Instead, he asked, "Know anything about the burglaries?"

"Only what I read in the papers," Max said, his voice carefully neutral.

"I need a short course on gold coins," Phil said. "Who collects them, what kinds of coins are collected, and why collectors keep them around instead of safely stashing them in a bank vault."

"I can do that," Max said.

"Name your favorite bar," Phil said. "I'll meet you there now."

"Can't do it tonight," Max said. "Full moon."

"Why? You'll turn into a werewolf?" Helen said.

"Something like that." Max gave an uneasy laugh. Phil shook his head and put his index finger to his lips.

"How about breakfast tomorrow?" Phil said. "Beer, steak and eggs on me."

"Only if Helen comes, too," Max said.

"Of course I'll be there," Helen said. "But I have to leave for work by nine thirty."

"Good," Max said. "If we meet at eight, we'll have enough time.

But I'll have to take a rain check on the beer. I can't drink. Ticker's acting up and my sawbones says no booze. He gets one more week and then I'm going back on the beer. Might as well be dead if I can't have a cold one."

"Sorry to hear that," Helen said.

"Thanks, doll. I'd like breakfast at my favorite neighborhood joint, but I'm not sure it's classy enough for you."

"If the food's good, I'll be there," Helen said.

"The food's spectacular," Max said. "Cuban home cooking. Frida and Sharo, a little joint on Fourth Avenue in Fort Lauderdale."

"Mustard yellow building by the Home Depot?" Phil said. "I know the place. See you in the morning."

After he hung up, Helen said, "Why did you want me to keep quiet? What's wrong with a full moon?"

"It's a smuggler's moon," Phil said. "I investigated Max years ago for a client who wanted to invest in Max's treasure-hunting ventures. The client wanted to know if Max ran drugs. He doesn't, but Max has played hide-and-seek with the Coast Guard more than once bringing in gold and Spanish treasure. I suspect tonight he'll be working on his retirement fund."

He yawned and said, "Bedtime for me."

The next morning was sunny and sticky. At seven fifty, Helen and Phil entered Frida and Sharo Cuban Cuisine, a one-story yellow building with a haunting blue mural on the side. Helen inhaled the scent of strong Cuban coffee and fried potatoes and heard rapid-fire Spanish. The brightly painted restaurant was packed with breakfasting workers and locals.

Max waved them over to a booth he'd commandeered by the window.

He looked like a piratical tourist: gray haired and tanned, with short, powerful arms and a barrel chest. Max's tropical shirt was so loud, Helen could almost hear the parrots on it squawking. His jewelry glittered in the morning sun. Max wore a shark's tooth on a heavy gold chain, a chunky gold pinkie ring with a square-cut emerald, and a gold-link bracelet with emeralds the size of postage stamps.

"Helen, you're even beautiful first thing in the morning," he said. "Order your breakfast at the counter. I've already paid for it."

"Thank you. That's so nice," Helen said.

"It's easy to be a big shot at these prices," he said.

"What are you eating, Max?" Helen asked.

"Cuban toast slathered with cream cheese, and *cortadito.*" He saw her puzzled face and added, "That's Cuban coffee with evaporated milk. To keep the doc happy, I have mango juice, too. Maria, the owner, picks the mangoes off the tree in her yard."

Helen ordered a large *café con leche*, mango juice, and *huevos con papas*—fried eggs, potatoes and toast. Phil wanted espresso and a Cuban sandwich with ham, cheese and roast pork.

Back in the big booth, Helen and Phil savored their breakfasts. "This is kind of like eating breakfast at home," Phil said, "except someone else does the cooking."

"Exactly," Max said. "Glad you like the joint."

"Who are Frida and Sharo?" Helen asked.

"They're the owner's pets," Max said. "Frida is a dog and Sharo is an African gray parrot. Maria came here as part of the Mariel boatlift in 1980 and worked at Home Depot—not the one around the corner, another one. When she lost her job in 2009, she took her 401(k) and started this place. It's a neighborhood hangout."

He finished the last of his juice and said, "What can I tell you about coins?"

"Everything," Phil said.

"I don't know everything," Max said. "But I know a little. The kinds of gold coins that people have these days are usually South African Krugerrands, Chinese pandas, American eagles, and Singapore lions."

"I've heard of Krugerrands," Helen said, "but not the others."

"Krugerrands are the most famous," Max said. "The name comes from the old white guy on the front—Paul Kruger, president of the old South African Republic. The other side has a springbok. That's like an African antelope. It's a national symbol. Here's a picture of one on my iPhone."

Max thumbed through his phone photos until he found a Krugerrand.

"They've been around since 1967. They're probably older than you," he said.

"I was born in 1975," Helen said.

"Back in 'sixty-seven, Americans couldn't legally own gold bullion," Max said, "but they could have foreign coins. Krugerrands were real currency in South Africa, so we could own them. It was like a gold rush. Gold buyers snapped them up. You can't believe how popular they were. By 1980, the Krugerrand was the number one choice for people who bought gold.

"It looked like there was no stopping the demand for Krugerrands. But five years later, Congress made it illegal to sell Krugerrands in the US. Because of apartheid. Krugerrands were illegal in a bunch of other countries, too. It was still okay for Americans to buy and sell the ones that were already here. I made a nice profit in those years."

Helen wondered if he'd smuggled in Krugerrands, but she kept quiet.

"South Africa finally stopped apartheid in, uh, 1994," Max said. "Yeah, that was the year. It was okay to buy new Krugerrands. But by then, Americans had switched to gold eagles. Newly minted American coins. I've got a picture of one here. I think all gold looks fine, but this is a pretty coin."

He thumbed to the next photo. "See, that's Lady Liberty, holding a torch and an olive branch. The other side has a bald eagle family. The father is carrying an olive branch to his nest, where the mother eagle has the babies."

Helen and Phil studied the gleaming coin's photo. "The bald eagle family is a good symbol," Phil said, "but you can't feed the kids with an olive branch."

"Lady Liberty looks like a strong woman," Helen said.

"The Chinese got into the act in 1982 with gold pandas," Max said, and showed them another photo. "One side has the Temple of Heaven—a sacred building—and the other has two giant pandas."

"The pandas are kind of cute," Helen said.

"The Singapore lion has a roaring lion," he said. "Another good-looking coin. There are other gold coins from different countries, but you get the idea. Each country that made them had a tidy profit because they could buy huge quantities of gold at a discount and the coins sold at a small premium over gold value, which was 'retail.'

"Each of these coins is one ounce of twenty-four-karat gold. The gold coins are bought and sold as a commodity, as long as they are kept uncirculated for the most part. They can be bought and sold pretty easily without a large spread between the buy and sell prices.

"These are not rare coins," Max said, "but they are valuable. If the price of gold is twelve hundred dollars an ounce, then a hundred one-ounce gold coins sell for a hundred twenty thousand dollars. They weigh about seven point five pounds. If you're stealing them, they're not much heavier than a laptop computer."

"Where can you buy gold coins?" Phil asked.

"At a coin store," Max said, "or from gold dealers, sometimes pawn-type places. That makes them easy to fence, if you know the right pawnshop.

"The thing is that folks who own these Krugerrands, pandas and such are not really collectors—they're gold hoarders. A real collector will buy numismatic-quality gold coins, rare dates or uncirculated early US gold pieces. One single coin can range in value from a couple of thousand right up to a million plus. So while Krugerrands would need seven point five pounds to make up a big amount, it would be real easy to have one or two US gold coins worth as much or even more."

"Do the gold coin collectors—I mean, hoarders—belong to clubs?" Helen asked.

"There are a lotta clubs," he said. "Some collectors belong to online forums where they go to brag or ask questions and other people in the community chime in. I don't participate in any of those because they are time eaters, but lots of people enjoy the online forums even though there is a lot of misinformation going around. I can tell you this much: A ton of Americans have their money stashed away in a closet or under the mattress in gold coins."

"But keeping gold in their condos makes hoarders targets," Helen said. "Why not put it in a safe-deposit box at the bank?"

"Gold hoarders keep the stuff at home because they do not trust banks, either for accounts or for safe-deposit boxes. Often, they are conspiracy-theory folks. Sometimes they will have a safe, but I have heard stories of hundreds of thousands of dollars in gold coins stuffed in closets, under floorboards, behind the molding, under mattresses, in plastic bags in the toilet tank.

"These coins can literally be a person's savings account. They're also a way to supplement your savings or pension, a neat little way to store it if you earned lots of tax-free money in your life. You can keep your savings in gold coins and cash one in from time to time as you need the money."

Helen wondered if Max was talking about himself.

"There's nothing like gold," Max said, his eyes bright. Helen watched him rub his heavy gold-and-emerald bracelet.

"The heft, the feel, the color. You feel better holding it. It's real treasure. You want your gold where you can put your hands on it. Visiting your money in a vault is like seeing a friend in prison."

CHAPTER 9

Helen heard small, whistling cries from the gaudy purple jacaranda tree near the Bonnet House gift shop.

Exotic birds?

The museum's thirty-five acres were alive with birds, from dazzling white swans to emerald-winged parrots.

She saw Liz, the soft-spoken Bonnet House staffer, holding a cup of cashews under the tree's purple canopy, surrounded by a flock of brightly colored tourists.

"The squirrel monkeys are here," Liz said, rattling the cup and making squeaky chirps. "They'll come down for cashews."

Two delicate white-faced monkeys with soft gray coats inched down the smooth bark, bright-eyed creatures no bigger than Chihuahuas.

"Were those Evelyn's monkeys?" Helen asked.

"They were never purchased by Mrs. Bartlett," Liz said. "They escaped from a bar outside the property and ended up living here, but she loved them and fed them when they came to call while she was sitting on her upstairs back porch swing.

"These are the last three monkeys living at Bonnet House."

"Can't they have babies?" a man in a yellow and blue Hawaiian shirt asked.

"I'm afraid these are three males," Liz said.

"What about artificial insemination?" Hawaiian shirt asked.

"Really, Kent," said his gray-haired wife in the orange sunhat. "How did you ever have two kids? You can't inseminate male monkeys!"

"Oh." Now Kent's red face clashed with his shirt.

One monkey took a cashew, examined it, and tossed it on the grass. "Hey, now, Mr. Picky," Liz said. "There's nothing wrong with that cashew." The monkey stared at her and dropped another broken cashew on the ground.

"These monkeys are so spoiled," Liz said proudly. "This one only eats whole cashews." All three monkeys were reaching for cashews with small paws.

Helen checked her watch: five minutes before her painting class started. She waved good-bye and crunched along the gravel path past the hibiscus garden, the orange-red blooms like ruffled dresses. She heard Liz tell the visitors, "Mrs. Bartlett started that garden when she was a hundred years old."

What a remarkable woman, Helen thought. After a full century, Evelyn Bartlett still craved life and color.

Then Helen was through the curlicued yellow wrought-iron gate and into the central courtyard. She passed a tawny lion carousel figure with an extravagantly curled mane and a red saddle. Whimsical animals lined the walkway: An absurd black and white ostrich with a white saddle stood against a wall. Two brown giraffes taller than Helen guarded a walkway arch.

The painting class's white folding tables were set up under a spinning fan. Cissy, buried in orange and purple fringe, waved. Helen was surprised to see Hugo, in a khaki green shirt, squatting like a toad at a table. Next to him, Annabel's empty seat yawned before Helen. She hesitated a moment, hoping she wouldn't have to sit beside horrible Hugo.

"Helen! Over here," Jenny called. "Come sit by me."

Jenny had set up her paints and a small canvas on an easel. Tubes of oil paint and brushes were arranged in plastic racks and a photo of a romantically weathered seaside cottage was clipped to Jenny's canvas.

"I don't have any supplies," Helen said, sitting next to Jenny. "I feel like an idiot."

"We'll buy some after class," Jenny said.

The art teacher, her fine-boned face crowned with blond braids, smiled a welcome. "Helen, you're here."

"Without any supplies," Helen said.

"Here's a list," Yulia said, pulling a white paper from a folder. "Today you can start by drawing. Pick something in the courtyard and sketch it." She tore a sheet off her sketch pad and gave Helen a black number two pencil.

Yulia held her thumbs and forefingers in front of her face to form a frame. "See the courtyard as a series of pictures," she said. "Look in the viewfinder."

Helen stared at the fountain through her "viewfinder" fingers and saw the fanciful octagon aviary, built by Frederic and painted peach, yellow and beige. The perspective would be too difficult, she decided.

Next, she looked at a section of wall with a red wooden bench made by Frederic, flanked by two of his youthful German paintings. Too lifeless.

She heard the fountain burbling in the center of the courtyard. Yes! Perfect.

"I'll draw the fountain," Helen said.

"Good," Yulia said. "Now, how will you frame it?"

Helen looked through her viewfinder again. "On the left are five small palm trees," she said. "On the right is a larger palm with two potted plants at the base."

The new number two pencil had a solid, first-day-of-school feel, Helen thought, but the blank cream paper had become a vast threatening expanse.

As she started sketching, Helen realized she'd picked the hardest subject in the courtyard. Her palm trees didn't sway in the summer breeze. They looked stiff and flat. Those trees have shadows, she thought. She tried to sketch them. Her palm fronds were still too straight, but at least she'd drawn the group.

The palm on the right side had a curved trunk. Helen thought her cross-hatching was pretty good. The potted plants she sketched weren't bad.

But that fountain. How could she draw the water that splashed off the three tiers? The bowl-shaped tiers were topped with a spout that looked, well, phallic. Except when Helen drew it, the fountain spout looked positively pornographic.

That's why pencils have erasers, she thought, as she rubbed out the carnal waterspout and tried again.

Yulia looked over her shoulder and said, "Contemplate the light, Helen. See where the sunlight is."

And get your mind out of the gutter, Helen thought. Or the bedroom. She studied the cluster of palms again and deepened the shadows on the trunks.

I'm too midwestern to be an artist, Helen thought. I grew up in staid St. Louis. A true artist doesn't block out sensuality. Frederic was from Chicago, but he painted those frisky Germans.

She sketched a veil of water splashing down the fountain, then made the ornamental grasses at its base with light strokes so they seemed to sway in the wind.

Yulia checked on Hugo, who was painting a black stallion. "Very bold, Hugo. But he needs shadows on his neck."

"I like it the way it is," Hugo said.

Yulia moved back to Helen. “Very good,” she said.

“But don’t quit my day job, right?” Helen said.

“No, you have a talent that is worth developing.” Yulia took a pencil and lightly traced a line down the center of the page. “Your fountain is crooked,” she said. “Leaning toward the right. But you’ve framed the sketch well.”

I’m bored, Helen thought. She was relieved when Yulia said, “Time’s about up,” and the class packed up their supplies.

“Follow me to Dick Blick’s art supplies on Federal Highway,” Jenny said as they walked to the parking lot. “It’s in the shopping center next to Whole Foods.”

Jenny’s bright red Tesla was easy to track in the Fort Lauderdale traffic. Helen had never been in an art supplies store, but she was dazzled by the colors.

“Rainbows everywhere!” she said. She saw rainbows of paper—tissue paper, construction paper, posterboard and sketch pads. Rainbows of colored pencils, and pots and tubes of paint.

“I love the color names,” Helen said. “Titanium White, Cerulean Blue Hue, Mars Black, Cobalt Blue, Brilliant Purple . . .”

“All you need for this class is Cadmium Yellow Medium, Cadmium Red and Ultramarine Blue—those are your primary colors,” Jenny said, “plus white and black. But throw in any colors that catch your fancy. My treat. I’m buying.”

“But—”

“You’re at this class because I hired you to find Annabel’s killer,” Jenny said, “and I saw you staring off into space. You’re bored silly.”

As they wandered the aisles, Helen said, “I read the old news stories about Hugo’s fling with his office manager and how Annabel told the private detective about the baby. Why did she do that?”

“Because Hugo was such a jerk,” Jenny said. “Annabel thought she had a happy marriage until the office manager turned up on her doorstep with a bouncing baby.”

“Sounds like a scene from a Victorian novel,” Helen said.

"You can't imagine the fireworks it set off," Jenny said. "Annabel and Hugo had been discussing whether they wanted children, and Hugo said he didn't. Annabel decided she didn't, either. She wanted a career. Then it turned out he already had a child by another woman. Hugo refused to acknowledge the child as his, and it got ugly.

"Hugo's affair with the office manager shattered his marriage. Annabel lost all respect for her husband when he tried to duck his responsibility. She divorced him, and it was bitter. Annabel was badly hurt by his betrayal."

"She certainly got her revenge when the detective showed up," Helen said.

"Yes, but Annabel really did believe her ex-husband wouldn't be a good CEO. That's why she told the detective about the messy scandal."

"And Hugo blamed her for ratting him out," Helen said.

"And Annabel was stuck with Hugo for the rest of her life," Jenny said. "If she went to a party, Hugo turned up and ruined her good time. When Annabel started painting and having shows, Hugo would find a way to be there and spoil her triumph. He even took this painting class to annoy her."

"How does he keep his job if he goes to a painting class in the morning?" Helen asked.

"He told his boss this is his lunch break," Jenny said. "Hugo devoted his life to ruining Annabel's happiness. He was bound to Annabel by a burning hate."

"And you think he killed her," Helen said.

"Yes," Jenny said. "Annabel's death finally freed Hugo."

CHAPTER 10

"It's me," said the girlish voice on Helen's cell phone.

Helen, juggling her new art supplies and her cell phone, didn't recognize the voice.

"Cissy. From art class," the woman said. "You skipped out today before I had a chance to talk to you. I have so much to tell you about Annabel. And the police interviewed me about her murder."

"Oh, right." Helen stashed her new supplies in the back of the Igloo and waved good-bye to Jenny. "When do you want to meet?"

"Now?" Cissy said. "We could have lunch. It's twelve thirty. We can go to Kaluz."

Helen whistled. "Fancy restaurant."

"So you know where it's at? On Commercial Boulevard right by the drawbridge."

"I've been there," Helen said. "Wonderful outdoor terrace."

"It's too hot to sit outside. I'll get us a table inside and we can watch the boats. My treat."

Kaluz's owners had turned an old Roadhouse Grill, a place where patrons could throw peanut shells on the floor, into a chic dark wood and steel restaurant.

Helen pulled up in the Igloo at the Kaluz valet stand. Cissy was vaping by the entrance, looking like a pile of old shawls. Most of the other customers wore expensive designer casual. Cissy's fringed outfit seemed out of place at the sleek restaurant.

Helen handed her keys to the valet and Cissy said, "I snagged us a table near the window. They'll make me sit outside if I'm vaping."

Inside, Kaluz was cool and dark, its two-story windows showcasing the Intracoastal Waterway. The Commercial Street drawbridge, pale gray with a sky blue clockwork underside, looked close enough to touch.

The hostess showed them to a table by the water, where a streamlined white Hatteras yacht was docking.

"This restaurant has valet parking for yachts and cars," Cissy said. "How big do you think that yacht is?"

Helen, who'd worked as a yacht stewardess, said, "I'd guess maybe seventy feet or so."

They watched a bronzed young man in a white uniform help a tanned, leggy blonde off the white boat. Her muscular husband—Helen saw his gold wedding band—carried a baby in frilly pink.

"Aren't they a perfect family?" Cissy said.

"It's fun to dine with the beautiful people," Helen said.

They both asked for white wine. Helen ordered the blue crab salad with mangoes, mandarin oranges, avocados and Key lime vinaigrette.

"I'll have a veggie burger," Cissy said, and Helen hid a smile. After the server left, Cissy asked, "What's so funny, Helen?"

"I was wondering what my meat-eating husband would think of something that had quinoa, beets, rice and black beans being called a burger," Helen said.

"That's why I'm glad I'm single," Cissy said.

Helen didn't see the connection. A red needle-nosed go-fast boat blasted under the bridge, setting off huge waves that rocked the tied-up yacht.

"Whoa," Cissy said. "He definitely ignored the no-wake warning."

"What's this about you and the police?" Helen asked.

"A Palmetto Hills detective interviewed me about Annabel's murder when I came home from class. Crimes against persons detective Burt Pelham. Do you know him?"

Helen shook her head. "What's he like?"

"Fiftysomething. Dyed blond hair. New York accent."

"Possibly a retired snowbird," Helen said. "What did you tell him?"

"Of course I mentioned Hugo and how he acted that day. I told Detective Pelham that Annabel was Hugo's ex-wife and he hated her. I can't believe he stepped right over that poor woman when she was dying in the parking lot and just took off. If anyone killed her, it's Hugo. He certainly had a good reason after she ruined his career."

"But that was years ago," Helen said. "Why kill Annabel now?"

"Because her career is taking off and he's on the fast track to nowhere. You know he follows her everywhere."

"I heard that," Helen said.

"He's like a stalker, except Annabel couldn't do anything about him. But I told Detective Pelham I'm not sure Annabel was murdered. I think she killed herself."

"Why would she do that, especially if her career was taking off?" Helen said.

"You know she had chronic fatigue syndrome. Some days it was so bad, she couldn't get out of bed."

"Lots of people live with it," Helen said.

"But Annabel was an artist," Cissy said. "She was unstable."

Helen looked at Cissy, her corkscrew curls bobbing, her fringe floating on the air-conditioning breeze, and said, "You're an artist, too."

"Yes, I am," Cissy said. "At least, I'm working on it. But Annabel's chronic fatigue syndrome left her depressed. She'd had a flare-up and was using a cane again. She'd been making the rounds of the specialists and a Miami doctor told her she might have something worse."

"What?" Helen asked.

"Myasthenia gravis, an incurable muscle weakness. It's horrible.

Annabel was facing weak arms and legs, double vision, drooping eyelids. She could have trouble talking, swallowing and breathing. That's what killed Aristotle Onassis, the richest man in the world."

"Myasthenia gravis isn't a death sentence anymore," Helen said. "I saw an article that said many people have it and live normal lives with occasional flare-ups."

"But Annabel was afraid her eyes were affected," Cissy said. "Both her eyelids drooped, and she had double vision. She couldn't be an artist if she couldn't see. I think she put nicotine in her iced tea and drank it."

"Did she make her own tea?" Helen asked.

"Yes, with so much honey I couldn't drink the stuff. But all that sugar would hide the bitter taste of nicotine.

"She didn't drink her tea in class that day," Cissy said. "She took the lid off her thermos and kept it next to her, but never touched it. She put the lid back on when we left class. Then, when I put away our art supplies in my car, she gulped down all her tea at once. Like she finally got the courage to do it."

Helen replayed the scene in her mind: She remembered Cissy trying to get Margery to smoke e-cigarettes. Jenny and Yulia wanted Helen to sign up for the art class. They'd all waved good-bye to Yulia. And Annabel drank down nearly a full thermos of tea.

"I can see where that's possible," Helen said.

"I told the detective I didn't think Annabel was murdered," Cissy said. "She killed herself."

A horn blast from the drawbridge interrupted their conversation. The halves of the bridge began to rise, blue metal meeting blue sky. A black-hulled sailboat was the first through the opening.

"I wish I had the talent to paint that scene," Cissy said. "The sun sparkling on the water, the sleek black boat with the white sails, gears as big as trucks under the bridge."

"Way beyond my skill level," Helen said. "Could Annabel have painted it?"

"Oh, yes. She was definitely talented," Cissy said. "She not only painted a scene, she made you feel it. But she'd changed so much in the last few months. She was depressed, bad-tempered and impatient with me and her husband. Clay noticed that her technique was deteriorating and advised her to take Yulia's art class."

"Did you agree with him?" Helen asked.

"It was good advice," Cissy said. "Clay knows what he's doing. He had a New York career before he came here. I could see that Annabel's art was becoming more abstract, almost like graffiti. That's the trend now. Clay felt she needed more grounding and recommended Yulia."

"Clay didn't feel Annabel should experiment to find her own style?" Helen asked.

"Of course," Cissy said. "But even Picasso had classical training. You have to know what the rules are before you break them. And Annabel wasn't afraid to break the rules."

"What do you mean?" Helen asked. The ethereal Annabel didn't look like a rule breaker, but Helen didn't know her.

Cissy lowered her voice and looked around, making sure no one was near their table. "Annabel was quite wild in her youth. You know she had a lesbian lover." Cissy waited for her bombshell to explode.

"I'm not sure a lesbian affair qualifies her as wild," Helen said.

"Well, aren't we broad-minded," Cissy said, her voice sharp. "I thought you were from the Midwest, where people have standards."

"I am," Helen said. "But what some call standards are an excuse for harsh judgments."

Helen was relieved when the server brought their meals. Both women admired the artfully arranged food, then ate in respectful silence.

When Helen's salad was nearly finished, she returned to the conversation. "I've met all kinds of people living here in South Florida. I'm more live and let live."

Cissy stabbed the remains of her veggie burger so forcefully,

Helen wondered if she was annoyed. I should have let that go, she thought. I'm supposed to get her to talk, not give sermons.

"Do you think Annabel was a lesbian?" Helen asked.

"She was very open about her past," Cissy said. "She was a classic femme, and Miranda, the woman she had the affair with, was very butch."

"Uh," Helen said. This was suddenly too much information.

"Miranda was extremely handy," Cissy said.

"Handy how?" Helen asked.

"She was good at fixing things," Cissy said. "Annabel appreciated that about her and said Miranda had a real sense that she knew what she was doing."

"Ah," Helen said, not sure what to say.

"Plus Annabel thought Miranda looked hot in a white ribbed tank top."

Cissy's smile was sly. Helen knew she'd enjoyed that payback for the "live and let live" lecture. "Annabel told me that experimenting with women helped her know more about herself. She enjoyed her time with Miranda and then it was over."

"How did Miranda feel?" Helen asked. "Used?"

"No, Annabel and Miranda parted on good terms. But you can ask Miranda yourself. Her name is Storings, Miranda Storings. She's settled down with another woman in Wilton Manors. They run the Women's Pride Lawn Service. You can look them up on the Internet."

"May I get you ladies coffee or dessert?" the server asked.

"No, thanks," Helen said. "This was delicious."

"Just the check," Cissy said.

"Along with a good lunch," Helen said, "you've given me a lot to think about."

CHAPTER 11

Miranda Storings was tinkering with a mower on a workbench in the Women's Pride All Organic Lawn Service. The lawn service was in a turquoise garage in Wilton Manors, Fort Lauderdale's mostly gay neighborhood. The garage's concrete floor was covered with tools and parts and smelled pleasantly of cut grass and oil.

Miranda's short, spiked brown hair looked like it had been styled with a WeedWacker. A cigarette butt dangled from her lips, and Miranda's sweaty white ribbed tank top showed off her toned arms. She had a rainbow equal sign tattooed on her right biceps.

"You're Miranda Storings?" Helen asked.

"Yeah," Miranda said, and ground out her cigarette butt on the concrete floor. "You need some yard work?"

"No, I'm a detective," Helen said. "I'm looking into the murder of Annabel Lee Griffin."

She watched Miranda's face. Not a flicker. She pounded the mower's engine with a wrench, tightened something, then said, "Yeah, I heard she'd died. How was she killed?"

"Nicotine poison," Helen said.

"Huh," Miranda said. "I always thought she'd be shot."

Helen tried not to look surprised, but she doubted that she'd succeeded. "Who would shoot her?"

"Hugo," Miranda said. "He's her ex-husband. You know about him?"

"I've been told Annabel destroyed his chances for a national career."

"Yeah, she screwed him up good. He was asking for it, but she ruined his career. Not saying he didn't deserve it, but sweet little Annabel crushed that man."

"Can I ask you a few more questions?" Helen asked.

Miranda wiped her hands on a rag, stuck it in a back pocket, and said, "I'm finished with this. Come into my office."

Helen followed her into the next room. The beat-up brown desk looked like a thrift-shop special. Miranda's chair creaked when she sat down and she put her work boots on the desk.

Helen sat carefully on a tilted office chair with a duct-taped leather seat and faced a vibrant oil painting of a Caribbean cottage, sunshine slanting across the green yard, hanging over Miranda's desk.

"I love your painting," Helen said.

"Thanks." Miranda looked pleased. "My fiancée, Lita, did that. She's got talent, doesn't she? But I hear Annabel did, too."

"You had an affair with Annabel for a while," Helen said.

"Affair, fling, whatever you want to call it. She moved in with me for about six months."

"Annabel told some people that she was experimenting with her sexuality," Helen said.

"That's right," Miranda said. "You'd be surprised by the number of women who like a little walk on the wild side before they settle down with hubby in the burbs."

"Was Annabel gay?" Helen said.

"Annabel was whatever she wanted to be. I don't put labels on people. We had some fun and then it was over. She wasn't the love of my life. Not like Lita. Do you believe in love at first sight?"

"Yes," Helen said.

"That's how it was when I met Lita. *Pow!* Like she'd slammed me in the head. I used to be uncertain about marriage. But I wanted to marry Lita. I proposed a month after we met. We're getting married at her parents' place at Christmas."

"Congratulations," Helen said.

"Thanks," Miranda said. Was she blushing? Helen wondered.

"Annabel and me, we didn't have anything like that. I was kinda relieved when she left me to marry Hugo. We parted friends. Mind if I smoke?"

"Help yourself," Helen said.

Miranda lit another cigarette, striking a kitchen match on the sole of her boot.

"You didn't feel used when Annabel left you?" Helen asked.

Miranda laughed and blew out a stream of smoke. "It would be hard to tell who used whom," she said. "We got along and then it was over and we both moved on."

"You didn't want to see Annabel punished?" Helen asked.

"Like I said, I was relieved when she left," Miranda said. "If I'd wanted her punished, marrying Hugo was punishment enough. From the moment I saw that man, I knew he was bad news. Annabel was wildly in love. She thought Hugo was forceful when he was inconsiderate and she mistook his rudeness for manliness. She married the bastard, and did she ever regret it."

Helen thought Miranda could barely hide her glee.

"They've been divorced for years now, but after the divorce, Hugo still made life awkward for her. I was at a group art show in Miami that had her work, and Hugo was there. He made a big deal about buying her most expensive painting. Even outbid her husband. Everyone could tell Annabel didn't want Hugo to have it, but he insisted. It was like he had to own a piece of her."

"The gallery ignored her wishes?" Helen said.

"The gallery is in business," Miranda said. "Paintings by unknowns rarely bring that much. The bidding war helped her reputation.

"When Annabel ruined Hugo, she underestimated her ex. Hugo was relentless. I heard he was even taking lessons at her art class."

"He was," Helen said. "In fact, Hugo sat at her table in class the day she died."

"And I bet she hated it," Miranda said. "I can see her, sitting all scrunched up so he couldn't touch her."

That was the scene exactly, Helen thought. "How did you know?"

"Because I know—knew—Annabel. And I could read Hugo like a book. She got her revenge, but he made it clear she couldn't get away from him. Well, she's free of him now."

There was an awkward pause when both women realized exactly what that remark meant. "She paid for her freedom with her life," Helen said.

"I didn't mean to be flip," Miranda said. "I really am sorry she's dead."

"Did Annabel have health problems when she lived with you?"

"You mean the chronic fatigue syndrome? Yeah, she had some bad days, but she didn't let it get her down. Annabel was a fighter."

"Do you think Annabel killed herself?" Helen asked.

Miranda gave a barroom guffaw. "Hell, no," she said. "She might drive people to murder, but she'd never kill herself."

"For someone who split with Annabel some time ago, you still know a lot about her," Helen said.

"The South Florida art world is very small and my fiancée, Lita, keeps me current on the gossip."

That was a lesson Helen was constantly relearning: Fort Lauderdale, despite its fluid society, is a big small town. The snowbirds and tourists come and go, but the full-time residents make the real difference.

"My fiancée has an art space in FAT Village," Miranda said.

"The Fort Lauderdale arts district?" Helen asked.

"That one. Officially, the Flagler Arts and Technology Village. Fun place. Lots of warehouse studios, food trucks, bars and restaurants. It's a happening place, but Lita says I sound old-school when I talk that way.

"Annabel was sharing a studio space with Lita in FAT Village, and Clay, her husband, didn't like that. He didn't like FAT Village, which attracts the young talent in Fort Lauderdale. Clay said the place was self-indulgent, nothing but jumped-up graffiti artists. Clay believes in art with a capital *A*. Personally, I think he's washed up, and I'm not the only one.

"Annabel and Clay are names in the South Florida art world," Miranda said. "They're the subject of a lot of gossip. Lita thought Clay was jealous of his wife's success. She said Annabel was getting restless and talking about divorce."

"What about you?"

Miranda shrugged. "I thought Clay was way too controlling, but Annabel liked her men that way."

"Would Lita let me look at her and Annabel's studio?" Helen asked.

"If I ask her. She's really busy. You just can't barge in on artists. Lita doesn't get that much free time. She's my partner in the lawn service, too. But I'll set up an appointment for you."

"Thanks," Helen said.

"Are you sure you don't need a good organic lawn service?" Miranda asked. "I'd give you a good price."

"Thanks, but my landlady does the yard work," Helen said.

"Does she use pesticides?"

"Only ones registered with the EPA," Helen said.

"Doesn't make them safe," Miranda said. "Even the EPA says no pesticide can be considered safe."

"I couldn't interfere with Margery's domain," Helen said.

"Okay," Miranda said. "But if you can't get your landlady to be careful about what she sprays in the yard, at least be careful about what you use in your house. You got ants?"

Helen hesitated, then nodded.

"Most Florida houses do," Miranda said. "You can get rid of ants in your kitchen with a little ammonia and water in a spray bottle. If you want to keep them away, make a barrier with cinnamon. Smells nice and won't hurt your pets or your kids."

Miranda tossed the cigarette into a big jar overflowing with them.

"You save your cigarette butts?" Helen asked.

"Yep. I use them to make an organic spray. Nicotine kills aphids, thrips, leafhoppers and scale. Only works on young, soft scale, though, but it works."

"How do you make cigarette butts into bug spray?" Helen asked.

"I boil the cigarette butts. Takes about a hundred to make a decent spray, but it's all organic. They die naturally," she said, and grinned.

CHAPTER 12

Did Miranda kill Annabel with her homemade nicotine spray? What about Hugo? Or did Annabel kill herself?

Helen pondered these questions as she headed home in the Igloo. Jenny and Miranda were convinced that Hugo had murdered Annabel. Miranda thought Hugo would shoot his ex.

Hugo's definitely a candidate, Helen thought. He could have put the nicotine in her open thermos during art class. If Annabel used as much honey as Cissy said, it could hide the bitter taste when she gulped down her tea.

But Cissy really thought Annabel had committed suicide. *I told the detective I didn't think Annabel was murdered. She killed herself.* Was that lunch with Cissy at Kaluz only today? Helen felt like the dead woman had taken over her life.

Annabel was an artist. She was unstable, Cissy had insisted. Annabel might have had myasthenia gravis and she'd been afraid her eyes were affected. Annabel couldn't be an artist if she couldn't see.

But that diagnosis wasn't confirmed, Helen thought. Would Annabel give up so soon? Myasthenia gravis sounded scary, but treatment could allow her to live a mostly normal life.

Miranda had called Annabel a fighter. How strong a person was she? Did Annabel lose heart and decide she couldn't face another debilitating disease?

If so, why would Annabel commit suicide while she was with her art class, a group who would—and did—rush her to the hospital? Was the poisoned tea a cry for help?

I don't know, Helen thought. But I believe the police: Annabel was murdered.

Hugo looks like the main suspect—but who were Annabel's family, friends and rivals? What about her husband, Clay, another artist? Miranda had suggested that Clay's career was on the skids, while Cissy admired his talent and bragged about his New York career.

Who was right? What kind of man was Clay? Who loved and hated Annabel?

I don't know enough, Helen decided.

Phil's ringtone sounded on her cell phone, and she pulled the Igloo into a parking lot to take his call.

"There's a police detective here who wants to see you," Phil said. "He's waiting in our office."

"Burt Pelham?" she said. "The crimes against persons detective from Palmetto Hills?"

"That's him," Phil said. "He's already talked to Margery."

"He's talking to everyone who was in Annabel's art class," Helen said. "I'm five minutes away."

"Good. Don't forget, you can't tell him you're working Annabel's case without Jenny Carter's permission. It's Florida law."

"Oh. Right." More than once, the two private eyes had had to call their lawyer, Nancie Hays, when a police detective wanted to know about an investigation.

"I'll call Jenny now and see if she'll give me permission to tell Pelham," Helen said.

"Do you want me to call our lawyer?" Phil said.

"No need to rile Nancie yet," Helen said. "I can probably settle this with a phone call. Let's hope I can reach Jenny. I'll call her and then come straight home."

Helen was relieved when Jenny answered on the second ring. "Helen," she said. "Did you get Hugo already?"

Helen heard the hope in her client's voice and quickly crushed it. "No such luck. Detective Pelham from Palmetto Hills wants to talk to me, probably about Annabel's death. Do you want me to mention that I'm working on the case for you?"

There was a long pause. Then Jenny said, "Do you have to?"

"No," Helen said. "Florida law says you have to give me permission to even mention that you hired me."

"Then no," Jenny said. "I don't want him to know."

"If we work together, it might help us find Annabel's killer faster."

"I know who killed her," Jenny said. "I told Detective Pelham it was Hugo and explained why. Her ex had motive, means and opportunity. Pelham brushed off my suggestion. He said Hugo was a respected businessman—and he's not. Then he said poison was a woman's weapon. Even if you tell him you're investigating Hugo, he won't do anything."

Helen decided to set the record straight now.

"Jenny, I am investigating Hugo, but I'm also looking into other suspects, in case Hugo's not the killer."

"But he hated her."

Helen took a deep breath and tried again. "He has good reason to hate Annabel, Jenny. But we know almost nothing about the other people in her life. I want to catch her killer. What if he turns out to be someone else besides Hugo?"

The silence stretched on, until Helen was afraid Jenny would fire her. Finally, she said, "No, I want Annabel's killer caught. But keep that detective out of your investigation."

"If that's what you want."

"It's exactly what I want," Jenny said. "He made me feel like a stupid woman. I don't want Cissy to know either, or Yulia, our art teacher. It will only make trouble for me."

"There's no reason to tell any of them," Helen said. "I'd like to talk to your friend Robert Horton at RH Gallery. Can you text me his number?"

"Of course. I'll call him, too," Jenny said, and clicked off her phone.

Five minutes later, Helen parked the Igloo in the Coronado lot next to what she guessed was Pelham's unmarked white Dodge Charger. The sporty model was replacing the boxy Crown Victorias on many forces.

Phil met her at the Coronado gate and said, "I'll go with you."

The PI pair hurried up the stairs and into the Coronado Investigations office. Helen was relieved to see that Phil had cleaned the papers off both their desks. She was sure Detective Pelham would snoop when he was left alone—she certainly would.

The Palmetto Hills detective had commandeered one of the black-and-chrome club chairs. Helen thought he was trying to separate them. Phil dragged his chair next to the yellow client chair and sat beside Helen.

"Ms. Hawthorne?" the detective said, and introduced himself.

Definitely a northeastern accent, Helen thought, but she wasn't sure what kind, except he sounded like he belonged in *The Sopranos*.

"Have a seat," he said, inviting her to sit down in her own office.

Detective Pelham's hair was the brassy blond of a bad dye job. Did he color it himself or pay someone to do that to him? Helen wondered. It certainly didn't make his red, creased face look younger. His mouth was thin and disappointed and his nose was too big, but she thought it gave his face character. He wore a dark gray suit, white shirt and blue tie with a handcuff tie tack. Even in the air-conditioned office, he was sweating.

"How can I help you?" Helen asked.

"I'm looking into the death of Mrs. Annabel Lee Griffin," he said.

"I understand you were present the day she took sick. How long did you know her?"

"I didn't really know her," Helen said. "I was never introduced to her. I was touring the museum with my landlady, Margery, and we stopped to watch the last part of the painting class. Annabel was part of that class. Then Margery and I walked out to the parking lot with the class and the teacher, Yulia."

"What did you notice about Mrs. Griffin?" he asked.

"Not much," Helen said. "I liked her painting. She sat next to a man I later found out was her ex-husband, Hugo, and she tried to avoid touching him. She had an open thermos next to her easel. She was very pale and walked with a cane."

"What did Mrs. Griffin talk about during class?"

"Very little while I was there," Helen said. "One of the other students said she wanted to paint as well as Annabel, and Annabel said she was still perfecting her technique. Then the class was out of time and everyone packed up their supplies and walked to the parking lot."

"The Bonnet House lot?" the detective asked.

"No, the lot down the street where some buildings had been torn down. It wasn't a real parking lot. The Bonnet House lot was too crowded, so we parked there. Jenny, one of the women in the class, and Yulia, the teacher, talked me into taking the art class.

"Annabel drank most of her thermos while we talked. Later, she said she felt terrible and collapsed, right there. Dropped her cane and everything."

"Then what happened?" he asked.

"It was kind of confused. I called 911 and stayed on the line so the ambulance could find us. Annabel was violently sick and I think she had a seizure. Margery and Jenny tried to help her."

"What about Narcissa Bellanca?"

"Who?" Helen said.

"I think she uses the nickname Cissy."

"Oh, Cissy. I didn't know her formal name. Before Annabel got sick, she'd been trying to talk my landlady into using e-cigarettes. Cissy likes to vape. Then she packed up her art supplies and Annabel's—I think they came in the same car. While Annabel was really sick, I think Cissy sort of hovered around on the edges, and then she called Annabel's husband, Clay. It took her a while to track him down. Then she followed Jenny and the ambulance to the Palmetto Hills Hospital."

"Where was the teacher, Yulia Orel?" the detective asked.

"She'd left by then," Helen said.

"And Hugo Hythe?"

"Annabel's ex-husband? He showed up while that poor woman was lying there and stepped right over her body. He didn't offer to help at all."

Helen left out the part about Margery keying Hugo's car.

"And what did you do after the ambulance arrived?"

"There was nothing I could do, except get out of the way," Helen said. "The paramedics took over. Once Annabel went off to the hospital, I gave Jenny my card, with my cell phone number. She and Cissy followed the ambulance. Then Margery and I went home."

"And when did you start investigating Mrs. Griffin's murder?"

"I—" Helen said, and Phil squeezed her hand. Whoa! She'd nearly fallen for the detective's clever question.

"You know the law, Detective," Helen said. "I can't tell you if I'm investigating a case without the client's permission."

"And you don't have her permission?" he asked.

"I can neither confirm nor deny that I am investigating a case," Helen said.

"Don't stonewall me, Ms. Hawthorne," he said. "I know you're investigating Mrs. Griffin's death. I don't want you interfering with my investigation."

Before she could reply, Phil squeezed her hand, and Helen kept silent.

"I've read all about you," Pelham said, "and seen the videos about Coronado Investigations on local television. You've got the media buffaloed, but you don't fool me. You've had some lucky breaks, but you're still an amateur."

Phil squeezed her hand again, but Helen shook it off. "Lucky breaks!" she said. "That was damn good detecting."

"I'm a detective," he said, getting out of his chair. "You're an amateur. Don't meddle in my case. Good day."

He shut the office door so hard the jalousie windows rattled. Helen and Phil waited until he was on the sidewalk before Helen said, "That jerk!"

"Hey, you handled him fine," Phil said, returning his chair to its proper place. "I'm going to aid and abet your meddling. I went to Silver Glade Condominiums today for a formal interview, to make it look like I was just another person looking for a security guard job. I found out Clay Griffin has a studio on the nineteenth floor, overlooking the ocean."

"A house and a condo?" Helen said. "How does he afford that?"

"Fort Lauderdale real estate prices seem cheap by New York standards," Phil said.

"Not that cheap," Helen said. "I think I need to talk to the grieving widower."

CHAPTER 13

"Hey, Helen and Phil," Markos called, waving to the private eyes as they locked up their office for the night. "Come on down. I have mojitos and Texas caviar for the sunset salute."

Helen saw the other Coronado residents, Margery and Peggy, stretched out on adjoining chaises. Peggy wore a fresh pink sundress that shouldn't have worked with her dark red hair, but did. Margery looked summery in purple clam diggers and a lavender cotton top.

Both women raised tall, cool glasses and Peggy said, "Hurry! We've started without you."

The setting sun painted the old art moderne building a delicate pink at this hour, and a light breeze stirred the purple bougainvillea and rippled the turquoise pool.

Markos had turned one umbrella table into a buffet and another into a bar. The Cuban American hunk's tight white shorts and white tank showed off his light brown skin and dark hair. One curl fell over his forehead. Helen, ashamed she was gawking, tried to focus on the drinks.

"I could use an ice-cold mojito," she said. "Especially after the day I've had."

"I'm building your drink now," Markos said, and smiled, showing his white teeth.

Damn, even his teeth are beautiful, Helen thought.

As she approached the bar, Helen caught the sharp, pleasant aroma of fresh mint and lime wedges. Markos was working on Helen's drink with his wooden muddler, which looked like a miniature baseball bat. He put the mint leaves on the bottom of the glass, then added the lime and extra-fine turbinado sugar.

Helen inhaled the scent. "Intoxicating," she said. "And you haven't even added the rum yet."

"The trick is not to shred the mint," Markos said. "Now I add the ice and the rum." He garnished the glass with a thin lime slice and handed it to Helen.

She took a sip, and the tense time with Detective Pelham was washed away in a refreshing rush of lime and mint.

"Perfection," she said, and raised her glass to the bartender.

"May I make you one, Phil?" Markos asked.

"No, thanks," Phil said. "I'll get a beer from my place. Beer, anyone?" Margery, Helen and Peggy all said no.

Phil returned shortly with a cold green bottle of Heineken. "Did you say caviar, Markos? Is it black or red?"

"It's kinda both," Markos said.

"Caviar," Phil said, drawing out the word. "Love that salty, fishy taste. Goes well with a little chopped hard-boiled egg and onion on toast points."

Phil's lean features were lit with a smile of anticipation. "It can't be beluga—that's too expensive for a sunset salute. But it's all good."

His smile disappeared as he examined the umbrella table. "I see some beans and stuff and a plate of lettuce," he said. "But no caviar."

"That's Texas caviar in the green bowl," Markos said. "Next to the endive."

"Endive," Phil said, his voice hollow.

"Texas caviar is made with black-eyed peas," Markos said. "They're actually a legume. It also has corn, tomatoes, green peppers, jalapeño peppers, onions and Italian dressing. Oh, and I forgot—avocado."

"Avocado," Phil said.

Helen thought Phil looked a little green.

Markos, gorgeously clueless, rattled on. "I thought you'd like Texas caviar better than eggplant caviar."

"They make caviar out of eggplant?" Phil sounded like he'd just learned there was no Santa Claus.

"Roasted eggplant," Markos said, still smiling. "But I know you don't care for eggplant. Texas caviar is so much healthier than real caviar, which is loaded with salt and cholesterol."

"And flavor," Phil said.

"Texas caviar is loaded with flavor, too," Markos said. "Try it with sour cream."

Phil stayed motionless, as if a live snake were on the table.

Markos abandoned his makeshift bar. "Here, I'll fix you one."

Markos piled a sneaker-sized endive leaf with Texas caviar and a generous dollop of sour cream. "Here," he said. Now Phil couldn't avoid the legume-laden endive.

Helen couldn't watch. She downed the rest of her mojito. Margery hid behind a Marlboro smokescreen. Peggy tried to turn a snort into a cough.

"Have another," Markos said, while Phil gulped down most of his beer.

"No!" Phil said. "I have to go to work at midnight."

"Midnight?" Peggy said. "You investigating the Little New York burglaries, Phil? Which condo are you working for?"

Phil stalled.

"There were three more burglaries at condos in Little New York," Peggy said. "I heard it on the radio when I was coming home from work. Once again, thousands of dollars in gold coins were stolen."

"Really?" Phil said, finishing the last of his beer. "Do you remember the condo names?"

"I think one was Ventura Towers. Another was Bay-something and the third was Bombay or Taj Mahal, some name from India."

But not Silver Glade, Helen thought.

Phil looked relieved. "I need to get ready for work," he said. "See you all later."

"India!" Markos said. "I forgot—I've scored some Rangpur limes. They should be ripe in a couple of days, and then I can make Evelyn Bartlett's cocktail."

"Now, there's a woman who liked healthy food," Helen said. "Our Bonnet House guide told us the Bartletts grew their own Rangpur limes, star fruit, and avocados and flew in eggs, vegetables and meat from their farm in Massachusetts."

"Then I'll have to make healthy appetizers to go with Evelyn's cocktail," Markos said.

Poor Phil, Helen thought. I can't let that happen. "Why don't I investigate what the Bartletts served for appetizers?"

"Just buy the museum cookbook," Margery said.

"Does Bonnet House have one?" Helen asked.

"Every museum has a cookbook," Margery said. "I think it's some kind of law."

"If I could make real Bonnet House appetizers, that would be . . ." Markos stopped. "Amazing."

He was staring at the glamorous vision in a yellow bandage dress. Valerie Cannata, the Channel 77 investigative reporter. Her complexion glowed, her makeup was perfect and her long dark red hair was frizz free in the humidity. Her lively face defied the usual TV personality blandness.

"Hi, Helen, may I come in?" Valerie asked. Her high-style black heels clip-clopped on the pavement.

"Introduce me to your friends," she said. "I know your landlady, the amazing Margery."

"I'm Peggy." The red-haired renter shook Valerie's hand. Markos nearly leaped over the table to say, "I'm Markos."

Helen thought there was an electric connection when the two shook hands. She remembered Miranda the lawn service owner saying, *Do you believe in love at first sight?*

Valerie shook her head slightly, as if recovering from a blow, and said, "Helen, I heard you're investigating the murder of the artist Annabel Lee Griffin. What can you tell me about it?"

"Valerie, you know better," Helen said, and smiled to take out the sting.

"Then you are," Valerie said, talking faster now, "but I know you can't say anything yet. Promise me I'll get the scoop when the time comes."

Helen said nothing.

"I'll take that as a yes," Valerie said. Her cell phone gave a *ping!*

"Excuse me," she said, and checked her phone. "Gotta run."

"Wait," Markos said. "Can you come back in two nights? I'm making a special treat for the sunset salute: Rangpur lime cocktails from the original Bonnet House recipe. Please?"

"I think I have that night off," Valerie said, reaching into her purse for a business card. "Text me. Now I really have to go."

She gave the tanned, toned Markos one last look and sprinted toward the gate.

After Valerie left, Markos said, "She is so hot." He began packing up the mojito bar while Helen wrapped up the Texas caviar.

"She's nearly twenty years older than you," Peggy said, then looked embarrassed.

"I know," Markos said. "I just hope such a beautiful, accomplished woman will be interested in me. Good night, ladies."

Helen helped him carry the sunset salute supplies to his apartment. When she rejoined the two women, Peggy said, "I shouldn't have said that. I don't know why I did."

"Not proprietary, are we?" Margery asked. "He's a fine addition to the Coronado. Helen was practically drooling when she saw him tonight."

"I was not!" Helen said. "I'm a happily married woman."

"Just because you're on a diet doesn't mean you can't look at the menu," Margery said. Helen saw her landlady's alligator grin through the cigarette smoke.

"Daniel and I get along fine," Peggy said, which made Helen wonder if that were true. She remembered how Peggy had stared at Markos when he was swimming. Daniel was a good man, but Markos was the stuff of dreams. Peggy looked a little tired and pinch faced, but maybe it was the slanting late-day light.

"Markos is handsome," Peggy said. "But why would a successful woman like Valerie go out with a food-service student? She's an award-winning broadcaster, a Fort Lauderdale celebrity."

"Markos is hot. Isn't that enough?" Margery said.

"And Valerie just got out of a relationship with an international correspondent who was always flying off somewhere exotic and missing important events," Helen said. "She won six Emmys last year and had to go to the awards ceremony alone."

"Maybe she wants someone hot, loving and uncomplicated," Margery said.

Peggy made a clumsy attempt to change the subject. "While we're talking about hotties, Helen, is Phil working undercover at a Little New York condo tonight?"

"You know I can't talk about that," Helen said. But Peggy was bound to see him in his uniform.

"I thought so," Peggy said. "I hope he's careful. That burglar is slipping in and out of those places like a ghost. He could get violent if he's surprised."

CHAPTER 14

Next morning, Yulia breezed into the Bonnet House art class, looking fresh off the beach in stylish blue shorts and a striped top that highlighted her blond hair.

"Good morning to you," she said in her charming, slightly stilted English, and unpacked her art supplies.

"Today is your first class, Helen. Have you painted before?"

"Just the walls in my condo," Helen said.

"What do you want to paint?" Yulia said. "Flowers, nature, people, architecture? What calls to you?"

"I need to think about that," Helen said.

"Start with something that you like," Yulia said, "then decide if you want to be realistic, or make an interesting design. Your assignment is to come up with a subject by the next class."

She pulled four art magazines out of her carryall and said, "These might give you some ideas. You can paint from a photograph in a magazine, or take your own photo, or paint from life. I've given you much to think about. If you need something, just ask. I have to see my other students."

The rest of the class was working on their canvases. Helen thought Hugo's black horse was lumpy and graceless, rather like the artist. Hugo's pink polo shirt made him seem even more porcine.

Jenny was frowning at her seaside cottage. Cissy was covered with strings of brightly colored beads, as if she'd hijacked a Mardi Gras float. She was still torturing her hibiscus. "I wish it didn't look so flat," she said.

That hibiscus looks like it's been run over by a steamroller, Helen thought.

While Cissy and Yulia discussed the best way to highlight the hibiscus and give it more depth, Jenny whispered, "I have news. I'll tell you after class."

"I do, too," Helen said.

They both jumped when Yulia asked, "Does anyone know when poor Annabel will be buried? Will she have a funeral or a memorial service?"

"I don't think her body has been released yet," Jenny said. "At least that's what Detective Burt Pelham told me when he interviewed me."

Hugo snorted. "Pelham! Some detective. He couldn't find his ass with both hands. He's an idiot."

"I didn't think Pelham was an idiot," Jenny said. "The detective seemed thorough but clueless."

Yulia said, "He talked to me yesterday. He was very polite when he asked me many questions. I am scared of police. In my country, you never want to talk to them. But he seemed respectful. He had a funny accent and I had trouble understanding him."

Helen saw Jenny hide a smile. Yulia's accent was endearing.

"I told him I thought Annabel's death was an accident," Yulia said.

"How do you accidentally drink nicotine?" Jenny asked.

"See, I told you he was an idiot," Hugo said.

Cissy quit trying to add dimension to her lifeless hibiscus and said, "Annabel's death was no accident. She'd been despondent about her health. That's what I told the police detective. She killed herself. She was tired of fighting a debilitating disease."

"You're smarter than you look," Hugo said. Cissy flushed the same color as her hopeless hibiscus but glared at Hugo. He didn't notice.

"I agree, Cissy," Hugo said. "Annabel committed suicide. She was always trying to get attention. Well, this time she's the star of the show. Too bad she can't enjoy it."

"Hugo!" All four women shouted that same shocked reproach.

"What a terrible thing to say about a talented artist," Jenny said, her brown eyes lit with angry fire. "The detective said she was murdered."

"Didn't you call him thorough but clueless?" Hugo said. Helen thought his acid comments could have burned the paint off his canvas.

"Detective Pelham didn't decide that Annabel had been murdered," Jenny said. "He's investigating her death. The medical examiner said she'd been murdered."

"Oh, come on," Hugo said. "Who would murder Annabel? I mean, who'd care enough to want to kill her?"

Now the silence was deafening. Helen heard the squeak of the overhead fan and the raucous squawk of a bird somewhere in the trees.

Jenny opened her mouth and closed it, then spit out the words, "You would, Hugo. You'd kill her. You hated your ex."

Oh. My. God, Helen thought. I can't believe Jenny said that. If Hugo is the killer, she's made my job a dozen times harder.

Helen tried to signal Jenny to be quiet, but Jenny would not be silenced. She rushed on, "You killed Annabel because she ruined your career."

Hugo's laugh was harsh and ugly. "Me?" he said. "If I was going to kill that bitch, I would have done it years ago. I didn't realize it then, but she did me a favor. I'm glad I didn't get that job. The CEO they hired lasted as long as a sneeze. They fired him and he's *still* out of work. They fired the next one and then brought in a third and he's been fired. I still have a job."

Not much of one. Helen could almost see those words floating over Jenny's head. But she said nothing and concentrated on the shadows in her seaside cottage.

"Please," Yulia said. "This is a painting class. Let us paint. Who has a question about their work?"

"Do you think I should tone down the yellow in my sand?" Jenny said.

Yulia rushed over and the two women discussed ways to give the sand depth and texture.

The class painted in silence after that until Yulia said, "We are out of time. I'll see you tomorrow."

"I won't be here," Hugo said. "My car will be in the shop. Some bastard keyed it."

Helen stared hard at the yellow shutters on the Bonnet House windows, afraid to look at Jenny. They both knew who'd damaged Hugo's car.

She heard Cissy tell Hugo, "I don't understand how the medical examiner could get Annabel's cause of death so wrong."

"Let me tell you what I think," Hugo said as the two walked out together, Cissy's beads clacking, their dislike for each other forgotten.

Yulia looked tired but relieved that class was over. Jenny packed up her things and said, "Ready, Helen?"

"Am I ever."

Helen followed Jenny through a curlicued iron gateway to the Bonnet House veranda and the same view that had enchanted Frederic and Evelyn: two regal white swans skimming across the pond.

"I needed to see this to calm myself," Jenny said. "How dare Hugo and Cissy say Annabel killed herself? She had everything to live for."

"Of course they're wrong," Helen said. "I'll prove it when I find Annabel's killer. What's your news?"

Jenny took a deep breath. "I'm calm enough to talk now," she said. "Annabel's husband, Clay, is going to be rich. He took out a big life insurance policy on his wife."

"How do you know this?" Helen asked.

"Annabel told me. It's no secret. She thought he should have lots of life insurance on her after she had a bad bout with chronic fatigue syndrome a year ago."

"How could she get life insurance?" Helen asked. "Didn't she have a preexisting condition?"

"You can get life insurance if you have CFS," Jenny said. "Annabel even researched the companies for Clay."

"Does Clay have life insurance?" Helen asked.

"I don't think so," Jenny said. "So tell me your news."

"Clay has a studio on an upper floor of the Silver Glade Condominiums in Little New York."

Jenny whistled. "Nice. That's a premier building, built in 1965."

"That's old for South Florida," Helen said.

"We prefer historic," Jenny said, and managed a smile. "I've sold a few units in there. Silver Glade has a putting green on the front lawn, twenty-four-hour security, valet parking, two restaurants and a health room with a—"

Jenny stopped. "Sorry," she said. "I slid into real estate–ese. The penthouse is for sale and I'd give my right arm to split the commission on it. The owner is asking six million."

"Would Clay's condo go for that much?"

"No, but it costs a pretty penny and has a spectacular ocean view. All the upper-floor condos do. It's a perfect studio for him, since he paints seascapes. Do you have time for an early lunch?"

"No, I have an appointment with your gallery-owning friend, Robert Horton. I'd better hurry if I'm going to find parking on Las Olas."

"Good. Robert can tell you where Annabel and Clay fit into the South Florida art scene. Are you going to talk to Clay?"

"After I speak to Robert, I want to see the new widower at his studio."

"The soon-to-be-rich widower," Jenny said. "Exactly how brokenhearted do you think he is?"

"That's what I'll find out," Helen said.

CHAPTER 15

RH Gallery Ltd. intimidated Helen. She was sure the owner, Robert Horton, could look at her and know her late mother had been an art collector: Dolores had had twenty-six Precious Moments figurines.

The gallery entrance was old-school elegant, with green and orange striped awnings, gilt lettering and double mahogany doors. Helen pressed the buzzer. A pale twentysomething brunette in a subdued pinstripe suit sized up Helen and said, "May I help you?"

After Helen introduced herself, Ms. Pinstripe said, "I'm Sara, Mr. Horton's assistant. He's expecting you. Please come in. You may look at our seascape exhibit, and I'll inform Mr. Horton that you're here." She moved soundlessly through a door to the back and left Helen alone with thousands of dollars' worth of paintings.

Helen saw the security cameras bristling in the corners of the gallery. The floor looked like it was covered with a thick gray cloud. The walls were a soft, comforting white that showed the canvases in ornate gold frames.

To Helen's untrained eye, most of the art looked pleasant but conventional, postcard-pretty paintings of silvery moonlit oceans and orange sunsets over the water. They reminded her of the art she'd seen in corporate law firms. Several had red dots on their frames, a sign the paintings had been sold.

She was studying one painting of a storm-tossed sea. The stiff gray-blue waves looked like cake frosting. There was no sense of the ocean's movement or danger. It could have been a paint-by-numbers work. No wonder it hasn't sold, Helen thought.

"Ms. Hawthorne?"

Helen turned and saw a tall man with sandy blond hair. His stylish suit was another work of art: double-breasted with a nipped-in waist and slim-leg pants. He had the broad shoulders to carry it off. The dark fabric wasn't shiny, but it had the shape and sheen of expensive, well-cut cloth.

"I'm Robert Horton," he said. His handshake was dry and firm, a friendly greeting, not a test of strength. "Jenny said you needed to talk to me."

"Thanks for your time," Helen said. "I'm investigating the death of Annabel Lee Griffin."

"Such a tragedy," Robert said, and sighed. "Annabel was talented, no doubt about it. Her death is a real loss to the art world. I know Jenny hired you to find her killer."

Good, Helen thought. That makes my job much easier.

"I'm trying to get a perspective on the local art scene," she said, "and how Annabel and her husband, Clay, fit into it. I understand he's an artist, too. Jenny said he paints seascapes."

"You're looking at one now," Robert said.

"Oh," Helen said. She didn't want to say anything critical about the clunky painting. She tried to think of how to praise it.

"It's very precise," she said.

"That's one way to describe it," Robert said. "Why don't we go back to my office where we can talk?"

Robert's office was a pale gray windowless room, dominated by a vibrant cobalt blue painting of humpback whales. Two black leather chairs were arranged in front of the painting, as if it were an exhibit at a seaquarium.

"Is that a Robert Wyland?" Helen asked.

"You know Wyland's work?" Robert looked pleased.

"I know he did a huge marine-life mural on a building in Key Largo," Helen said.

"The four-story building at Mile Marker ninety-nine point two," Robert said. "Stunning. It's part of Wyland's one hundred Whaling Walls." He smiled proudly. "This is my own whaling wall. I look at it every day and dream I'm at the ocean. Would you like some coffee?"

"That would be nice," Helen said. "Black, please."

Robert filled two white china cups from a carafe on the credenza and handed one to Helen. They each took a black leather chair by the huge Wyland.

"Now, what do you want to know about Clay?"

"Is he a good artist?" Helen asked.

"His work is precise, as you said, but it's . . . well, lifeless," Robert said. "There's no passion in his art. With Wyland, you can feel his love of the sea and its creatures."

"But you carry Clay's work," Helen said.

"For now," Robert said. "If his painting doesn't sell at this show, I won't be representing him anymore."

Helen must have looked startled. Robert said, "I've already discussed the issue with Clay, Ms. Hawthorne. He knows."

"I heard that Clay had a New York career," Helen said.

"He got off to a good start," Robert said. "He was in New York for many years, represented by a Chelsea gallery. Then he got dropped. His work wasn't exciting or innovative enough for New York. He moved here and became a big frog in this very small pond. He had some success in Fort Lauderdale for a while—anyone with New York connections will sound impressive in Fort Lauderdale, but Clay hasn't taken his art to a new level. He's gotten comfortable and paints the same picture over and over."

"What's the next level?" Helen asked. "Should he try to get back to New York?"

"Clay is smart enough to know that door is closed unless he has a really lucky break. He should be trying for shows at Miami galleries. Miami is the gateway to South America and a major player in the art world. There are a lot of rich collectors who haunt those galleries. Are you familiar with Art Basel in Miami Beach?"

"A little," Helen said. "It's a big art show held there in early December."

"It's a big *international* art show that brings in major collectors from around the world."

"The exhibits look like fun," Helen said. "Phil and I saw the giant rubber duck."

"Miami artist Alexander Mijares wrapped the giant rubber duck at the SLS Hotel, and then filled the swimming pool with painted replicas."

"And that's taken seriously?" Helen asked, then wished she hadn't. She sounded like a rube.

"Absolutely," Robert said. "Art Basel in Miami Beach has contemporary artwork from all over the world, and nearly a hundred thousand international visitors—artists, collectors and curators. It's exciting. You've seen Clay's work. It's too . . ." He hesitated.

"Conventional?" Helen finished, though that described most of the work in Robert's gallery. Still, the gallery owner must be doing well if he could afford a huge Wyland.

"Uninspired," Robert said.

"Clay can't make it to the international level," Helen said. "He doesn't take chances. He plays it safe."

"Yes," Robert said. "That's it exactly."

"Can Clay make a living in Fort Lauderdale as an artist?" Helen asked.

"No, but very few artists can," Robert said. "Clay teaches at Fort Lauderdale Junior College."

"That must be quite a comedown," Helen said.

"Not really," Robert said. "There's no shame in it. Most artists need either a rich spouse or a day job. They teach workshops and college classes to survive.

"Clay was luckier than most. His junior college post doesn't pay much, but he works forty hours a week, so he has health insurance, and he needed that for his wife. Annabel was his student, you know."

"No, I didn't," Helen said.

"Everyone went to their wedding on the beach. Annabel was a beautiful bride. They had the reception at his studio in Blue Heron Crescent."

"How could Clay afford an expensive condo studio," Helen asked, "plus a big house in Coral Ridge Country Club Estates when he had a sickly wife?"

"I'm not sure he can," Robert said. "Clay told me he'd sold his New York co-op for a nice chunk of change. He couldn't believe how cheap Fort Lauderdale real estate was."

"Cheap? You're kidding," Helen said.

"Compared to Manhattan, real estate is cheaper here. But Clay said that when he first moved here. I think the costs were getting to him. I know he's been trying to get extra money teaching workshops and master classes."

"Besides his full-time job at the junior college?" Helen asked.

"Exactly. He's giving dreary lessons at country clubs and women's clubs. He complained it left him little time for his own work. Frankly, it showed. He needs to get out from under his financial burdens.

"Clay took some of his work to the Huffington Gallery, where he has to pay to display his paintings," Robert said.

"Is that like vanity publishing?" Helen asked.

"Not exactly," Robert said. "Some artists pay galleries to show their work and that's a legitimate move. But the Huff—I call it the Huff and Puff—is for artists on the way down. It's a desperate attempt to keep a career going. Once artists show in a place like the Huff, their careers rarely bounce back."

"That's very sad," Helen said.

"What's sad is the person with the real talent was his wife, Annabel. We carried her work and it sold. I had trouble keeping her oils in stock."

"I've seen only one of her paintings," Helen said, "and it wasn't finished. I've heard they're good."

"I have one I'm holding for a client who's in Italy right now," Robert said. "Too bad I sold it before she died. Now I can't raise the price. I'll show you. That sounded awfully crass, didn't it?"

He came back with a medium-sized canvas with a black crow perched in a flame tree. The colors glowed.

"Gorgeous," Helen said.

"Her work was starting to get more abstract and playful. She was finding her own style," Robert said. "Annabel used to paint at their home, but then she rented studio space in FAT Village."

"So Annabel was on her way up," Helen said.

"To the very top," Robert said. "She was invited to join a prestigious group show in Miami and her work did well there. Her prices were starting to go up, and I can't charge my clientele that much. I was going to ask her if she'd paint some smaller pieces for me. Some artists won't compromise, but I'd hoped she would. If she'd kept going, she would have been at Art Basel in another year or two."

"They take local artists?" Helen asked.

"A very few, but there was talk she might be one of them."

"If Annabel was so good, why was she taking lessons at Bonnet House?"

"Her husband convinced her she needed to work on her technique. Clay told her that Picasso couldn't succeed at Cubism until he became an accomplished representational painter. 'The bones have to be there,' he said."

"Did you agree with Clay?" Helen asked.

"I thought he was stifling a major talent," Robert said. "But then, I wasn't married to him."

CHAPTER 16

Little New York was perfectly named, Helen thought. Someone set a slice of Manhattan on a South Florida beach. Too bad they missed the point.

Florida architecture is light and playful, sun drenched and colorful.

Little New York buildings were grim gray slabs, with no subtropical softness. They looked like they were wearing business suits to the beach. The only concessions to Florida were grudging balconies and huge windows overlooking the ocean.

Silver Glade Condominiums was on the curve of Blue Heron Crescent, the official name for Little New York. The condo looked like every other building, except for that peculiar putting green. But then, New Yorkers convinced themselves that worn patch of green known as Central Park was a real city park.

No wonder Clay Taylor Griffin moved here, Helen thought as she pulled into the condo's circular drive. He probably felt like he was still in Manhattan.

A white-uniformed valet hurried over to park Helen's car and a uniformed doorman with more braid than a marching band opened the silver doors with a flourish.

The Silver Glade lobby was high ceilinged and metal cold, with steel chandeliers and a polished marble floor. The reception desk was a swirl of black marble manned by a security guard with a Brooklyn accent. He was Billy, according to his name tag, but this guard was no gray-haired retiree. Helen guessed his age as mid-forties, and his narrow eyes were shrewd.

"May I help you?" Billy asked.

"I'm here to see Mr. Clay Taylor Griffin," she said.

"Is Mr. Griffin expecting you?"

Helen stalled. She didn't think she could charm her way past steely-eyed Billy. How can I get upstairs without an appointment? she wondered. Better play dumb.

"Mr. Griffin is a famous artist," she said. "I'm supposed to see him about his paintings. He said he wants to paint me."

Is the guard smirking? Helen wondered. She wasn't sure in the lobby's dim light.

"Mr. Griffin's wife just died, ma'am," Billy said.

"Oh," Helen said. "I'm so sorry. Is he home? I'd like to pay my condolences."

"He's making the arrangements for Mrs. Griffin's funeral," Billy said, his voice as cold as the wind off the East River.

"Of course," Helen said. "I'll come back later."

She was glad to escape Billy's disapproval. Outside, the valet held open the Igloo's door. She climbed inside and switched on the radio, catching the afternoon news.

The announcer's voice was solemn. "The Gold Ghost burglaries turned deadly last night," he said, "when an elderly man was killed during a break-in. Alexander Woodiwiss, age ninety-two, was beaten to death in his condo on the nineteenth floor of the Exeter Arms Condominiums in Blue Heron Crescent.

"Mr. Woodiwiss, who lived alone, was discovered by his cleaning woman at eight o'clock this morning when she showed up for work.

"A police spokesperson said the victim, dressed in pajamas and slippers, had been fatally attacked with a lamp in his living room sometime after midnight," the announcer said. "Police believe the victim was awakened when the thief made a noise and went to investigate. More than twenty thousand dollars in gold coins are believed to be missing from Mr. Woodiwiss's condo. No other units were robbed at the Exeter Arms last night."

The Gold Ghost took the money and ran, Helen thought. But not before he beat to death a defenseless old man. Now Phil will really feel the heat. He has to catch this creep before someone else gets killed.

Helen hadn't taken the burglaries seriously before this news. She didn't have much sympathy for gold hoarders. But bashing an unsuspecting old man with a lamp was pointless and cruel. This burglar was a dangerous hothead.

She hurried home to tell Phil the news and found him in his apartment, dressing for work. Helen sat down on his bed and said, "You've heard about the murder at the Exeter Arms?"

"Just heard," Phil said. "Silver Glade was already in an uproar over the break-ins. That poor old man's murder has them terrified."

"Did the Silver Glade manager call you?" Helen asked.

"Yep," Phil said. "Victor said everybody knew Alex Woodiwiss. He played golf with some of the residents at Silver Glade, and a couple of the condo widows had their eye on him. Alex was six feet tall, a good dancer, and he could drive at night."

"So he was a senior hunk," Helen said.

"Definitely. Victor said golf made Alex surprisingly strong. Victor thinks Alex put up a fight. He was a decorated World War II veteran. Mrs. Cassidy, who went dancing with him Friday nights, was distraught. She stormed into Victor's office as soon as she heard the news, leading a brigade of outraged residents. They wanted to know what Victor planned to do to protect them.

"The condo board is holding an association meeting at seven tonight to discuss the issue. I have to go into work now and talk to Victor. Maybe we can set some kind of trap for the Gold Ghost. The problem is, if we do come up with a plan, we can't discuss it at the meeting. We'll have to give vague assurances that won't satisfy anyone."

"Why? Are you worried about gossip?" Helen asked.

"That's one reason," Phil said. "A condo is a small village. Everyone knows their neighbors' business: who has visitors, who drinks too much, who fights with their spouse and who has money trouble.

"Besides, we suspect these burglaries are inside jobs."

Phil shooed Thumbs off his navy uniform pants. Helen brushed the cat hair off the dark fabric while Phil buttoned his medium blue uniform shirt. She thought that color looked good on her silver-haired spouse. The tailoring accented his broad shoulders and slim hips. Phil had pulled his long hair back into a ponytail. She was glad Silver Glade didn't make him cut it.

"Are you worried that Silver Glade will be hit next?" Helen asked.

"It's bound to happen eventually," Phil said. "The burglar is getting bolder. I want to force the issue and make it happen, before more people get hurt."

Helen looked at her husband in his uniform: straight shoulders, slightly crooked nose, blue eyes. Phil looked confident. Overconfident, Helen thought, and felt a stab of fear. One well-placed blow, and that burglar could smash their life.

"I'm worried about you," she said, wrapping her arms around him.

"You worry too much," he said, kissing her.

Helen held him and said, "I stopped by Silver Glade today to see Clay. The guard, Billy, said Clay was planning Annabel's funeral."

"Billy's an ex-cop," Phil said. "I haven't met him yet, but I learned some things about Clay while I was on rounds with Jimmy, the graveyard shift guard."

"Tell me," Helen said, pulling away.

"Jimmy says Clay has an eye for the ladies. He brings art students to his studio for extra instruction."

"Maybe he does," Helen said.

"Jimmy said the women never have any art supplies, sketch pads or portfolio cases."

Like me, Helen thought. That's how I showed up today.

"So that's why Billy was smirking at me," Helen said. "I didn't imagine it. He thought I was one of Clay's cookies."

"And you were chasing Clay when his wife was barely cold," Phil said. "You hussy." He grinned at her.

"That rat, cheating on his sick wife."

"The staff liked Annabel, but they can't stand her husband. He talks about being a New York artist and brags about what a good observer he is. Clay doesn't realize the elevators have cameras, so the guards can see him doing the wild thing with his so-called students on the way up to his floor."

"Poor Annabel," Helen said. "She was a good artist but had no talent for picking men."

Like me, she thought, before I met you. "I miss you," Helen said, kissing Phil's ear. "I don't see much of you now that you're working the late shift. I was asleep when you left last night, and you were asleep when I got up this morning. We don't get a chance to talk."

"Or anything else," Phil said, kissing her back. "If I didn't have to leave right now . . ." He pulled away, and Helen rubbed her lipstick off his ear.

"Is it boring working the graveyard shift?" she asked.

"We had some excitement: Jimmy and I got a call that a visitor's car was parked in a resident's spot."

"You don't think that was the burglar?" Helen asked.

"No, it was a resident's grandson. Grandma vouched for him and he moved his car to a legal spot. Oh, and I have an admirer."

"Already? That was fast."

"Jimmy says Nancy admires anyone in a uniform. She's single and hangs around the reception desk. She brought me homemade lasagna for dinner." He patted his flat stomach.

"Quite the welcome wagon," Helen said.

"That's the problem," Phil said. "Jimmy warned me that Nancy can be a cougar."

Helen's eyes narrowed. "How old is this single woman?" she asked.

"Jimmy says she's sixty-five," Phil said.

"So nothing for me to worry about," Helen said.

"Don't be so sure," Phil said. "Caitlyn Jenner was the hottest woman in America at age sixty-five."

Helen threw a pillow at him, and Phil ducked.

"I'll walk you out to your car," she said.

Out by the pool, Markos was setting up his mojito bar on the umbrella table. "Hey, Helen and Phil," the resident hunk said. "Have a mojito and some collard greens rolls with *umeboshi* paste."

"What's *umeboshi* paste?" Helen asked.

"Dried pickled green Japanese plums," he said. "There's nothing like it."

"I bet," Phil said. Helen gave Phil a light kick on the shin.

"Wish I could," Phil said. "But I have to go to work."

"I hope you'll make tomorrow's sunset salute," Markos said. "The Rangpur limes will be ripe and I'm making Evelyn Bartlett's famous cocktail."

"I'll make the Bonnet House appetizers," Helen said quickly. She could pick up the museum cookbook when she went to her art class. She wanted Phil to enjoy the rare cocktails with food he could eat.

"Fix me a mojito, please, Markos," she said. "I'll be right back."

As Phil climbed into his dusty black Jeep, Helen said, "Be careful. The Gold Ghost is dangerous. He's killed once."

"I'm not worried about that coward," Phil said. "The real danger is the old codgers at Silver Glade. Victor said they're roaming the halls with weapons.

"Mr. Thornton in 717 had a Luger he'd liberated from the Nazis.

"Mrs. Cassidy wanted to patrol the lobby with her late husband's shotgun until Billy convinced her to keep it upstairs. She said she was a crack shot, but Billy questioned her until she finally admitted she hadn't been to a firing range in twenty years."

"It's not funny," Helen said. "What if you're shot by some gun-slinging senior?"

"Not a chance they'll hit me," Phil said. His last kiss was hot, but his words chilled her.

CHAPTER 17

Helen heard a key rattling in the lock and sat up in bed. She'd slept in Phil's apartment last night, comforted by his familiar coffee-and-citrus smell on the sheets.

"Phil?" she said.

"It's me," he said.

Helen came running into the kitchen and threw her arms around her tired-looking husband. "You're safe!"

Phil laughed and kissed her. "Of course I'm safe."

"I was afraid you'd be shot by a pistol-packing senior," Helen said.

"They were all in bed by nine o'clock," he said. "Mr. Thornton came down at five o'clock this morning, but without his World War II Luger. He told me there were no gold coin burglaries during the night. His grandson is on the force. Maybe Alex Woodiwiss's murder scared off the burglar."

"How was the condo meeting?" Helen said.

"As we expected. The residents are scared and angry. They didn't buy our reassurances that management has a plan in place."

"Do you?" Helen said.

"Victor and I are working on one. You look like you didn't sleep a wink."

"I didn't," Helen said. "I was too worried."

He kissed her again, harder and more insistent. "You need to go to bed," he said. "Right now."

"Don't you want some food?" she said between kisses.

"Later," he said. He picked her up and carried her into the bedroom.

"You swept me off my feet," she said, and giggled.

"You talk too much," he said, climbing into bed with her, and for a long time, they didn't talk at all.

Afterward, Helen fell asleep in Phil's arms, then woke up suddenly at eight thirty-four. The bed was empty and the apartment perfumed with coffee. Phil breezed into the bedroom wearing the blue robe that matched his eyes and handed her a mug of coffee.

"Morning, sunshine," he said and smiled.

"Coffee! You saved my life," Helen said. "I have to run to my art class."

"Not for another hour," Phil said. "You have time for a cheese omelet. I'll make it while you shower."

Helen sang while she showered. Phil was home safe, and all was right in her world. The omelet, oozing cheddar, was ready by the time Helen was dressed.

Thumbs the cat yowled when she came into the kitchen. "I already fed him," Phil said. "He's panhandling for a second breakfast."

Helen finished her food and gathered her art supplies. Her blank white eight-by-ten canvas glared at her. I don't have a subject yet, she thought. I'm about to fail my first assignment. All the way to Bonnet House, she wondered what she should paint.

My cat? Too ordinary, Helen decided. Phil? She thought her husband looked like a Regency dandy, but she didn't have the skill to capture his elegant face. She parked the Igloo at Bonnet House and studied the flowers and trees on the path to the yellow-painted gift shop, hoping for inspiration. Nothing.

She had time to buy the cookbook for the Rangpur lime cocktail party appetizers. At the gift shop register was a slender woman with high cheekbones, ivory skin and silver hair the same color as Phil's. Up close, Helen guessed her age to be sixtysomething. Maybe I need to take that Silver Glade cougar more seriously, she thought. Maybe this woman is another example of that predator.

"Do you have a cookbook?" Helen asked.

"Absolutely," the gift shop cougar said. *"Entirely Entertaining in the Bonnet House Style."* She pulled a slim volume off a bookshelf.

"Does it have appetizers?" Helen asked.

"Appetizers, soup, main courses, desserts, even Mrs. Bartlett's Rangpur lime cocktail. They grow the limes here, you know. We have some in that basket. You can donate a dollar for one."

"Really?" Helen said. "Can you cut one open?"

"Of course." The gift shop cougar disappeared into the small kitchen behind the register and returned with a lime sliced into quarters.

Helen studied the juicy orange-red fruit. She remembered last night's mojito, frosty cold and crowned with mint.

She imagined Evelyn's cocktail as it would be served tonight: rum, maple syrup, and this shimmering juice in a short glass. Liquid inspiration. Now she knew what she would paint.

"Perfect," Helen asked. "I'll take the book and six limes, including the cut one."

The cougar bagged the limes. On the short walk to art class, Helen decided she was unfair. Not every attractive older woman was a man stealer.

Helen took her seat at the art class next to Jenny. Her friend was still working on her beach cottage. Hugo, who looked like a frankfurter in a red polo shirt, was still dabbing at his black horse. Cissy, a mass of loops and whirls in a beige cotton crocheted outfit, was still struggling to unflatten her flower.

Yulia looked especially somber in black shorts and a baggy gray top, and when she greeted the class, Helen knew why.

"I have an announcement," Yulia said. "Annabel's memorial reception will be tomorrow morning at ten o'clock at her husband Clay's studio in the Silver Glade Condo. Do you all know where that's at?"

"Everybody knows where Little New York is, especially after the burglaries," Jenny said. The others nodded.

"Out of respect for Annabel, we will not have class tomorrow. I will be too sad to work."

"Me, too," Cissy agreed.

"Will Annabel be buried in Fort Lauderdale?" Jenny said.

"She's being cremated," Yulia said. "Her ashes will be sent home to her aunt in Connecticut. She has no other family."

"Except for Clay," Jenny said.

Who doesn't want his wife's ashes, Helen thought.

"Clay told me that Annabel's aunt Ruth is eighty-five and too old to fly alone," Yulia said. "She wants to bury Annabel's ashes next to her parents. Aunt Ruth also plans to be buried there, and she wants to keep the family together. From what Clay said, it won't be long before the old woman is reunited with her family. I just hope that detective finds Annabel's killer soon and gives her poor aunt Ruth some closure."

"Fat chance with that detective," Hugo said. "He couldn't catch a cold."

"Someone will get her killer," Jenny said. "Even if the police can't."

"Really?" Hugo said, glaring at her. "Now, who's gonna do that, huh?"

"I—" Jenny said.

Helen gently elbowed Jenny to remind her to keep quiet.

"I just know," Jenny said.

"Yeah, you really know," Hugo said. "You think I killed her. But your precious detective doesn't. He interviewed me and moved on. He's still looking, and he's so stupid, he'll never find the killer. No one will."

"We have to find Annabel's killer," Jenny said. "It will comfort her poor aunt."

"Her aunt needs to accept that Annabel took her own life," Cissy said. "She was so unwell and so depressed."

Helen thought Jenny made a small growl, but she didn't say anything as Cissy babbled on, "I hope death brought her peace."

"It's certainly brought me peace," Hugo said.

Once again, Hugo had shocked the class into uneasy silence. Yulia broke it when she stopped by Helen's table. "So have you decided on a subject to paint?" she asked.

"A still life with Rangpur limes," Helen said. "In honor of Evelyn's favorite cocktail." She produced the bag of limes. "I have a title, too. 'Still Life with Rangpur Pyramid.'"

"Sounds mysterious," Cissy said.

Yulia held Helen's small canvas so it was first vertical, then horizontal. "And which way will you use your canvas?" the art teacher said.

"Uh, I hadn't thought about that," Helen said.

"You're working with shapes in two dimensions, not three," Yulia said. "How will you use your shapes? You have the limes, but what else will be in your picture?"

"I want to use a fat-bellied glass pitcher from home," Helen said. "I like the shape. I'll fill the pitcher with that cocktail, then have the short glasses and maybe a bucket of ice along with the pyramid of limes."

Helen could see the drink ingredients shimmering on her canvas. She could almost taste them.

"Good," Yulia said. "Remember that painting is about light against dark. Think about where you will have your light and how you will balance your shapes. You don't have to draw anything today. Thinking is important."

The teacher moved on to Jenny. "Your sand has excellent texture," Yulia said, then glided over to Hugo and his tormented horse. The creature was turning into a misshapen blob.

"A few highlights would improve your work," Yulia said. "May I?"

With a few deft strokes, she was transforming Hugo's hunchbacked horse into a high-stepping animal, until he shouted, "Get your freaking hands off my work."

His face was as red as his shirt and he was literally spitting mad. "It's my horse and I'll paint it the way I want, without interference from some foreigner who barely speaks English."

"I'm sorry, Hugo," Yulia said, her pale face pink with embarrassment. "I asked permission."

"And did you hear me give it? I'm outta here." He threw his paint tubes into his carryall and dumped his turpentine brush cleaner into the plants along the loggia. "Don't expect me back!"

Helen hoped Yulia would say, "Good," but she looked stricken. "Hugo," she said. "I'm sorry. Please come back."

But he stomped off, holding the wet painting against him. Helen hoped the oil paint would ruin his shirt.

No one in the class stopped him. Helen thought she could feel the class's relief when he passed through the curlicued wrought-iron gates.

"It's my fault," Yulia said. "I should have never touched his work. That was unforgivable."

"Bull!" Jenny said. "You touch up our work all the time. That's why we're in this class. Hugo's a jerk and I'm glad he's gone."

He's more than a jerk, Helen thought. That man has a hair-trigger temper. No wonder Jenny thinks he killed Annabel.

CHAPTER 18

"Have you been avoiding me?" Cissy asked.

"Me?" Helen said, her voice a guilty squeak. She'd been hoping to escape Bonnet House without running into Cissy. Now she was trapped. Cissy was smoking her e-cigarette by the Igloo, blocking Helen's way to her car.

"I want to talk to you about Annabel," Cissy said. "I know you agree with Jenny, but Hugo and I believe she killed herself."

"You agree with him?" Helen said. She couldn't hide her contempt. "After that scene in class today?"

"I know he behaved badly," Cissy said, and blew out a puff of smoke. "But he's an alpha male."

"There's no such thing," Helen said. "Don't excuse his behavior."

"I'm not," Cissy said. "But people aren't black-and-white. Hugo can be extremely kind."

"He can?" Helen's disbelief was obvious.

"Let me tell you about it at lunch—and about Annabel, too," Cissy said. "My treat."

I'm a detective, Helen told herself. I can't interview only the people I agree with. I have to find Annabel's killer. Cissy gave me good information about Annabel before. She could hold the key to this case.

"Lunch it is," Helen said. "Where do you want to go?"

"If you like Mexican, we can go to Casa Frida. It's not your usual taco joint, although Frida's serves those, too." Cissy was almost pleading now.

"Sure," Helen said. "That's the restaurant on Federal Highway, two blocks north of Commercial."

"See you there," Cissy said. She ran for her car, curls and crochet bobbing lazily in the heavy air.

The hot sun bleached the sky white. Once again, Helen was grateful for the Igloo's air-conditioning. She heard the *ping* for a text message on her cell phone.

Miranda, the lawn service owner and Annabel's former lover, had texted, *Lita can C U @ 2 PM 2day*, and included her fiancée's phone number and FAT Village studio address. Helen confirmed the appointment with Lita, then headed for Casa Frida. After passing endless strip shopping malls, she sailed right past the restaurant and had to make a U-turn.

Inside, Casa Frida was a small, brightly painted restaurant honoring Mexican artists Frida Kahlo and her husband, Diego Rivera. Framed prints of their art, as well as Day of the Dead figurines and grinning skulls, gave the restaurant a cheerfully morbid charm. Cissy waved to her from one of the last empty tables. She was drinking a Mexican beer and eating chips and salsa. "This place fills up fast," Cissy said, proud of her culinary discovery. "Have some pico de gallo and chips."

Helen took a scoop of the salsa, fragrant with cilantro, and read the menu. She ordered Mayan roasted pork and iced tea and Cissy had the ceviche Caesar salad.

They dipped corn chips into the flavorful red sauce and talked between crunches. "You were going to tell me about Hugo's good deeds," Helen said.

"Yes," Cissy said. "I've seen them. Hugo's mother, Linda, is a widow with Parkinson's disease."

"That's tough," Helen said.

"It is. Linda can still get around without a walker, but she's a little unsteady. She lives a few doors down from me, off Bayview."

"Lots of big houses there," Helen said. "Does she live alone?"

"Linda didn't want to leave the home she's had all her adult life, so Hugo lives with her since he split with Annabel."

Rent-free, Helen thought.

"The house is huge, and it needs constant upkeep," Cissy said. "Hugo handles everything: the yard service, pool service, and repair people. He has the house power washed for mold and freshly painted."

So he earns his keep, Helen thought. Their lunch arrived and they admired the artfully arranged food. Helen's roasted pork was orange-red from the achiote paste and bitter orange juice marinade. Cissy photographed her salad with her cell phone. They savored their meal in silence until Helen prompted, "So Hugo takes care of the house for his mother."

"He does more than that. He keeps up on the latest advances in Parkinson's treatment. He heard about a clinical trial sponsored by the Michael J. Fox Foundation."

"He's the actor with Parkinson's, right?" Helen said.

"Right. He still acts, too, even with his disability. His foundation is supporting a clinical trial to treat early stage Parkinson's patients with nicotine patches."

"The patches people take to quit smoking," Helen said.

"Right," Cissy said. "There's no proof yet, and Hugo's mother couldn't get into the study, but he gets her nicotine patches. I think a sympathetic doctor is helping him. Hugo told me the patches seem to help his mother a little. He takes her to see all sorts of doctors and pays for everything that's not covered under Medicare.

"So Hugo can be dislikeable, but he's good to his mother," Cissy said.

Helen wasn't sure that proved anything. She'd read about serial killers who loved their sweet old mothers. And he was getting a free home. Rather than say anything, Helen sampled her red pickled onions and beans and rice.

"Clay, Annabel's husband, is another unsung hero," Cissy said.

"He is?" Helen asked. That's not what Robert Horton thought. She decided she couldn't say anything if she had a mouthful of pork. She had to be careful if she wanted to learn more about Clay.

"Annabel's depression and her illness made her difficult to live with," Cissy said.

"How?" Helen said, reaching for a tortilla.

"Whiny, short-tempered. She'd stay in bed all day and expect Clay to wait on her. But he never complained. He encouraged her to get up and work on her art and gave her helpful suggestions to improve it.

"Clay and Annabel could have lived in his art studio—it's certainly big enough."

"You've been there?" Helen asked.

"For lessons," Cissy said. "It has a fabulous view of the ocean. It inspired him. But Clay kept that big house in Country Club Estates because Annabel loved painting nature. She said she needed the flowers and birds in the yard for inspiration. That poor man wore himself out trying to pay for that huge house and his studio. And then she turned around and rented a FAT Village studio."

"Was their marriage happy?" Helen asked.

"At first," Cissy said. "But then they started growing apart. He spent so much time taking care of her and teaching class—you know he's been teaching full-time at the community college to get health insurance for her?"

"That's good of him," Helen said.

"It is," Cissy said. "Too good. He's neglected his own career to build hers."

"Do you think they would have stayed together if Annabel had lived?" Helen asked.

Cissy lowered her voice. "Yes. Clay was devoted to her. But Annabel knew he was unhappy, and that's why she killed herself."

"That's a ri–" Helen started to say "ridiculous," then quickly changed it to "romantic idea. Was Annabel that selfless?"

"I think she was," Cissy said. "She's the one who suggested he take out a big life insurance policy on her. She even researched which companies would let him get it with her preexisting condition. She knew he would never desert her, but if she died, he would be free."

"But Annabel's career was on the way up," Helen said. "She was starting to command big fees, wasn't she?"

"Not enough money to live on—especially with no health insurance. Once she suspected she had myasthenia gravis and her sight was going, she lost the will to live. That's what her friends, like Jenny, can't face: Annabel was a realist. She was on her way to a big-time art career and suddenly she was losing her eyesight. Fate was too cruel. She couldn't live with that."

"That would be cruel," Helen said, "but nothing was confirmed yet. Annabel was a realist, but she was also a fighter. When her marriage to Hugo fell apart, she had the good sense to get out of it. How did she live when she left Hugo?"

"She moved in with her parents," Cissy said. "That's how she met Clay. Her parents wanted her to take something practical at the community college, medical billing or something like that, and she did. But it was so boring, she also took an art class. She was Clay's student. She fell madly in love with him. He guided her art career, and when she got sick, he started teaching full-time and that's when his own career started failing."

Helen thought Clay's career was already failing when he left New York.

"I understand the creative temperament," Cissy said, shaking her corkscrew curls.

Does she think wearing wacky clothes makes her an artist? Helen wondered, and bit back a reply.

"One reason Annabel and I bonded is because we had so much in common," Cissy said. "Like her, I had to divorce my first husband. I'm better fixed financially than she was, thanks to a good lawyer, but it still takes courage to walk out. It's one thing to decide a marriage isn't working and another to actually leave it."

"It's a big step," Helen said. "It certainly was for me."

That's all she wanted to confide to this gossipy near stranger.

I'll never tell her that Rob was unfaithful from the start: He'd had an affair with my maid of honor. I was so blinded by love I didn't see my husband was a dog until I caught him years later with our next-door neighbor. And when the divorce judge gave Rob half of my future income I swore my ex would never see a nickel of mine and took off on a wild, aimless zigzag cruise around the country, until I wound up at the Coronado in South Florida. That's where Margery became my surrogate mother and Phil saved me from becoming another bitter, sun-blasted divorcée.

"So you're divorced, too," Cissy said, and leaned forward, mouth slightly open, like a baby bird begging for nourishment.

"Fortunately, my second marriage is a success," Helen said, "and I'm living happily ever after." She smiled.

"You're in love," Cissy said.

"Definitely," Helen said.

"I am, too," Cissy said. "I met the man of my dreams on the beach here. One look, and I knew he was my soul mate. He's so protective. It's sweet. He even persuaded me to stop smoking and switch to vaping."

"What's he like?" Helen asked.

"He's an artist," Cissy sighed. "That's why I'm taking this class, so I'll be able to communicate with the man I love. And taking it at Bonnet House is so inspiring. I want to live like Evelyn Bartlett.

"Evelyn had a terrible marriage to Eli Lilly, just like my first marriage, but she comforted Frederic Bartlett while he was mourning his second wife's death, and they had a long and happy marriage. They were artists together. Frederic called Evelyn his greatest discovery and helped her find herself. Their house became the beautiful symbol of their love. Frederic's first two wives were sickly, but he found true happiness with Evelyn. Frederic and my true love are both real artists. They're so creative. They love Florida. They even share a name."

Frederic? Helen wondered.

Then she remembered Frederic's full name: Frederic Clay Bartlett.

Cissy is talking about Clay Taylor Griffin, Annabel's husband.

Now Helen felt cold in the bright Mexican restaurant with the grinning skulls. Frederic's second wife, beautiful, talented Helen Louise Birch, died of cancer.

Did Cissy kill Annabel so she could marry the man she loves?

CHAPTER 19

The woman was six feet tall and covered with a lumpy rash from her bald head to her bare feet. As Helen approached the sculpture, she saw that it wasn't a rash—those were women's breasts. Orangey pink breasts with darker pink nipples, like cherry-topped pastries.

"Her name's Barbie," Lita said. Miranda's fiancée was a striking woman in her early twenties with milk white skin, wide blue eyes, and ruler-straight raspberry hair. Helen thought she looked like a manga heroine.

Helen studied Barbie. The sculpture had a mannequin's face, blank blue eyes, a nipple for her mouth, and breasts on her cheeks. Large shoulder-pad breasts were over her collarbone, small breasts like headphones were her ears, and she had a bunlike breast at the base of her neck. The breasts on her chest were the size of flour sacks.

"Barbie is part of my series Unreal Reality," Lita said.

"Fascinating," Helen said. The quirky artwork should have been repellant, but Helen thought it looked oddly playful. "And quite a statement."

"It's all men see when they look at women," Lita said.

Some men, Helen thought, not my man. But she wanted to talk about Annabel, not debate men and their merits. "How did you make the breasts?"

"I didn't," Lita said. "Those are silicone gel implants from China. I get them in sizes from A to double Es, and different shapes, from round to teardrops. They're surprisingly cheap, which is another statement."

"But these implants have nipples," Helen said.

"These aren't actually implanted under the skin," Lita said. "Women who've had mastectomies but don't want reconstructive surgery wear them in their bras for a natural appearance. So do cross-dressers."

More symbolism, Helen thought.

Behind Barbie, Helen saw three light-drenched oils: a Caribbean cottage, a secluded beach and a banana plantation.

"Are these yours, too?" she said.

"That's my representational work," Lita said. "I painted those on vacation."

"I like them," Helen said.

"I do, too, but I've outgrown that style," Lita said. "I keep reaching for the next level. I'm also working with charcoal."

She showed Helen four charcoal abstract nudes set up on easels. Each was a different view of a large, muscular woman, her powerful curves executed in tender detail.

"This is my fiancée, Miranda," Lita said, as if she was introducing the woman herself.

Helen hoped she wasn't blushing. Sometimes her midwestern upbringing asserted itself at inopportune times.

"I talked with Miranda at the lawn service office," Helen said. "She really guards your working time."

"She understands I have so little creative time," Lita said. "I help her out, but I can't wait until the business is doing well enough that she doesn't need me."

"It must be hard working in the Florida sun when you're so fair-skinned," Helen said.

"I have to wear a shitload of sunscreen, long sleeves, a hat that covers my neck, and heavy gloves. I'm suffocating. But I promised I'd do it until Miranda gets the business going. That's one reason why we're getting married at my parents' house. It will save a lot of money."

"Congratulations on your wedding," Helen said.

"Thank you," Lita said, and Helen saw her pale skin turn pink. Lita was a blushing bride. "I'm counting the days. Annabel was going to be a bridesmaid."

She wiped away a tear.

"I'm sorry," Helen said.

"She was better than any of us," Lita said. "Dammit! It's such a waste. She was on her way to the top!" Lita's face was almost red, but this was the color of rage.

"Do you have any of Annabel's work?" Helen asked.

"That bastard she married came the day after she died and took everything—all her paintings, even her supplies, down to the last tube of paint. I kept one painting hidden under a drop cloth. He would have taken it if he knew about it, but she gave it to me. It's all I have left of her."

"May I see it?" Helen asked.

"It's on an easel, behind my charcoals," Lita said.

Helen wondered how she could have missed the glowing oil. A pale pink female figure with large breasts and a look of ecstasy was sprawled across the canvas, her raspberry hair fanned out in a joyous swirl.

Helen stared at the painting again and realized that it was a very naked Lita.

"It's amazing." Helen said, and she meant it. The painting was colorful, sensual and sophisticated.

But as she studied its seething sexuality, Helen wondered just how kinky Annabel had been. Some men liked to have affairs with mothers and daughters or two sisters. Did Annabel have an affair with Miranda and then her fiancée? Were the two women notches on Annabel's bedpost?

When Helen had asked Miranda if Annabel was gay, she'd said, *Annabel was whatever she wanted to be. I don't put labels on people, Ms. Hawthorne. We had some fun and then it was over.*

Helen brushed away that thought as if it were an annoying fly and said, "The painting is both abstract and figured—is that the right word?"

"I know what you're trying to say," Lita said. "Annabel was trying to break out of the representational straitjacket and find her own style. That's why I hid this painting. I wanted something to remember her by." Lita sounded wistful. "*He* would have never understood it. Did you see that crap he painted? The sea never stops changing, but he painted the same picture over and over.

"Clay!" Lita's lips twisted into a sneer. "That's the right name for him. His work looks like modeling clay done by an untalented ten-year-old."

"You worked with Annabel. Did she talk about her marriage?" Helen asked.

"All the time," Lita said. "What do you want to know?"

"I've heard that after her marriage to Hugo fell apart, her parents sent her to junior college to take a medical billing course."

"They weren't bad people," Lita said, "but they didn't understand Annabel was an artist. Her mom and dad didn't think she could earn a living as an artist."

"You can't, can you?" Helen asked.

"Annabel was that rare exception. In another year or two, she would have been able to support herself. But I can see why her parents wanted her to be able to support herself. Men didn't treat Annabel very well. Have you met Hugo?"

"A real piece of work," Helen said.

"Exactly," Lita said. "Annabel loved her parents. She took the practical courses they wanted, but she was bored. So she took a life drawing class, too. About that time, Annabel's father died of a heart attack. She was devastated. One day he was fine and then he was gone. Next, her mother developed cancer. That was another blow. They were close.

"Annabel spent all her savings going back and forth to Connecticut to be with her mother. Her aunt Ruth lent her money, too.

"Annabel was alone and vulnerable, and she fell in love with her art teacher, Clay. He's an attractive man." Lita paused, and Helen could almost hear the unspoken part of that sentence: *if you like men.*

"Clay did his 'I had a studio in Chelsea' routine and dropped big New York names. Annabel was impressed. When her mother died, Clay was there. Her mother's illness had eaten most of her parents' savings. After Annabel sold their house, there was only a few thousand left.

"Clay proposed during this time. He promised if she'd marry him, he'd help Annabel become an artist. She loved him—or at least she convinced herself she did—but Annabel was still under the spell of those New York names. She also loved the idea of advancing her own art career.

"Either way, the marriage worked for a while. Clay was a good teacher and he guided her career steadily upward. Clay was happy to have an adoring wife, but after a while, Annabel's adoration turned into respect."

"Did she still love her husband?"

"I don't know," Lita said. "I'm not sure she knew. Annabel was struggling to find her identity as an artist—and maybe as a woman."

Helen longed to ask if Annabel had had an affair with Lita.

"Who do you think killed Annabel?"

Lita didn't hesitate. "Clay," she said. "Annabel knew about his students—the ones he took up to his studio for special classes. He killed her because he was jealous. She was going to leave him and he didn't want to lose his meal ticket. If she died, he'd collect that life insurance. A million dollars. You know about that?"

"Yes," Helen said. "But I didn't know it was that much."

"Annabel died of nicotine poisoning," Lita said. "That's another reason why I think Clay killed her. Do you know he gave up cigarettes for her? The smoke bothered her, but he still needed his nicotine fix, so he switched to e-cigarettes. Those little bottles of e-liquid are full of nicotine, and he smoked the strongest level: twenty-four milligrams of nicotine in something the size of a bottle of nail polish.

"All Clay had to do was dump that liquid in her iced tea, and it would kill her. She drank her tea so sweet it made my teeth ache."

"Your fiancée thinks Hugo killed Annabel because she'd ruined his career," Helen said.

"Miranda never liked Hugo," Lita said, "and that flap over his CEO job was years ago. Hugo sorta stalked Annabel—he went to her art show and bid up her painting, and she was upset when he took her art class, but Hugo enjoyed annoying her. He lived with his mom and so far as I know he didn't date much after Annabel divorced him."

"Do you think Annabel might have killed herself?" Helen asked.

Lita laughed—a surprisingly raucous guffaw. "Suicide? Annabel? Of course not! She was a born fighter."

"But her doctor thought she might have had myasthenia gravis," Helen said.

"Annabel was staggered when she first found out," Lita said. "But then she did her research and realized it wasn't a death sentence anymore."

"Wasn't it affecting her eyesight?"

"Yes, but her sight was getting better," Lita said. "Her art was her reason for living. She wasn't afraid of myasthenia gravis—not once she got used to the idea. She would have kicked its ass."

Helen thanked Lita for her time and started to go, when she saw Annabel's painting, glowing like a ghost in the studio.

"Did Clay ever see that painting?" she asked.

"No," Lita said. "She didn't want him to see it. He wouldn't have understood a nude study. He was jealous. He was a typical patriarchal male."

But men aren't the only ones who can be jealous, Helen thought.

She thought of Miranda, with the rainbow equal sign on her biceps, telling Helen, *Do you believe in love at first sight? . . . That's how it was when I met Lita.* Pow! *Like she'd slammed me in the head.*

What would Miranda do if the love of her life had had an affair with another woman?

CHAPTER 20

Helen's head was spinning when she left Lita's FAT Village studio. After all those interviews, she had no idea who'd poisoned Annabel.

Did Miranda kill the artist because she'd had an affair with Lita? Were Annabel and Lita lovers? Helen didn't know, but that sensuous nude of Lita proved Annabel knew Lita very well indeed. Lita hid the painting from her fiancée, as well as Annabel's husband.

What other secrets was she hiding?

Then there was Cissy, so caught up in the romantic tale of Frederic and Evelyn Bartlett, she wanted to relive their love story. Did she poison Annabel to become Clay's next wife and live her dream?

Hugo, seething with hate and anger, was another possibility. But so was Clay, the high-flying artist whose career was nose-diving.

Helen did know one thing: Annabel didn't commit suicide. Too many people said she was a fighter. The private eye agreed with the medical examiner: Annabel was murdered. And every one of Helen's suspects had access to nicotine.

The bright sun stabbed Helen's eyes. She needed coffee. She

blasted the Igloo's air conditioner as she drove to the FAT Village coffeehouse, Brew Urban Cafe Next Door on Northwest First Avenue. She saw *Entirely Entertaining*, the Bonnet House cookbook, on the seat and remembered she'd volunteered to make authentic appetizers to go with Evelyn's Rangpur lime cocktail.

Helen could smell Brew Urban before she entered. The air was fragrant with coffee. The dark interior soothed her sun-dazzled eyes. She felt at home carrying a book. Behind the counter, a wall of books reached to the warehouse ceiling.

Helen ordered a French press and a muffin, then settled into a pillowy overstuffed chair. She enjoyed the funky decor: an old gilt chandelier, an oriental carpet, and the back end of a classic Airstream trailer sticking out of the wall.

She sipped her coffee and paged through the Bonnet House cookbook, hoping Evelyn's appetizers weren't too complicated. The Bartletts had had a cook and Helen could barely open a can.

Under "Favorite Recipes of the Bartletts," she found caramelized bacon. Now, that was simple: thick slices of bacon sprinkled with brown sugar and baked.

I can do that, Helen thought. I have both ingredients, too. And Phil will love it.

The blue cheese puffs looked almost as easy. They needed a can of refrigerated biscuits, butter, and blue cheese.

Evelyn didn't worry about cholesterol, Helen thought. Those Rangpur lime cocktails were magic potions. But I should make something healthy for Markos.

Here's one: sesame chicken wings. It's a bit complicated. I'll need a bunch of ingredients, including gingerroot, sesame oil and red pepper flakes, but I know Markos will like it. So will Phil.

Helen took a last sip of her coffee, then swung by the supermarket for the ingredients. At home, she stopped at Phil's apartment and tiptoed inside. As she expected, he was asleep, with Thumbs snoring on his feet. Helen longed to kiss him but knew he needed his rest.

I hope the Gold Ghost is caught soon, she thought. I hardly ever see my husband. Thumbs woke up and padded after Helen to her apartment.

She spent the afternoon preparing appetizers and patting herself on the back for her domestic skills. The hardest part was keeping Thumbs away from the food, but she bought him off with treats.

It was nearly six o'clock and Helen had the caramelized bacon arranged on a platter, the blue cheese puffs cooling on a rack, and she was checking the sesame chicken wings broiling in the oven.

Phil knocked on her door. "Come in," she called, poking a chicken wing with a fork to test for doneness.

"Mm, what smells so good?" Phil said.

"Appetizers for tonight's sunset salute," Helen said. The wing felt sort of rubbery, but she thought it was done.

"Love this bacon," Phil said, filching a piece. "And looky, looky, what have we here on the rack?"

"Blue cheese puffs," Helen said, wondering if the wings would burn if she left them in longer. Better not risk it, she decided, and pulled out the pan with pot-holdered hands.

"Yum!" Phil said, and reached for another cheese puff. "My favorite food groups: calories, cholesterol, fat and sugar."

"I knew you'd like them," Helen said. She smiled as she set the wing pan on another rack. Then she saw Phil, and the smile slid off her face. "You're wearing your uniform."

"I have to leave here at six fifteen," Phil said. "Victor called. There was another burglary in Little New York after all."

"At Silver Glade?" Helen asked.

"No, the Hazleton, at the south end. The condo owner came back from a trip about two o'clock this afternoon and found his coin collection gone. Silver Glade is in an uproar. Victor asked me to come in early and brainstorm."

"You'll miss the Rangpur lime cocktails," Helen said.

"Duty calls," Phil said, eating another cheese puff and reaching for a chicken wing. "Besides, I'm a beer drinker."

"Let me fix you a plate so you don't get grease on your uniform," Helen said. She piled a dinner plate with appetizers. "Beer?"

"I'd better not report to work with alcohol on my breath."

"Then I'll make more appetizers when you can drink," Helen said, and poured him iced tea.

She arranged the rest of the appetizers on platters and carried the cheese puffs and chicken wings out by the pool. Markos was setting up his bar at an umbrella table.

He's clearly dressed to impress, Helen thought. That fitted white shirt with the black cuffs that end just below the elbow shows off his muscles. So do those well-tailored (okay, tight) black pants.

"You're stylin'," she said.

"I'm tired of dressing like a kid," Markos said.

Helen saw the red creeping up his neck.

"I've wiped down that table there if you want to use it," he said, switching the subject. "Are these the Bonnet House appetizers?"

"Straight from the cookbook," Helen said, and described the three she'd made.

"Old-school but interesting," he said. "I didn't realize they had chicken wings back then. I've mixed the first batch of cocktails. Would you taste test it? I'll bring out the pitcher."

He flashed Helen a dazzling smile.

"Let me get the bacon," Helen said. She felt sweat trickling down her shirt and hoped it was the heat.

Phil was finishing his appetizers when Helen returned to the kitchen. "More food?" she asked him.

"No, I have to leave," he said. "I'll feed the cat and go."

By the time Helen had the appetizers out and set the table, Markos had returned with a fat-bellied pitcher filled with a deep orange liquid. Beads of condensation rolled down its smooth sides. Markos filled a short glass with ice and poured Helen a drink.

She sipped cautiously. She'd expected Rangpur limes to taste like oranges, but this was definitely a lime flavor. "It's good but a little tart," she said.

"Let me add more maple syrup to your drink," he said.

"Too late," Helen said. "I drank it."

"I'll add more syrup to the pitcher," he said.

It took two more tries before Helen said the cocktail was "Rangpurrrfect." When Markos offered her another drink, Helen said, "Just a splash," except it came out, "Jusha splash."

By that time, Margery had glided out in a long, cool dress banded with purple. She wore her amethyst pendant and a light wrap of Marlboro smoke. She appraised Helen with a knowing eye.

"Have some appetizers, Helen," she said. "In fact, have a lot of appetizers."

Helen put three pieces of bacon on her plate, but they slid off into the cheese puffs. "Ooopsh."

"Sit down," Margery said. "I'll bring you some food."

Helen sat down in a chaise. Actually, she fell into it. "Hi, Peggy," she said as their red-haired neighbor joined them. "You look chic and mysterious in black. Do you have a date with Daniel?"

"A dinner date," Peggy said, "so I'll skip the appetizers. Are these the famous Rangpur lime cocktails, Markos?"

"Try one," Markos said, handing her a cold glass. Margery gave Helen a plate mounded with appetizers but kept Helen's cocktail and drank it.

"Mm, this is fabulous," Peggy said.

"Markos, I salute you," Margery said, raising her glass. "No wonder Evelyn lived to be a hundred and nine. She stayed here for these cocktails. You can't get these in heaven."

"Of coursh you can," Helen said. "It wouldn't be heaven without them. I can see Evelyn up there, wearing wingsh, and shlipping these." Her tongue kept tangling.

"You're probably seeing pink elephants," Margery said. "Keep eating."

That's when Phil appeared. "Doesn't he look handsome in his uniform?" Helen said, and giggled. Phil looked uncomfortable.

"Would you like a cocktail, Phil?" Markos asked.

"Thanks, Markos, but I have to go to work."

"I knew you were working undercover at a Little New York condo," Peggy said. "Which one?"

"I can't say," Phil said. Helen knew the patch on his shirt said SILVER GLADE CONDOMINIUMS, but Peggy didn't notice. Daniel, her date, had arrived and she hurried to meet him.

Right behind Daniel was Valerie. The TV reporter wore a curve-hugging black dress so simple Helen knew it cost a fortune. Her long hair fell to her shoulders and her red heels looked so hot they should have blistered her feet.

Helen heard a small sound like a gasp or a sharp intake of breath. She'd read romance novels where the lovers locked eyes, but Helen had never actually seen it. Now Valerie and Markos acted as if no one else was at the pool. The TV reporter floated over the sidewalk to the handsome bartender.

"May I fix you a drink?" he asked.

"I wouldn't miss it," she said.

The pitcher shook slightly as he poured. "I love the color," Valerie said, holding up her drink.

"I love your color, too," Markos said. "Of your dress. That color. It looks good on you."

Valerie sipped her cocktail. "Amazing," she said. "This is my first time. That I've had a Rangpur lime cocktail, I mean." Now she was as embarrassed as Markos.

Helen had never seen the reporter lose her cool. Markos and Valerie stared at each other as if they were starving. The air around them sizzled. Finally, Margery took pity on them.

"Well, thank you, Markos," she said, standing up. "These cocktails were a once-in-a-lifetime experience. Now, why don't you and Valerie go to dinner?"

"Dinner would be nice," Valerie said, her voice soft.

"I should clean up," Markos said, as if in a trance.

"Helen and I can put everything away. It's no big deal," Margery said. "Go ahead. Leave."

The couple left, hand in hand, feet hardly touching the walkway.

"Good night, Margery," Peggy and Daniel said. They walked together, but Helen thought there was a distance between them.

After they left, Helen said, "Do you think there's a slight coolness between Peggy and Daniel?"

"Now, there's a sobering thought," Margery said. "Glad you finally had one. If you take the appetizers back to your apartment, I'll put away the bar."

By the time Helen had put away the appetizers, Margery had cleared the bar. She handed Helen a bottled water and lit another cigarette and they settled into adjoining chaises.

"Have you found out who poisoned your artist?" Margery said.

"I'm stalled," Helen said. She told her landlady what she'd learned, while Margery smoked and listened.

When Helen finished, Margery said, "You have two women attracted to one man, Clay. Annabel used to love him and you think Cissy loves him now. And he's quite the Casanova with his students."

"I prefer hound, but yes, he plays around," Helen said.

"What else do you know about him, except he's a failed artist?"

"Very little," Helen said. "I've never even seen him. I'll meet him tomorrow at Annabel's memorial service."

"He's the key," Margery said. "Know him and you'll know what happened."

CHAPTER 21

Helen awoke to the soft rumble of thunder and patter of rain. Good, she thought. I'm glad it will be raining for Annabel's memorial service. The harsh subtropical sun always feels wrong when people are mourning.

Helen sat up and the room tilted. She clutched the sheet, as if that could stop the movement. It didn't help.

The revenge of the Rangpur lime, she thought. Helen had even more respect for Evelyn Bartlett. But maybe that grand old woman didn't down three cocktails on an empty stomach.

Phil was snoring gently beside her. She must have been asleep when he came home earlier this morning. Helen's bedside clock finally came into focus: Nine o'clock.

I can make Annabel's ten o'clock memorial service if I hurry, she thought.

She drank hot coffee to skin the fur off her tongue, fed Thumbs so the cat wouldn't wake Phil, and donned a subdued black skirt and gray blouse.

By nine forty-five, she was dodging the raindrops and running through the doors of the Silver Glade Condominiums, the perfect setting for a memorial service. The lobby was a mausoleum.

She saw the members of her art class signing in at the reception desk. They made a somber trio: Yulia in deep black, her blond hair a beacon. Jenny in sleek navy Armani, her face solemn. Cissy in a frumpy black dress. The rain turned her springy curls into a frizzy mass, struggling to escape her beaded scrunchie.

Helen was surprised to see Hugo slouching a few feet away, hands in the pockets of his gray pants. He wore a black long-sleeved polo—Florida mourning.

What's he doing here? Helen wondered. Would he make a scene at his ex-wife's funeral?

The rest of the art class gave Hugo the cold shoulder. Jenny waved Helen over, and the group greeted her with subdued smiles and awkward small talk. "A sad day," Cissy said.

"Even the sky is crying," Yulia said.

Nobody mocked her. The rain was pounding, drops rolling down the lobby windows like tears. The women waited for Hugo to sign in and take the elevator. Then Helen checked in with the security guard.

"The memorial for Mrs. Griffin is in 1917," he said, "on the nineteenth floor."

The women's heels clacked across the marble and they were swallowed by the steel elevator.

"I never expected to see Hugo here," Yulia said, pressing the button. "He would not look at me. I guess he is still mad."

"Who cares?" Jenny said. "Our class is better without him. I hope he doesn't say something awful at Annabel's memorial service."

Helen hung on to the elevator railing. Its rapid ascent made her queasy.

The steel doors chunked open, and they followed the sound to 1917. A string quartet playing something mournful—Helen thought it was "Pavane for a Dead Princess"—was overlaid by subdued chatter.

The door to Clay's art studio was open and mourners spilled out into the hall, clutching drinks and small plates of appetizers. Helen passed a plate loaded with smoked salmon and her stomach flip-flopped.

Clay's condo was massive—a corner unit with two walls of windows overlooking a greasy green ocean. The string quartet played in what was probably a dining room. White-gloved caterers were setting out trays of fresh fruit, mini quiches, smoked salmon and shrimp. A tiered tray held tiny cupcakes. Next to the desserts was an open bar.

"Helen, I'm Robert Horton." The gallery owner held out his hand.

"You don't have to remind me, Robert," Helen said, shaking it. "I remember you." And your exquisite suits, she thought. This one was charcoal, with the same rich sheen and slim cut.

"Big crowd," she said.

"Everyone who's anyone in the South Florida art world is here," he said. "May I get you a drink?"

"Club soda, please," she said, then added, "without lime."

While Robert fetched her drink, she surveyed the vast apartment. Clay's work desk, covered with tubes of paint and brushes, had been pushed into a corner, along with other supplies, blank canvases, and a paint-spattered easel with a partly finished seascape.

The widower was receiving condolences in a salon next to the kitchen, and the line wrapped around the room. Helen saw Clay standing beside a poster-sized photo of Annabel and a vase of flowers.

Helen thought Clay had the romantic good looks that would appeal to impressionable young women: He was a well-muscled thirtysomething, at least six feet tall. His longish blond hair fell over his forehead, hiding his eyes. Helen thought his mouth looked weak but wondered if she was being perceptive or prejudiced.

She watched him listen to a curvy redhead and thought Clay held her white hand just a fraction too long.

"Here you go," Robert said, and handed Helen a club soda. She gulped it.

"There's a slide show of Annabel in that room there," Robert said, and they crossed to a darkened room where photos flashed on a large screen.

Helen saw photos of Clay with an adoring Annabel wrapped around him at their beach wedding. She looked younger and healthy in that photo. Her pale skin glowed and her long hair was fine silk. Next was a photo of Clay shaking hands with the Fort Lauderdale mayor. Annabel was barely in the picture. Then Clay was accepting a plaque while Annabel applauded in the background.

"Did you notice that these photos are all about Clay?" Helen whispered.

"Wait till you see the so-called art exhibit," Robert said. "But we should pay our respects first."

As they made their way through the crowd, Helen saw Miranda, the lawn service owner, in a gray pantsuit, with a glass of wine and a plate of appetizers. Her fiancée, the raspberry-haired Lita, was striking in a black-and–hot pink dress. The women gave Helen and Robert subdued smiles.

The condolence line was down to one person, Hugo. He was talking softly to Clay, but as she got closer, Helen heard Hugo say, "Nice piece of real estate you got here, Clay. Musta cost a fortune."

Robert raised an eyebrow and Helen tried not to look shocked. Hugo was incredibly crass.

"This condo was cheap by New York standards," Clay said.

Now Robert's eyebrow was hovering up by his hairline.

"How cheap?" Hugo asked.

"Only three million," Clay said, his voice smug.

"You must be doing okay with those ocean pictures," Hugo said.

"I do all right," Clay said.

"Lemme know if you want to sell this," Hugo said.

"Not for sale," Clay said. "I'll be living here full-time now. But if you'd like to buy a nice house in Country Club Estates, I'll be putting it up for sale shortly. I can't live there anymore. Too many memories."

"Not interested," Hugo said. "I live in a house not too far away in the Landings."

Hugo's cell phone played the first bars of Sinatra's "My Way."

"Sorry, gotta take this," Hugo said, and clicked on his phone. "Hey, Mom, you okay? What? You can't find your cane? Did you check the hall closet? What about your bedroom? Don't worry, Mom. I'll come home and help you look for it."

He hung up the phone and said, "Sorry, Mom has Parkinson's disease. She was doing real good but now she's had a bit of a relapse and can't find her cane. I gotta go, Clay. I'm sorry."

Helen wasn't sure if Hugo was sorry he had to leave or sorry that Annabel was dead, but neither man seemed too interested in her.

"I understand," Clay said. "You go be a good son. And thanks for coming."

He turned to Robert. "So glad you came," he said. "Did my painting sell?"

"I'm afraid not," Robert said. "But you can pick it up at your convenience. I'm so very sorry about Annabel. She was as talented as she was beautiful."

"Indeed," Clay said. "I never expected her to commit suicide, but she carried a terrible burden." He shook Robert's hand and slyly shoved him on so he could talk to Helen.

She introduced herself and said, "I'm from Annabel's art class. Your wife was a talented artist."

"Yes, she was," Clay said. "You can see some of her paintings in that room there." He nodded at the connecting door to another large salon.

That's when Cissy interrupted. "Clay, you poor man. How are you holding up?"

"Uh, fine, Cissy," he said. "I need to show Ms. Hawthorne something."

He steered Helen to the next room and lowered his voice. "I have to get away from that woman," he said. "I met her on the beach once, and ever since she's been stalking me. She has this crazy idea that we're soul mates."

"That's what she told me," Helen said.

"Ms. Hawthorne, that woman was after me to leave Annabel. I told her I couldn't do that. I loved my wife and I was faithful."

"You were?" Helen said.

Clay looked uneasy. "In my heart, I was always faithful. But Annabel was sick and a healthy man has needs."

As a detective, Helen wanted to know more. As a woman, she was disgusted by his lies.

"The more I said I wouldn't leave my wife, the more determined Cissy was to marry me. She would show up at the most inopportune times."

"What about Cissy's friendship with your wife?" Helen asked.

"Cissy only befriended Annabel at that art class," he said. "Cissy confessed to Annabel that she'd lost her head over me, but she'd regretted her rashness. Annabel said she understood. She believed her."

"Really?" Helen said, not bothering to hide her skepticism. Clay was sweating now. The sun had come out, but the room wasn't that hot.

Clay looked over his shoulder. "Thank God, she's gone," he said. "Take your time, Ms. Hawthorne. Enjoy Annabel's art. Have a drink and some nibbles."

He left Helen in front of a painting of a wild parrot in a lemon tree. Helen knew it was Annabel's by the jewel-like colors.

"One of Annabel's early works," Robert said, rejoining her. "In fact, that's all I see displayed here: four of her very early paintings on easels. They show she had undeniable talent, but she hadn't fully developed her voice."

"Well, there's plenty of Clay's work," Helen said. "I count at least eight seascapes, all with plaster of paris waves."

"He's displayed more of his art than Annabel's," Robert said.

They both fell silent, and Helen caught murmured comments.

"She had a lovely eye for color, didn't she?" . . . "We've lost a great natural talent." . . . "If you ask me, the wrong artist died." . . . "Sh!"

All at once, everyone went quiet. Even the string quartet was taking a break.

Helen heard Lita ask Clay, "Where's Annabel's latest art?"

"It's with her," Clay said.

Helen could feel all the mourners straining to listen.

"What do you mean?" Lita said, her voice rising. Miranda interrupted, "Come on, honey, this is not the time."

"Yes, it is!" Lita said. "I want to know what happened to Annabel's paintings."

"I put them in her casket," Clay said.

"She was cremated. *You burned her best work!*" Lita screamed. Everyone stared.

"No, I put her work with her. The galleries wanted to exploit it. This is more romantic. It will be with her forever."

"You destroyed it," Lita said. "Like you destroyed her!"

That's when Lita's fiancée dragged her out of the room.

Helen saw Miranda's hand gripping Lita's shoulder possessively, as if she were escorting a prisoner.

CHAPTER 22

"Ladies and gentlemen," Clay said, as he stood at a podium near the window. A feedback screech from the microphone stopped him for a moment, until he adjusted the mic and began again.

"Dear friends and colleagues of my beloved wife. Please excuse the emotional display from one of Annabel's friends. I know that this is a difficult day for all who loved Annabel. We will begin our memorial service shortly."

Clay appeared unruffled by Lita's accusations. He smoothly spackled over her harsh words. The memorial guests chatted and refreshed their drinks, while the string quartet played a transcription of a Bach fugue. The sound seemed to drive the last traces of Lita's dark words from the room as the remaining storm clouds scudded across the sky.

Helen stood in line for another club soda and found herself behind Burt Pelham, the Palmetto Hills crimes against persons detective.

"Ms. Hawthorne," he said. "How are you on this sad occasion?" His tone was oddly formal and his New York accent fit right in at the Silver Glade Condominiums.

"Detective," Helen said. She nodded and felt her sludgy brain shift in her skull.

"I'd like to speak to you," he said. "Later today if possible." Helen thought his cheap, brassy blond hair was a jarring note with his well-tailored dark suit. Men never seemed to get dyed hair right.

"I'll be happy to meet with you, Detective, but I'm not sure there's anything I can say."

"Then perhaps you'll listen to what I have to say," he said. "Four o'clock, then? At your office?"

"I'll be there, Detective," Helen said.

She spotted Robert Horton across the room, drinking white wine and admiring the panoramic view from the high windows. The gallery owner seemed an oasis of calm command after Lita's ugly scene.

The sun was out now, dancing on the impossibly blue ocean, filling the room with dazzling light. A rainbow lit the sky. Clay stepped up to the podium again and said, "I feel that Annabel is smiling on us all. The Reverend Patti Zgorski will lead us in a prayer."

A small woman with a brown bob and a dark suit stepped up and said, "Our Father, who art in heaven . . ."

After the simple, moving prayer, Clay was back at the podium.

"I will miss my lovely wife, her courage, her talent, her love of nature. One of the last things she said to me was, 'Clay, we've been so happy together. I can't thank you enough for all you've done. I hope you'll remember that, no matter what happens.'

"I didn't realize," Clay said, and his voice wobbled to a stop. He took a deep breath and tried again. "I didn't realize she was telling me good-bye. I didn't pay enough attention to her suffering. I didn't understand that she had reached the end of her strength. I thought it was limitless.

"Annabel, as you know, had a troubled life, mentally and physically, despite her great talent—maybe because of her tremendous talent. The two do seem to go hand in hand.

"But she was always a fighter. And after she was diagnosed with myasthenia gravis, I thought she would continue the battle. We researched this terrible disease together. We talked about how it was no longer a death sentence. She knew she wouldn't face the same terrible end as Aristotle Onassis, its most famous victim. That poor man had to have his eyelids taped open.

"Annabel knew how many great talents had this dreaded disease, but she also knew they had major careers. She loved movies and the theater. Laurence Olivier had myasthenia gravis, but he lived to a ripe old age and died of something entirely different. She knew that Karl Malden, who was in classic Brando films like *A Streetcar Named Desire* and *On the Waterfront*, also had it. But Karl died of old age.

"And I thought my Annabel would also die of old age after a long, successful career. But she didn't."

Clay paused, as if trying to find his own strength to continue. The room listened in rapt silence. Helen heard a small sob and sympathetic murmurs. The woman next to her wiped her eyes and smeared her mascara.

"I never expected," Clay said, "that my lovely wife would give up after fighting so bravely for fifteen years. But for some reason she felt she could no longer go on. I blame myself for her death. I should have listened to her more. I should have realized she was tired of fighting. But I wasn't there for her. I wasn't there and her death is my fault!"

Robert looked so startled, he spilled wine on his suit, then dabbed at it with his handkerchief.

Clay wiped away tears and left the podium, comforted by the pretty redhead whose hand he'd held a little too long in the receiving line.

Under cover of the string quartet's "Clair de Lune," Robert whispered, "Do you think Annabel killed herself?"

"Of course not," Helen said, "and neither does that man over there. And he's the one whose opinion counts."

"The dude with the bad dye job? Who is he?" Robert asked.

"He's the Palmetto Hills detective investigating Annabel's death as a murder."

"Oh," Robert said.

"And the way I heard it, Annabel's diagnosis of myasthenia gravis wasn't confirmed yet."

"Then why would Clay say that she killed herself?" Robert said. "Wouldn't it be easier to accept his wife's death as murder rather than suicide?"

"You'd think so," Helen said, "unless he has something to hide."

"Do you think Clay killed Annabel?" Robert asked.

Helen watched the creamy-skinned redhead patting Clay's shoulder.

"I think he had several good reasons to kill her," Helen said, "but he's not the only one."

She thought of Hugo, seething with hate, and Cissy, so in love with Clay that she couldn't see he thought she was a nuisance. And Miranda, who might have lost the woman of her dreams to Annabel.

"This was a very odd memorial," Robert said. "It was more about Clay than his wife. She deserved better."

"A better husband, or a better memorial?" Helen asked.

"Both," Robert said. "I hope that detective finds out who killed Annabel. And if there's any way I can aid your investigation, Helen, please don't hesitate to call. This is my private number." He handed Helen an engraved business card.

A server came by to collect their glasses. The string quartet was packing away their instruments and the guests were leaving. Annabel's service was over. As Helen said her good-byes, she heard her cell phone buzz.

While she waited for the elevator in the hall, she checked a text from Phil.

It read, *Outside w TV & Valerie. Don't b surprised. DNC.*

DNC was their code for "Do not call." Phil was a fanatic about not discussing business on a cell phone. But what was he doing outside now? He worked the graveyard shift. When did he come to work? He was asleep when she left home this morning.

I'll find out shortly, she thought.

The elevator dinged open and Helen joined the crush inside. She was taller than most of the passengers, but she still felt the walls closing in.

The Silver Glade lobby was brighter now that the sun was out. "Is that a Channel Seventy-seven TV truck outside?" asked a woman in a black pantsuit.

"Don't tell me this condo has been hit by the Gold Ghost," said her companion, a stylish brunette with too much perfume and a dramatic black hat.

"This is about the only condo in Little New York that hasn't been burglarized," Black Pantsuit said.

Phil! Helen thought. That's why he's here. The condo has been robbed. This is terrible. It could hurt our reputation. I just hope no one's been hurt. Her heart was beating faster as she pushed toward the entrance, passing the two women. Now she was behind a handsome older couple who could have stepped out of a Cialis commercial.

"Isn't that Valerie Cannata, the TV reporter?" asked the man. He had beautifully cut gray hair and a firm jawline.

The woman—Helen guessed she was his wife—had perfectly coiffed and tinted shoulder-length silver hair and a little knife work done on her eyes. "She's my favorite local reporter," she said. "I like her dress. Green is definitely her color. But why is she talking to an Arab? He certainly is handsome."

Fort Lauderdale was an international city, but Helen wasn't used to seeing an Arab in a long-sleeved white robe and a white headdress with a gold band to hold it in place. Sunglasses completed the ensemble. There was something stagy about his outfit—more *Lawrence of Arabia* than Saudi Arabia.

"He's not my type," joked the man, "but his Rolls-Royce is outstanding."

"How old is that car?" the wife asked.

"I'd say it's a 1960-something Rolls-Royce Phantom," he said. "A classic."

"Beautiful," she said. "They both are." She grinned at her husband. "You can keep the car."

Helen gently pressed through the crowd and was out the door, blinking in the sun. She heard Valerie say, "You've bought the penthouse, Your Highness."

"Abdul, please," the Arab said. "I am pleased to be in your beautiful city." He had a slight, pleasant accent and golden brown skin.

"But why are you here in South Florida?" Valerie asked.

"Fort Lauderdale is known as the Venice of America," he said. "I will be taking delivery on my new yacht here."

For some reason, that Arab looks familiar, Helen thought.

"You are the sixteenth-richest person in the world," Valerie said.

"Only the twenty-first," he said. "The price of oil has fallen." Even wearing that robe, there was no hiding that His Highness was hotter than a Saudi summer.

"But you're known for your gold coin collection," Valerie said. "Doesn't gold appreciate?"

The Arab smiled at her. "Many people collect gold coins," he said. "It's a popular hobby, you know."

Odd, Helen thought. She was no expert on foreign accents, but his seemed more Cuban than Arab.

"Your collection is way beyond the scope of the hide-a-few-thousand-under-the-mattress crowd," Valerie said.

"I don't know what other people collect," he said.

"You do know there's been a problem with gold coin burglaries at the Blue Heron Crescent condominiums," Valerie said. "Aren't you concerned about a break-in? There's been one murder."

Helen could imagine the local chamber of commerce screeching when Valerie said that, but she didn't pull any punches.

"Not at all," the Arab said. "Management assures me they have the best security in Fort Lauderdale."

Helen saw five Silver Glade security guards, shoes shined and uniforms crisp, lined up behind the ostentatious Rolls-Royce. Phil was on the far end. He winked at her.

That's the entire security staff, Helen thought. All six guards are here, from the three shifts. Five out here and the guard at the reception desk.

"So you have no fear of burglary," Valerie said.

"No fear whatsoever," Abdul said. "This is one of the few condos in Blue Heron Crescent that has never been hit by your Gold Ghost. That is his name, correct?"

"So you have been following the stories," Valerie said.

"Of course," Abdul said. "Security is important to me. My staff has researched this area thoroughly. Silver Glade Condominiums have never been burglarized. I believe they are a safe place to stay until my yacht is ready."

He smiled at Valerie. Helen saw the handsome man's white teeth, and everything fell into place. She knew him. This was no Arab prince.

Markos was wearing those stagy robes.

CHAPTER 23

Helen was seething as she waited for the Silver Glade valet to bring her car.

What the hell is Phil doing? she asked herself. He's behind this. He has to be. Phil loves disguises. That sneak hired Markos as an undercover operative without asking me. My PI partner is sending Markos alone—and untrained—to that huge penthouse suite.

Security will be twenty stories below, sitting at a desk. No way can a guard shoot up the elevator in time to help Markos. And he sure can't run up the stairs. Markos will be stranded.

Phil should have consulted me, Helen thought as she paced the rain-washed pavement by the valet stand. She must have radiated anger. Some of the memorial service guests waiting for their cars backed away from her.

Helen wanted to scream. She wanted to run over and shake her clueless PI partner. This sitcom scheme was too dangerous.

Furious questions darted through her troubled mind: When did Phil get this bright idea? Why didn't he let me know? He could have woken me up when he came home this morning. Instead, all I got was a coded text when it's too late to do anything.

How did he even contact Markos *and* Valerie? The last time I saw those two, they were running off to dinner after the sunset salute. Did he track them down last night or see them early this morning?

And where did Phil get that ridiculous Arab getup for Markos?

Markos isn't going to a costume party. He's bait in a dangerous game. Phil's letting a college student deal with a wily crook. A burglar who's slipped through high-level security multiple times. The Gold Ghost who's never appeared on the security cameras or left behind evidence for the police. A crook who kills when he's cornered.

Sure, Markos is young and muscular—but he's no match for the Gold Ghost. The way he slithers in and out of scary situations, this gold thief must have special-ops training. Maybe he's some sort of ninja.

Either way, Markos is no match for him. The Coronado hottie can disembowel a Brussels sprout, but he can't defend himself against a trained killer.

"Careful, lady!" said a soberly dressed man, and Helen realized she'd nearly plowed into him. The memorial service guest eyed her warily.

"Sorry, sir," she said, and wondered if she'd been mumbling to herself.

Helen took several deep breaths and tried to stay still in the line. A calming thought crept in, but she quickly squashed it: Markos did work undercover for us before. Once. But both Phil and I were there, and close enough to protect him if the setup went south.

Besides, we had an armed police detective with us and a couple of uniformed cops at the back door. Markos did fine, but he was clearly scared. He's too honest to be a really good actor. He's too open and easy to read.

Helen looked across the circle and saw her husband in the security guard lineup, arms crossed on his chest, watching Valerie interview Markos with a satisfied smirk. Even from this distance, Helen could see the pretend potentate was bewitched by the television star. Markos looked like he was dazzled by the desert sun.

Valerie was the only one with any sense—or acting ability. She was lobbing softball questions at Markos that Helen suspected had been scripted by Phil.

"Do you have your own security guards, Your Highness?" Valerie asked, her face perfectly deadpan, her demeanor impeccably professional.

"Yes, but not now. They will be joining me when . . ." Markos stopped and stared at the sky as if the answer were written on a cloud. "When my yacht is ready. Yes, my yacht. Which I'm waiting to take delivery on. So I don't need my security yet."

"And you're not worried?" Valerie batted her eyelashes, and Markos puffed out his manly chest. Helen thought he'd dive off the twentieth floor to prove he was fearless.

"I've been assured by my advisers that Fort Lauderdale is perfectly safe," he said. "Much safer than Miami, and I have my driver when I go out. I am not worried."

You should be, Helen thought. You should be scared spitless. Thanks to this interview, a big neon sign is flashing on your penthouse roof: CLUELESS COIN COLLECTOR HERE! ALONE! COME AND GET IT, BURGLAR!

Phil has done everything but send the Gold Ghost an engraved invitation to rob you. I can't believe he didn't check with me, his wife and business partner. It's time for me to take charge. Markos is not staying alone in that penthouse tonight. I'll be there with him.

But I can't march into the building and go up to the twentieth floor. Even with Phil working the graveyard shift. How am I going to get into Markos's penthouse?

I'll have to come up with an idea—fast.

That's when the Igloo appeared and the suntanned valet hopped out. "Sorry for the delay, miss," he said. "Your car was parked on the other side of the circle, but that TV truck is in the way. Took a while to get around it."

"That's okay," Helen said, and tipped him. "I was watching the show."

"What do you think of an Arab prince moving into Silver Glade?" the valet said.

"Unbelievable," Helen said, climbing into her car.

Helen decided to take the highway home. She thought better when she was roaring down I-95 with the radio playing.

The Igloo rode a little bumpy coming out of Silver Glade, but the street was potholed. The ride smoothed out when Helen turned onto Commercial Boulevard, a six-lane artery.

Ten minutes later, the Igloo was barreling down the interstate at seventy miles an hour in the fast lane, and Helen was singing along to "Born to Be Wild." She was slightly over the speed limit, but so many cars passed her in the next lane, Helen felt like a model driver. The *I* in I-95 should stand for insane, not interstate. Its drivers were daredevils and lane-switching speeders.

A black Beemer zigzagged through the heavy traffic, the twit behind the wheel flipping off slower drivers as he surged past them. A bug green beater with a coat hanger antenna rumbled past the Igloo, muffler blurping and farting. A teen in a Mustang moved restlessly from lane to lane, trying—and failing—to pass this clot of traffic.

As she sang, Helen wondered how she could go up to Markos's penthouse. Maybe His Highness could order a pizza and I could deliver it. Except I'd have to sign in at the desk and come back downstairs again. Even Phil couldn't get around that. The security cameras would record me the moment I drove through the Silver Glade entrance. Ditto for any other delivery service.

I can't be a housekeeper, either. Nobody gets their condo cleaned in the middle of the night. Maybe I . . .

Thump, thump, pop!

The Igloo swung wildly and Helen hung on to the steering wheel, fighting to control the car. She heard flapping sounds and the car listed heavily on the right side.

I've blown a tire, Helen thought. I have to get my car across four lanes of crazed traffic to the shoulder.

Honk! Honnnk! Hoooooonnnk!

The woman in the next lane had seen Helen's tire blow out. She slowed her own white car, honked loud and long, and put on her flashers, signaling to the drivers behind her that something was wrong.

Traffic began to slow down as Helen steered the thumping, bucking Igloo to the other side of the road. She was safe.

She sat in her car, hands shaking so badly she couldn't open her door. The traffic whizzing past reminded her how close she'd come to an accident.

She switched off the radio and in the sudden silence tried to figure out where she was. Up ahead, she saw the green Davie Boulevard exit—and a white car parking in front of the Igloo. Helen recognized her roadside angel. She could see that the honking rescuer was a thirtysomething Latina with rich brown hair. The woman cautiously emerged from her car and ran to Helen's, tapping on the passenger-side window. Helen powered down the window.

"Are you okay?" the woman shouted over the rumble and roar of the highway traffic.

"Yes, thanks to you," Helen said. "I'm a little shook up, but not hurt."

"Turn off your car," the woman shouted, "and put on your flashers."

"Oh, right." Helen followed her commands. Her hands still shook.

"Do you have AAA?" her rescuer asked.

Helen nodded.

"You should call them," the woman said.

With fumbling fingers, Helen found her AAA card and her cell phone. She tried to open her door, but too many cars zoomed past. She crawled across the seat and got out on the passenger side.

"Thank you again," Helen said.

"You're very welcome," the woman said. She was dressed in white eyelet lace, like a real angel, and her dark brown eyes were kind. "Now call AAA."

"Let me see the damage first," Helen said.

The shoulder was bristling with treacherous bits of rusty metal, rocks, and red plastic from broken taillights. Helen walked shakily to the back of her car. The Igloo's steel-belted radial was shredded. She'd been driving on the wheel rim.

Helen called AAA and shouted to the operator, "I've just had an accident. I'm not in a safe place. I'm on the side of I-95." Helen described where she was and the operator said they'd send out a truck.

"Do you want to alert the highway patrol, ma'am?" the operator asked.

"Yes," Helen said, and the operator switched her to the highway patrol. Helen assured the officer who answered that no one was hurt.

"Help is on the way," Helen told the roadside angel and thanked her again.

"Then I'll go now," she said, and waved good-bye.

As Helen watched the woman drive away, she realized she'd been too rattled to get her name. She saved my life with her quick thinking and she stopped to check on me, and I don't even know who she is.

The AAA truck arrived a few minutes later, driven by a burly thirtysomething African American. He kneeled down and checked the battered tire.

"Your wheel rim's safe to drive on," he said, then dug out the spare tire and checked the air pressure.

He jacked up the wheel and said, "That's one flat tire. What happened?" He loosened the lug nuts to remove the damaged tire.

"I don't know," Helen said. "I was driving along, the road felt bumpy and then I heard a pop. Luckily another woman realized what happened. She honked and put on her flashers and made such a racket, she slowed down the traffic and I steered my car over here. But I don't know why it blew. It's a new tire."

"It still has plenty of tread," he said.

"Guess I ran over a piece of debris and the tire exploded," Helen said.

He pulled the tire off the wheel rim and said, "What's this?" The repairman pulled a shiny, pointed metal object out of Helen's damaged tire.

"Looks like a little knife blade," Helen said.

"It's an X-Acto blade," he said. "I bought a set of these for my daughter. She's an artist—goes to the Art Institute of Fort Lauderdale."

"Maybe the tire picked up the blade accidentally."

"At that angle? That's a steel-belted radial, ma'am. Whoever did this jammed the knife into the sidewall with considerable force, and then unscrewed the knife and left this blade.

"This was no accident," the repairman said. "It was done on purpose.

"You got any enemies?"

CHAPTER 24

Helen slowly drove her car home on the side streets. The Igloo felt different with the new tire. Now the car was far safer than when she'd been sailing down the highway at seventy miles an hour, but she'd lost the sureness that made driving an effortless pleasure.

The street route took Helen through an iffy neighborhood on the edge of downtown. At a stoplight, Helen saw a homeless man in a wheelchair panhandling on the concrete median by McDonald's. Across the street, a badly worn blonde in a grubby yellow tank top commandeered the other median, holding up a cardboard sign for truck drivers.

One driver read the sign, then refused to look at her. She waved it and pushed out her substantial chest, but he kept his eyes glued to the stoplight. Helen studied the desperate woman and *Wham! Bam!* she suddenly realized how she could get into Markos's penthouse tonight. Thank you, ma'am, Helen thought as the light changed.

Finally, she was at the Coronado Tropic Apartments, safe at last, surprised it was only three thirty. Helen had half an hour before Detective Burt Pelham showed up to talk about Annabel's murder.

Margery was weeding the flower beds by the pool, ripping out trespassers with gusto and tossing them in a plastic bucket. Her burning cigarette was balanced on the edge of the sidewalk. The landlady wore a stretched-out lilac T-shirt and disreputable purple pants.

Margery looked up and said, "What happened to you? You look like you've been hit with a hurricane."

"I was nearly hit by a car," Helen said. "Several cars, in fact." She told Margery about the tire blowout while her landlady took a long drag on her cigarette.

"I'll get you some iced tea and a sandwich," Margery said. "We can have lunch by the pool."

"Good," Helen said. "I'll change into something comfortable. A Palmetto Hills detective is coming to interview me at four o'clock."

"We've got time," Margery said. She abandoned her bucket of wilting weeds and charged into her apartment.

Helen changed into cool cotton pants, a fresh shirt and sandals. By the time she'd set the umbrella table, Margery had arrived with a plate of chicken sandwiches and a pitcher of tea. A light breeze rippled the pool's turquoise water and purple bougainvillea blossoms drifted on the surface. Helen could feel the tension leaving her neck and back as she told Margery about Annabel's odd memorial service and then the tire blowout.

"So after Annabel's memorial," Helen said, "I took the highway home. I wanted to blow off some steam."

"Instead you blew a tire," Margery said. "I thought you just had a tune-up and bought four new tires."

"I did," Helen said. "The repairman told me someone stabbed my tire with this." She fished the X-Acto knife blade out of her purse. "His daughter is an artist and she uses these."

"Looks like a new blade," Margery said.

"Anybody else use X-Acto knives besides artists?" Helen asked.

"Lots of people," Margery said. "Cake decorators, for one."

"How?"

"They use the knives to shape fondant roses, leaves and other cake trimming. Quilters, ice sculptors, model airplane makers. Supermarket box jockeys use them to slice open cardboard boxes."

"I don't think there were many box jockeys or ice sculptors at Annabel's memorial," Helen said. "But the place was crawling with artists."

"And you think one of them stuck a knife in your tire?" Margery said.

"Yes," Helen said. "Valet-parked cars are in an open lot. Anyone could have stuck that knife in my tire. Everyone I suspect was at that service: Hugo, Annabel's ex. Cissy, her good friend who thinks Annabel committed suicide. Miranda, the woman who owns the lawn service. Miranda's fiancée, Lita, made a scene when she found out Clay had cremated Annabel's paintings along with her body."

"With her fiancée there? That must have been awkward."

"It was, but I don't blame Lita. Clay destroyed his wife's legacy. Even he could have slipped downstairs and stabbed my tire."

"Are you afraid someone will stab you next?" Margery said.

"That's kind of the message, isn't it?" Helen said.

"Maybe the message is you're getting too close," Margery said.

"To what?" Helen said. She poked at that thought while Margery lit another cigarette.

When Helen was tired of worrying the subject, she asked, "Did you see Markos on the Channel Seventy-seven noon news?"

"Didn't watch it," Margery said. "I've been working in the yard. The weeds are easier to pull when the ground's wet. Why would Markos be on TV?"

Helen sat up straighter. She could picture the scene outside Silver Glade—Valerie interviewing Markos in his Arab robes, Phil smiling smugly as he stood by the rented Rolls. She felt herself getting angry all over again.

"I think Phil's got him mixed up in some crazy scheme," Helen said. "He had Markos dressed up like Lawrence of Arabia. Valerie interviewed him about his supposed gold coin collection and her questions told me she was in on it. Phil is using Markos for bait, Margery! And he didn't tell me. Just sent me a coded text while I was at the memorial service, so I couldn't answer him. I don't even know how Phil found Valerie and Markos."

"Together," Margery said. "They were having breakfast out here at seven this morning. Markos fixed Bellinis and eggs Benedict with portabella mushrooms."

"What a romantic breakfast," Helen said. She could almost taste the peaches and champagne in the Bellinis.

"Very," Margery said.

"It was thoughtful of Markos to substitute low-cal mushrooms for the high-calorie English muffins in the eggs Benedict. Valerie has to watch her weight because she's on-camera."

"He made a low-cal sauce, too," Margery said. "They politely invited me to join them, but I would have been a third wheel. Valerie had a glow you could see from outer space. Phil stopped to talk to them when he got home from work this morning."

"Oh," Helen said.

"Oh? Aren't jealous, are we?" Margery grinned at her and unleashed a long spiral of smoke. "You're not seeing much of your man lately."

"I'm not jealous," Helen said. "But those two didn't waste any time."

"Why should they?" Margery said. "Two beautiful single adults. If I were younger, I'd jump Markos's bones."

She looked at Helen. "Don't go all midwestern on me. Ditch that disapproving look."

"I'm not," Helen said. "I'm worried about Markos. Phil's plan to trap the Gold Ghost is risky. If Markos gets hurt, I'll kill Phil."

"I wouldn't say that too loud," Margery said. "I think that's your detective at the gate." She stubbed out her cigarette, picked up the sandwich plates and disappeared into her apartment.

Even on this rather mild day, Detective Burt Pelham looked hot in his dark gray suit. His red tie hung limp around his neck and his brassy blond hair was sweaty.

"Ms. Hawthorne," he said, giving her a formal nod.

"Let's go up to my office," Helen said, and he followed her upstairs into the chilled air of Coronado Investigations. "Would you like a bottle of water?"

"No, thanks," he said.

"Well, I would. I'll be right back."

When she returned, Detective Pelham was sitting in her black-and-chrome chair, and Helen knew this was a territorial battle. She shoved the yellow client chair aside and pulled the other black chair around so she was sitting in front of the detective. Their knees were almost touching and he looked uncomfortable.

Good, she thought, opening her bottle. Round one to me.

"Ms. Hawthorne," he said. "I'd like to ask you some questions about the murder of Annabel Lee Griffin."

"As you know, I am a licensed private eye, Detective, and anything I've learned is confidential between me and my client under Florida Statute 493."

"Who's your client?" he asked.

"That's also confidential," Helen said. "You know that."

"And you know your client can waive that right."

"I asked my client and my client did not want to waive that right," Helen said.

"Very carefully stated," the detective said. "You're good, Ms. Hawthorne. You and your partner have done a pretty good job with some difficult cases."

Helen was not about to be patronized. "Better than 'pretty good,' Detective. We solved some cases the police couldn't." She took a long drink of water.

"I'm sure they would have, given time," he said.

Helen refused to be verbally patted on the head. "Are we going to spend the afternoon debating that?" she said. "I have another appointment and I'm sure you're busy, too."

"We're both busy," he said. "We can agree on that. So let's cut to the chase. We both want Mrs. Griffin's killer caught, but we could catch him faster if we pooled our knowledge."

Him? Did the detective suspect Hugo or Clay? If she knew which man, Helen could quit spinning her wheels and gain some traction on this case. She wanted it solved, but she couldn't reveal any information without Jenny's permission.

"All I'm asking is that you talk to your client again," Detective Pelham said.

Nice little trap, Helen thought. But I'm not falling for it. Most of the Florida detectives I've dealt with were dumb—retired snowbirds who came down here for an easy job. Pelham seems smarter than that.

"I will ask my client, either him or her," Helen said. "I'll call that client in the back office to keep our conversation confidential."

"I'm willing to wait while you make a call," he said.

Helen went into the back office, a former bedroom, shut the door and called Jenny. She was relieved when her client answered.

"Hi!" Helen said, too brightly. "I'm with Palmetto Hills Detective Burt Pelham." Please get the hidden message, she thought.

"So you can't really talk," Jenny said.

"That's right," Helen said. "Listen, Detective Pelham is asking you to release me from our confidentiality agreement. I think it would help solve the case faster and save you money. Some of the detectives I've dealt with in the past were dumber than a box of hammers, but this one seems smart. I think we should trust him."

"He didn't seem all that smart when I talked to him," Jenny said. "I told him Hugo killed Annabel and I explained why in great detail."

"But what if Hugo didn't kill Annabel?" Helen said. "Are you willing to let the real killer go free because you want him to be Hugo?"

"Hugo *is* the real killer," Jenny said. "And it's your job to prove it."

"No," Helen said. "Read your contract. It's my job to catch the killer of Annabel Lee Griffin."

"And that's Hugo," Jenny said. "Same thing. I don't want you to share any information with that police detective, including my name. Especially my name."

"If that's what you want," Helen said, trying to hide her annoyance. "But your decision goes against what I think is in your best interest."

"*I'm* the client," Jenny said. "*I'm* paying. Do your job." Jenny hung up.

Helen wanted to throw her cell phone across the room. Cooperating with the detective would have given her a convenient shortcut to end this case.

She shut the door to the back office a little too hard. While she was on the phone, Detective Pelham had scooted his chair back a couple of inches.

Helen sat down and slid her chair forward, so they were once again almost knee to knee, and watched him lean back when she invaded his space.

"I'm sorry," she said. "My client has refused. I wish I could cooperate, but I can't say anything."

"Then I have a hypothetical question for you that might help both of us," he said.

"Let's say a woman was poisoned when she drank iced tea laced with nicotine. One of the chief suspects is her husband. He was unfaithful, had taken out a big life insurance policy on her, and was jealous because her career was rising faster than his."

Pelham is smart, Helen thought. He suspects Clay, not Hugo.

"Furthermore, this hypothetical woman was thinking about divorce but hadn't taken any steps yet, except to mention she was unhappy to one or two people.

"If this hypothetical woman died, her husband would get a substantial check from her life insurance. If she divorced him, he'd get nothing."

Pelham has dug up exactly what I have, Helen thought.

"That's a fascinating story," Helen said. "But aren't those circumstances enough to get the husband arrested for her murder? Hypothetically, of course."

"No," he said. "Suspicion alone is not enough. There's no evidence the husband killed his wife. If he was arrested now, the speedy trial rules would apply. A smart attorney would do nothing to delay the proceedings. If the husband wasn't brought to trial within one hundred eighty days, the prosecution would automatically lose and it would be very difficult to charge the husband again for that crime.

"Hypothetically, if a private detective investigating the same case knew of any evidence, then the husband could be arrested."

"I see," Helen said. "Hypothetically, I would say that detective doesn't have any evidence."

"Does this hypothetical detective know what happened to Mrs. Griffin's thermos when she was taken ill in the parking lot?"

"No," Helen said. "Not a clue. The victim was drinking from it while her friend loaded their art supplies into the trunk of her car. The next thing I knew, the victim was deathly ill and I was calling 911. That's all I can say. Hypothetically, of course. The detective has no personal knowledge of what happened to the thermos."

But maybe I should start asking about it, Helen thought.

"I'm done playing games, Ms. Hawthorne," Detective Pelham said. "If you can't give me a straight answer, I can go to a judge to compel you to talk."

"I would if I could," Helen said. "But my client won't let me and I don't know any more than you do. Uh, hypothetically speaking."

Those last two words were pathetic pasties. They couldn't hide that she'd nakedly betrayed her client. Worse, Pelham didn't believe her.

He was still talking. "The judge could order you to talk or he could hold an in-camera hearing. That means the judge and you would have a very confidential meeting, usually with a court reporter. Then he or she would interview you and ask questions. Because this is a murder case, you would most likely be compelled to testify about the murder of Annabel Lee Griffin.

"The judge would rule on this, Ms. Hawthorne, and you'd be bound to disclose any information or evidence you have."

"There is no evidence," Helen said.

"Right," he said. He stood up and walked out, slamming the door so hard the glass rattled.

Helen was alone with her double failure: She'd failed her client and herself.

CHAPTER 25

"What the hell were you doing?" Helen shouted when Phil came home at five o'clock that afternoon. She'd been pacing in his apartment, rehashing her grievances and growing madder by the minute.

"Bringing home the bacon," he said, handing her a warm, grease-spotted pizza box. "Actually the pepperoni and mushroom. That's your favorite."

He smiled his cute little-boy smile. This time, his innocent act didn't work.

"I'm not talking about pizza," Helen said, glaring at him. His smile melted like snow on a sunny spring day. Phil looked tired this afternoon. This morning's bold, super-starched security guard had a wrinkled uniform. His long hair looked oily and in need of a wash. Helen wished she didn't want to hug and strangle him at the same time.

"I meant that charade at Silver Glade with Markos dressed like the sheik of Araby."

"The what?" Phil said.

"Markos!" Helen said. "In the flapping white robes and headdress. The Cuban Arabian."

"He looked good, didn't he?" Phil said. Helen wanted to slap that smile off his face. Phil refused to get angry, which only made her more furious.

"Why didn't you tell me about this plan?" she said. "I'm your partner. I'm your wife! I have a right to know." Helen fought hard to keep the hurt out of her voice, but she didn't quite succeed. She was afraid she'd start crying and hoped her anger would burn away the tears.

"I was going to tell you when I came home this morning," Phil said, "but you were sound asleep. You looked so cute, I didn't want to wake you."

"Sleep! I had to get up at eight anyway," Helen said. "If you're so worried about my sleep, what about the sleep I'm going to lose over this escapade?"

"You worry too much," Phil said.

"And you don't worry enough," Helen said. "How the hell did you rope Valerie into this scheme?"

"I promised her an exclusive, the way we always do," Phil said.

"Hah!" Helen said. "Valerie will do anything for an Emmy."

"Hey, hey," Phil said, trying to soothe her. "That's not fair. We owe our success to Valerie. Those stories she did about Coronado Investigations when we were starting launched us."

"And won Valerie how many Emmys?" Helen asked.

"So it was mutually beneficial," Phil said. "Thanks to her, we've never spent a penny on advertising—and look where we are today."

"On the verge of having our first dead operative," Helen said.

"Like me, Valerie believes that Markos is a grown man."

"He's a college student," Helen said. "If you want someone to gut a grapefruit, he's your man. But he has no experience in self-defense."

"We've used him as an undercover operative before," Phil said.

"And we were both with him," Helen said. "And we had armed police with us."

"He did a terrific job," Phil said.

"And almost collapsed when it was over," Helen said.

"So, that's how it works. You get high on the adrenaline and then you feel like someone pulled the plug and you want to sleep for a week."

"When did you come up with this scheme to use Markos as bait?"

"He's not bait," Phil said. "He's an undercover operative, making double the usual pay. I got the idea late last night. Victor, the Silver Glade manager, called me into work early and said I had to come up with something or else."

"Or else what?" Helen asked.

"He'd have to let us go. He can't afford to keep me on the payroll forever and the condo owners give him more grief every time there's another burglary. They're in his office all day long asking what he's doing to stop the burglaries.

"We can't afford to lose this contract, so I told Victor I'd come up with something that night, and I wracked my brains for a solution. I was on my rounds in the building when I got the inspiration: I realized the penthouse is empty—and likely to stay that way. The residents tell me it's way overpriced. It's fully furnished and the price includes all this overdone custom-made furniture.

"I thought we could stage a sting operation and lure the Gold Ghost up there.

"When we catch the burglar, that Silver Glade penthouse will get tons of publicity. It's already started. You didn't stay for the best part of the interview. Valerie went up there with a camera crew and they shot the whole place, all ten thousand square feet. It's fantastic, Helen. It even has a Jacuzzi and an indoor pool with a waterfall. It's like *Lifestyles of the Rich and Famous*."

Helen groaned. "Did the TV crew video the bedrooms?"

"All six of them," Phil said. "The master bedroom has the Jacuzzi and this big canopy bed with a gold headboard. It's right off the balcony."

"So you showed the Gold Ghost exactly where he can find Markos," Helen said.

"That was misdirection," Phil said. "Markos will be sitting in the living room with the lights off. It will be easier to take down the Gold Ghost in there."

"How?" Helen said.

"There are two mahogany chairs right by the entrance to the room. Markos can slug him with a chair and knock him out. If he misses, there's a heavy cut-crystal ashtray on the side table. He thunks the Gold Ghost with that and it's bye-bye."

"A chair," Helen said, her voice flat. "And an ashtray. Yep, that's real protection, Phil. What caliber ashtray do you carry on your rounds? Me, I prefer a good Waterford .44-caliber vase, but other people prefer the protection of the .22-caliber Baccarat fruit bowl."

"You don't have to be so sarcastic," Phil said. "I'm licensed to carry. You know that."

"And how do you know the Gold Ghost doesn't have a gun?" Helen said. "It's Florida! Everybody here has a gun. The whole state is gun-happy. Our lawmakers up in Tallahassee want people carrying concealed weapons on college campuses. Markos is probably the only person in Florida who doesn't have a gun."

"Besides you," Phil said.

"Right," Helen said. "Now tell me about your grand plan to catch the Gold Ghost."

"I thought if Markos dressed up as a rich Arab, he could say he had a fabulous gold coin collection. That interview would lure the Gold Ghost into a controlled situation, and *boom!* We'd catch him."

"Or *boom!* It blows up in our faces," Helen said.

"If I may continue," Phil said. "I called Victor at home and told him my plan."

"You woke up the condo manager but didn't call me?" Helen said.

"I didn't wake up Victor. It was six in the morning and he was already awake. He loved the idea and approved it. He didn't even mind that I rented the Rolls."

"Did you rent it from the same place we got that Rolls when we used Margery as an operative?"

"Of course," he said. "And may I add, you didn't mind my using a seventy-six-year-old woman as an operative."

"Margery is tougher than both of us," Helen said. "And she knows how to think on her feet."

"Maybe," Phil said. That's all he was going to concede. "I rented Markos's costume, too. I got the Deluxe Arab Prince. Victor said to spend whatever I needed to make the plan work.

"When I came home, I saw Markos and Valerie eating breakfast by the pool and knew my plan was meant to be."

"Really?" Helen said. "You're supposed to be a hardheaded private eye, not some New Age gooney looking for signs and portents. You do realize the Gold Ghost has already killed one person?"

"A defenseless old man," Phil said. "The poor guy wandered out of his bedroom and got whacked with a lamp. Have you seen the muscles on Markos? Of course you have—I've seen you drooling over him."

"I wasn't drooling," Helen said, but she felt her own stab of guilt. "I was noticing. Yes, Markos is muscular, but can he stay alert all night? What if he falls asleep in that plush playhouse and the Gold Ghost sneaks up on him?"

"He won't fall asleep," Phil said. "I'll make sure of that. Markos will check in with me every half hour. If I don't hear from him, I'll come upstairs and check on him.

"Markos is strong. He can take care of himself. And I'll be on duty."

"Twenty floors away!" Helen said. "He'll be dead by the time you get to his penthouse. What are you going to do? Fly up there? There's no way Markos is going to be left alone in that huge place. I'll be there with him."

"You!" Phil said. "What can you do? You don't like guns. You're sure not trained in the martial arts."

"I have pepper spray," Helen said. "I've used it before."

"If I recall, the last time you used it, you got shot in the face with your own spray," Phil said.

"So? I survived. And the killer got caught. I'll put up with a little discomfort to save Markos from getting killed.

"If the Gold Ghost gets in, I'll call you or dial 911—or both—and get help in a hurry. This is a two-person job, Phil. The thief could sneak up on Markos before he calls for help. I'll be there tonight."

"And how are you going to get into the penthouse suite?" Phil asked. "We've already established that Markos is supposed to be from a foreign country. We strongly suspect the thefts are inside jobs and someone is watching the victims' condos.

"What excuse will you use to visit our phony prince? You're with the local Welcome Wagon? Those women don't stay the night."

"Call girls do," Helen said. "I'll be from an escort service. That way I can stay with him all night."

"A call girl?"

"That's an expensive condominium," Helen said. "I assume that security is used to dealing with visitors from escort services. Well?"

"The other guards say they see them," Phil said. "Especially on Wednesday nights."

"Why Wednesdays?" Helen asked.

"Social Security checks are automatically deposited on the second, third or fourth Wednesdays every month. That's your tax dollar at work."

"Make love, not war," Helen said. "I'd rather have my money spent on pretty women than on some of the other ways the feds waste it."

"Not all the escorts going to the building are women," Phil said. "There's a man on the ninth floor who has a lot of 'nephews' visiting. They all look alike: blond, tanned, slightly sneery and squeezed into tight shorts."

"So it won't be a problem for me to get into the condo," Helen said. "Especially if you're on duty."

"No," Phil said. "It's too dangerous."

"Oh, so you admit this assignment is dangerous. And it's okay to sacrifice Markos?"

"Yes! No! It's not the same. Besides, what are you going to do once you're upstairs? Club the Gold Ghost with your four-inch heels?"

"No, call girls carry big bags. I'll have sensible clothes and shoes stashed in mine."

"You're making some ugly cultural and sexist assumptions," Phil said.

"I'll live with them," Helen said. "Just so Markos isn't hurt."

"Let's say you do this crazy plan," Phil said.

"I *will do* this," Helen said. "Got that?"

"Okay, but how are you going to get to the Silver Glade?"

"Drive," Helen said.

"In the Igloo? You've been there several times already in your car. The valets might recognize it. It will show up on the security footage."

"Then I'll take a taxi." Helen picked up her purse and headed for the door.

"Your pizza's getting cold," he said. "Where are you going?"

"Shopping," Helen said. "I don't have the right clothes or shoes to look like a high-class escort. And we have an expense account."

"But what about the pizza?" Phil said.

"It's even better when it's reheated," Helen said. "Bye."

CHAPTER 26

At the stroke of midnight, Helen was transformed into a lady of the evening. She slung her soft leather bag on her shoulder and stepped into the moon-silvered night. The air was fragrant with flowers and a faint whiff of cigarette smoke.

Margery's sitting out here in the dark, Helen thought. She saw the red eye of her landlady's Marlboro glaring by the pool. Margery whistled when she saw Helen. "You look like a million bucks," she said.

"Close," Helen said. "I'm supposed to look like forty thousand a night."

"You're that good, huh?" Margery said, and grinned up at her from the chaise. "Governor Eliot Spitzer paid forty-three hundred a night for Kristen."

"He was a cheap politician," Helen said. "I'm a high-class escort. Forty thousand a night is what we command during the Cannes Film Festival. Plus we go to all the A-list parties."

"We?" Margery said. "And what do we do for that kind of money? Besides the obvious, of course."

"We're high-maintenance," Helen said. "A working girl has to invest in her main assets. A couture bustier is two thousand dollars. It's expensive to look good: We have to eat right, hire fitness trainers and be perfectly groomed. I spent hours getting my hair, nails and makeup done for tonight."

"Good paint job," Margery said. "Took ten years off you."

"The false eyelashes feel like lead weights," Helen said.

"You did some serious shopping," Margery said. "You aren't dressed like a Lauderdale working girl."

"A high-class escort has a more subdued style than a common streetwalker. This is a Herve Leger bandage dress."

"Looks more like a tourniquet," Margery said. "Shows off those long legs. How much?"

"Almost eight hundred dollars," Helen said. "But you have to spend money to look like money."

"Whose money are you spending?" Margery said.

"The client's, of course," Helen said. "Unlimited expense account."

"Those ankle-strap spikes are killer," Margery said.

"Jimmy Choos. Twenty-five hundred dollars," Helen said. They were killer. The double band wrapping her ankles had a faint hint of bondage. Helen wished she was stepping out with Phil in those hot shoes instead of babysitting Markos.

She felt as shaky as a newborn colt walking in her glittering stilettos. "I'd better keep moving. My cab will be here any moment."

"You need help walking on those stilts? I'll walk you to the gate," Margery said, stubbing out her cigarette. She lit the way with the flashlight app on her cell phone.

"I feel kind of ridiculous in this outfit," Helen said. "But I wanted to look fit for a king."

"I thought he was a prince," Margery said.

"Actually, I'm not sure what Markos is supposed to be, but I'll be glad when I can ditch this getup and put on jeans and sneakers."

"You look very nice," Margery said, and patted Helen's bare arm.

Helen tried not to tear up. She wished her own mother had told her that. But Helen's hyper-religious mother would have condemned Helen to the everlasting fire for dressing like this. Dolores even disapproved of Helen divorcing her unfaithful husband.

I can't cry, Helen thought. My eyeliner will run. She saw headlights approaching the Coronado.

"That's your cab," Margery said. She grinned wickedly. "Maybe the driver will mistake me for a madam."

"Margery!" Helen said. But she was laughing when the driver pulled up and pleased to see how quickly he jumped out of the cab to hold the door for her. Helen tried to fold herself discreetly into the backseat. Margery winked and waved good-bye.

The Silver Glade Condominiums valet tripped over his feet scoping out Helen. She sashayed across the slippery marble floor, aware that Phil's eyes were glued to her figure. Like many wives, she sometimes wondered if her husband took her for granted. But not tonight.

"Helen," Phil said, his voice an awed whisper. "You look fantastic."

Helen decided to keep in character. "I'm here to see Prince Abdul in the penthouse apartment," she said. "Please let him know I'm here."

"Sure, sure," Phil said. "Just sign the visitors' book. And you're getting out of that dress right away, aren't you?"

"Such a personal question!" Helen said.

Phil was not in a joking mood. "I mean, you're not going to hang around upstairs dressed like that, are you? You won't be able to help Mark—uh, Abdul if that Gold Ghost shows up."

"I'll get out of the dress as fast as I can," Helen said, "but I might need help unlacing these heels."

"Helen!"

Phil looks miserable, Helen thought. Good. Even the best husband needs a little waking up.

"While we're gabbing," she said, "the Gold Ghost could sneak past and be upstairs. I see Markos every day. If I wanted an affair, it would have started months ago. You either trust me or you don't."

"Of course I trust you," he said. "I've been calling Markos every half hour. The next check-in is at twelve thirty, in about ten minutes."

He started to kiss her, but Helen shook her head. "The security camera is running," she said.

"I love you," he whispered. "Please stay safe."

"I love you, too," she said, and she wished she'd kissed him as the elevator swallowed her. She was on her way to confront a killer. Who knew what could happen.

The elevator opened directly into the penthouse lobby, where Markos waited for her in jeans and a black T-shirt.

Helen blinked when she saw the penthouse. It looked like a wedding cake dipped in gold. The furniture and curtains were heavy red velvet and the Oriental rug was as big as Bahrain.

"Wow!" Helen said.

"Back at you," Markos said. "You look amazing."

"So does your penthouse," Helen said.

"Can you believe all this red velvet?" Markos said. "In Florida?"

"I'm glad you ditched the Arab outfit," Helen said.

"I was afraid I'd trip over the robes," he said. "Besides, I don't think real Arabs dress like that."

"Where can I change my clothes?" Helen said.

"You've got your choice of five guest rooms. You've gotta see the one on the right."

The room was adorned with swags of royal purple and gold with a curlicued gold bed shaped like a giant swan. The headboard was the swan's tail feathers and the bird's head was at the foot of the bed. The teardrop mattress looked uncomfortable.

Helen couldn't figure out how to perch on the swan's wings, so she sat in a gold-and-purple velvet chair. It was a relief to take off those heels—they left marks on her ankles. She slipped on her jeans, a blue shirt, and her black Chuck Taylor sneakers, then slid her pepper spray canister into her shirt pocket and shut the door on the nightmare swan.

"I'll give you a quick tour," Markos said. "Then we'll turn out the lights, so the Gold Ghost thinks the prince is asleep."

Markos led Helen through a cloying display of crystal, gold and velvet until she felt like she'd eaten too many bonbons. At last, they were in the kitchen, a surprisingly homey room with honey-colored cabinets and designer appliances.

"This kitchen is the size of my apartment," Helen said, "but it's the only livable room in this sky mansion."

"Phil had supplies delivered," Markos said. "I've been cooking all day."

Helen almost said, "I'm sorry," before she remembered cooking was Markos's idea of a good time. She also realized she was hungry. That pizza was hours ago.

"I've made espresso to keep us awake," he said. The platters lined up on the granite counters looked like art in a gallery. Markos described each one. "Those are mini lamb kebabs," he said. "That's chickpea and walnut falafel. That's real hummus with tahini, and this is baba ghanoush, made with roasted eggplant, garlic and tahini sauce."

"Yum," Helen said. "I've had it before, but what is tahini sauce?"

"A paste made from crushed sesame seeds, lemon juice and garlic. You can buy it, but I like to make my own. It's creamier but doesn't have the fat of a cream sauce."

A salsa ringtone erupted from Markos's cell phone. Helen jumped. Markos clicked on his phone and said, "Hi, Phil, all is well. Helen and I are about to have some snacks in the living room. Okay, talk to you at one o'clock. Yes, yes, I'll tell her you love her, but she knows that."

Helen smiled and helped carry the snacks into the garish living room and set them on the coffee table, an absurd gold Egyptian sphinx with wings and King Tut's head.

Helen checked the area around the balcony. The sliders were hidden behind yards of thick red velvet. The balcony opened onto two doors: One led to the master bedroom, the other to the living room.

Two chairs flanked the living room entrance off the balcony, the backs carved into stylized suns. Helen figured the daggered sun rays could inflict serious damage. Next to each chair a round gold table held a cut-crystal ashtray the size of a hubcap.

I'll stick with my pepper spray, she thought, but these could make good backup.

"Time for His Highness to turn in," Helen said.

Markos doused the lights and flipped a wall switch to open the red velvet curtains, revealing twenty-foot tall windows. Silver moonlight made a shining path across the wrinkled silk sea, and the black velvet sky was scattered with stars.

"How could anyone cover up this stunning view?" Helen said. "The moon's so bright we don't need lights."

"I wish Valerie was here with me," Markos said, then added, "Sorry, Helen, nothing wrong with you . . ."

"But I'm not Valerie," Helen said, "and you're not Phil."

"She's wonderful, isn't she?" Markos said, his voice soft. "Beautiful, talented, intelligent, strong. What does she see in me?"

"Someone who's equally talented," Helen said, "and strong and handsome." She scooped up warm hummus with a pita triangle, then polished off a lamb kebab spiced with garlic and oregano.

"This is fabulous," she said between bites.

"Thank you," Markos said. "But I haven't achieved what Valerie has. I'm afraid I'm no match for her."

Helen nibbled on the baba ghanoush, then left it alone. It was a little too vegetably for her taste. "I've known Valerie for several years," she said. "Like most strong women, she dates equals."

Including my husband, before I knew both of them, she thought. But Markos didn't need to know that bit of ancient history.

They both filled their plates with more snacks and ate until Helen broke the awkward silence. "Where did you eat on your date the other night?"

"I wanted to take her someplace special on Las Olas, but she wanted a casual dinner. We picked up lobster tacos at the Mobstah Lobstah food truck and a bottle of champagne and sat on the beach."

"Sounds romantic," Helen said. She was feeling sleepy from the food and took a drink of espresso with two cubes of sugar in the tiny porcelain cup. The sugared caffeine should keep her awake.

"It was. We couldn't have alcohol on the beach, so I poured the champagne into water bottles. We sat on the sand and talked for hours about everything—her job, my plans to open my own restaurant, her family, my family. We came back to the Coronado about three in the morning and talked some more. I fixed her breakfast the next morning and we ate by the pool. That's when we saw Phil and he asked me to be an operative."

"If you talked to Valerie for hours, then you're her equal," Helen said. "You kept up with her and didn't have to struggle for conversation." If you spent the time at your place talking, she thought, and shooed that thought away.

"But what about my age?" he asked.

"What about it?" Helen said. "For a young man, you're awfully old-school. What's Valerie say?"

"She was afraid I wouldn't find *her* attractive. She's—she's perfect!"

"Then there's your answer," Helen said. "The age issue is only a problem for you."

Helen was relieved when the phone interrupted. It was time for Phil's one o'clock check-in.

"All's well, Phil," Markos told him.

Helen checked the balcony while the two men talked. It wrapped around the outside of the vast penthouse. This corner was littered with wrought-iron furniture, and the red-flowered cushions looked like an explosion in a flower shop. She counted two settees, two chaises with side tables, and a small dining table with four chairs. The railing was lined with white pots planted with tough, leathery-leaved shrubbery.

Markos hung up his cell and asked, "How's the case going with the poisoned artist, Annabel Lee Griffin? Have you found the killer?"

"How did you know about the case?" Helen asked.

"I heard you talking to Margery," Markos said. "Now that I'm an operative like she is, you can discuss it with me. I won't talk."

"Not even to Valerie?"

"She understands we have to keep our professional lives separate," he said.

So Helen told him about her (unnamed) client who insisted that Annabel's killer was the loutish Hugo.

"And you don't think he is?" Markos said, reaching for more hummus.

"I'd like him to be, but I suspect Annabel was killed by Miranda, the jealous fiancée of the woman who shared Annabel's FAT Village studio. Or Clay, Annabel's husband.

"I think the police detective believes Clay killed her, but we don't have any proof. And Cissy, Annabel's good friend, thinks she committed suicide."

"But you think she was murdered," Markos said. He polished off the last lamb kebab and all the baba ghanoush.

"Yes. I agree with the professionals: The medical examiner ruled Annabel's death a homicide, and the detective agrees. Clay was unfaithful, he needed money and he resented his talented wife. He even burned her paintings."

"How?" Markos asked.

"He stashed them in Annabel's coffin when she was cremated."

"That doesn't make sense," Markos said. "Are her paintings valuable?"

"They were getting to be," Helen said. "Her work was starting to sell for three to five thousand dollars a canvas."

"How many paintings did Clay burn?" Markos asked.

"Ten, according to Lita. That's how many he took from Annabel's studio."

"Why would a man hard up for money burn more than fifty thousand dollars?" Markos said. "Who sets fire to a stack of cash?

Maybe he said he burned them but he actually sold them. Didn't a local dealer handle her work?"

"I don't think Clay would have sold Annabel's paintings to Robert Horton, the Las Olas art dealer," Helen said.

"Would Robert tell you if he'd bought them?" Markos said. "It's kind of a questionable deal."

"Maybe I'm naive," Helen said, "but I trust Robert."

"Then why don't you check with him?" Markos said. "Robert would tell you where they could be sold. Then you might want to check with the crematorium and see if the paintings really were in Annabel's casket."

"Wonderful idea," Helen said. "Markos, you're a natural PI. I'd kiss you if you didn't belong to another woman."

Clunk! Scrape!

"What was that?" Helen whispered.

Markos rolled off the couch and looked out the window.

"A noise," he said. "A chair was knocked over. On the balcony."

CHAPTER 27

"It's just the wind," Markos whispered.

He and Helen were crouched in the dark living room behind a red-velvet barge of a couch. Both had a clear view of the moonlit balcony.

"It really whips around when you live near the water," he said. "I've been listening to it all day. See that bush moving there?"

"Yes," Helen whispered back. "I also see the other bushes aren't moving. The wind doesn't rustle one shrub."

A tense silence stretched between them as they watched the shrub suddenly stop shaking.

Helen stared into the darkness, trying to distinguish shapes in the moon-stark shadows on the balcony, the foliage, and the wrought-iron furniture.

"See that weird shadow by the table?" she whispered. "Next to the wrought-iron chair?" Markos nodded.

"The shadow's moving this way!" Markos said.

"Shadows don't crab crawl," Helen said. "That's a man. Check out the head."

"The Gold Ghost," Markos said. "We're the first people who've ever seen him."

Except for the man he killed, Helen thought. Her heart was pounding and she felt like she was moving underwater. Her vision locked in on that low-slung black shape, moving like a predatory beast straight for the balcony sliders. The killer was less than twenty feet away.

Markos's open, boyish face was alert, his massive muscles tensed. He smiled, and Helen wanted to tell him to take this seriously. This wasn't a TV show. This adventure could turn deadly.

She felt sick. Garlic, lemon juice and espresso rose in her throat. Why did I pig out on all that food? she wondered, but she knew the answer. She ate when she was nervous.

Helen felt a flash of anger at her husband. Oh, Phil, why did you get Markos tangled in this? Hell, why didn't I open my big mouth? I didn't have to go along with Phil's crazy scheme. I could have stopped it anytime today. I'm as much to blame as my husband if anything happens to Markos.

Helen couldn't let that happen.

"I'm calling Phil," she whispered. "Now."

"Do we need him?" Markos asked. "The Gold Ghost doesn't look that big. I can take him out. I've got more muscles than he does."

"Careful! The wiry types can be dangerous," she said. "You don't know if he's armed. That's why they used to call guns 'equalizers.' It doesn't matter how big he is if he has a gun."

"I can grab his wrist and turn his weapon on him," Markos said.

Helen wanted to wipe that smug smile off his handsome face. This wasn't a video game. This was life and death, and so far, the Gold Ghost's record was 1–0.

"He's already killed one person," she said.

"An old man," Markos said.

Helen wasn't going to debate the issue. "Is that balcony slider locked?"

"Yes, but the lock is so simple a two-year-old can pop it," Markos said.

"At least it will slow him down a little," Helen whispered as she reached for her phone. "I'm calling for backup."

She texted Phil the number 666, their silent code for the Gold Ghost, then crawled along the soft, thick carpet to the hall with the guest bedrooms so she could talk to the 911 operator.

As her fingers fumbled with her phone, she wished she could answer her own questions: How did the Gold Ghost get on the balcony tonight? Did he climb the side of the building? If so, why didn't the exterior cameras catch him?

Where was Phil? He'd notice someone climbing the side of the condo. So would the residents of Little New York, even at this hour. They had all been sleepless since the Gold Ghost first struck.

She wished she and Phil had agreed to a confirmation text, so she'd know he'd gotten her message. I'd better call him, she thought, and speed-dialed Phil's cell phone number. It rang and rang until she heard Phil's voice mail recording: *"Hi, I'm Phil Sagemont. Please leave a message and I'll get back to you."*

A terrible thought slammed through Helen's soul: What if the burglar had attacked Phil? He could be bleeding out on that cold black marble lobby floor right now. This recorded message will be the only way I'll ever hear his voice again.

Oh, cut the drama, she decided. That strapping blond valet is downstairs, too. Phil's fine. The Gold Ghost killed an old man. He won't take on two healthy young ones.

She longed to run downstairs and check on her partner and husband but knew she couldn't. It's up to me to protect Markos. Who knows when the cops will get here? Never, if I don't dial 911.

"Nine-one-one. What's your emergency?" the operator answered.

Helen found her flat, emotionless voice oddly comforting. Its passionless tones told her, *Reason reigns here. Bad things will be fixed. People will be saved. That's what we do.*

"I need help," Helen said, her voice low and breathless. "A man is trying to break into the penthouse at the Silver Glade Condominiums." She rattled off the address. "I think he's the Gold Ghost. The man who's been burglarizing condos in Little New York."

Helen expected the 911 operator to respond to this information, but she kept asking questions. She's trying to size up the situation, Helen decided.

"Is the intruder breaking down your front door?" the operator asked.

"No, he's on the balcony," Helen said.

"How did he get there?"

"I don't know," Helen said. "Somehow he climbed twenty stories."

"Are you in danger, ma'am?' the operator asked.

"Yes," Helen said, then stumbled. "I mean, not yet, but I will be. He's already killed once."

"Did he kill someone in your apartment? Do you have a deceased individual?"

"No, he killed an old man. In another condo building. Two days ago, I think. He's the Gold Ghost. I'm sure of it. Call the police. Get law enforcement here, please, before he hurts someone again."

"Are you alone?"

"There's one other person with me."

"Are you armed?"

"No," Helen said.

"Is the assailant armed?"

"I don't know," she said. "He hasn't attacked yet."

Helen heard a soft scraping sound. What was that? Warm, soggy air poured into the air-conditioned condo. Did the Gold Ghost break the glass on the balcony slider? Last winter, local burglars put bricks through slider doors for quick, easy entry. But breaking glass would make more noise, wouldn't it?

This was a different kind of sound, a metallic drag-scrape. Helen had to see what was happening.

She peeked around the corner and saw the intruder had popped the locked slider out of its track with some kind of tool—a flathead screwdriver? Phil had told her that's how experienced burglars got around locked sliders: They removed the whole door.

She saw the Gold Ghost lift the slider effortlessly out of the track, as if it were cardboard instead of glass, and lean it against the other slider.

"Ma'am?" the 911 operator asked. "Are you still there?"

"Can't talk," Helen said in a stripped-down hiss. "He's inside. Hurry! Please!"

"Don't hang up, ma'am," the operator said. "Help is on the way."

Helen dropped her cell in the hall and ran into the living room, grateful for the soft, thick carpet that silenced her footsteps, and for the bright moon that lit the room.

Now she was in a black-and-white horror movie. The moon showed her the nightmare: A spidery black figure stepped over the threshold. Helen saw his body silhouetted against the moon-bright sky. The killer was dressed in black, like an executioner: black shoes, pants, and long-sleeved shirt.

He had no face. He had no hair. A black balaclava tightly covered his head and neck, except for an eye slit. Like a letter box to hell. There was nothing behind the slit. It was shielded by some kind of mesh.

The killer's nose was a small, anonymous tent. He had no lips. He had no race: Helen couldn't see any skin at his neck, wrists or ankles. Even his mouth was covered.

He's a ninja, Helen thought. A professional killer. She could see his hands, covered with thin, flexible black gloves.

No wonder he leaves no traces. He really is a ghost.

At his feet Helen saw a black lump the size of a hump-topped tombstone. What was that? Ah, a backpack. That's how he carries out the gold.

She heard the *zirpppt!* of a zipper and watched him stash the flathead screwdriver in the backpack.

Helen held her breath. Was the killer taking something out of the backpack? Did he have a weapon? No.

She almost relaxed. Then she wondered: Does he need a weapon? Can he kill with his bare hands? He's outnumbered two to one up here by an unarmed student and a pepper sprayer who'd shot herself with her own weapon.

Don't panic, Helen told herself. Markos's life depends on your next moves. So does the future of Coronado Investigations. And your marriage. You'll never forgive yourself—or Phil—if that talented young man dies because of your overweening pride and careless ambition.

She watched the killer shoulder the backpack, then look both ways, like a preschooler crossing a busy street by himself.

He couldn't see Markos, poised at the doorway to the living room, holding the heavy mahogany chair high. He looked ready to bash the intruder in the head.

The muscles bulged in his arms.

Helen felt for her pepper spray. She made sure the nozzle was pointed away from her.

Her ears strained for the sound of the elevator. Where was Phil? Where were the police? Why wasn't anyone here?

The Gold Ghost checked both doorways, then entered the living room. Markos swung the chair, but the man ducked at the last minute and crouched down. Markos launched himself at the killer, but the backpack hit him in his gut. Whatever was in it knocked the breath out of Markos.

He recovered quickly and reached for the huge crystal ashtray. Markos tried to slam the killer in the face, but the Gold Ghost dodged it and took the blow on his shoulder, where the backpack absorbed most of the force.

Helen hovered uselessly in the background. She couldn't spray the killer in the face—he didn't have a face. Besides, Markos was in the way.

Markos was strong, but not strong enough to subdue the sinewy killer, who slipped from his grasp again.

The killer sat back and kicked Markos in the cojones.

Markos shrieked and gripped his crotch. Helen grabbed the crystal ashtray and brought it down on the killer's head as hard as she could.

The Gold Ghost slumped back on the floor. Helen hoped he was out cold. She kneeled down beside the still body and ripped off the black hood.

Helen saw buzzed bleached hair framing a heart-shaped, tanned face. And turquoise lipstick.

Lipstick?

The Gold Ghost was a woman.

CHAPTER 28

Dark blood dripped from the Gold Ghost's head wound. She was still out cold on the carpet, her turquoise mouth slack and her eyes shut.

Who wore lipstick to commit a burglary? Helen wondered. Especially when her face was covered with a balaclava?

Helen had subdued a killer, but she couldn't keep her thoughts in order.

She clutched her pepper spray canister and wondered: Should I shoot the Gold Ghost in the face? She looked helpless, her head surrounded by a hellish red halo.

Poor Markos was curled on the floor in a fetal position, a waterfall streaming down his cheeks. Helen looked away, knowing he would be ashamed of those tears. She suspected he'd be out of commission for a while, thanks to the mule kick of this woman.

Hurting Markos was one of the Gold Ghost's lesser sins. This harmless-looking creature had terrorized Blue Heron Crescent, robbing all the residents of their sleep—and taking some of their carefully hoarded gold.

Worse, she'd brutally beaten to death ninety-two-year-old Alexander Woodiwiss, golfer, dancer and World War II veteran. Killed the man in his condo on the nineteenth floor.

Helen could see the much-loved senior in her mind, dying without dignity on his living room floor, pale, scrawny legs poking out of his striped pajamas.

The Gold Ghost had cruelly left Alex to be discovered the next morning by his hardworking housekeeper, and turned that woman's pleasant memories of her employer into a horror show.

What kind of monster was this turquoise-lipped creature?

Helen guessed her age at mid-twenties. She's too young to be so callous, she thought.

And what about Phil, who still wasn't up here? Did the Gold Ghost hurt him, too? She looked easy to underestimate. Helen could see Phil and the valet dismissing this woman with the mermaid makeup. She could walk right past them and into the elevator, where she'd pull the balaclava over her head.

But how did the Gold Ghost get on the twentieth-floor balcony? Helen knew she didn't ride the elevator into the penthouse. That meant she had to have climbed down from the roof.

The woman's face had a weathered, outdoorsy look and her hair—what there was of it—was blond. Maybe the Gold Ghost's hands would give Helen a clue to her identity.

She felt the gloves: thin black leather, unlined, with no damp spots or blood crusts. Good.

She stripped off the Ghost's left glove and examined her limp brown hand. No rings, including an engagement ring or a wedding band. Her short nails were painted the same turquoise as her lips, but her small hands were hardly decorative. The moon was so bright Helen could see that the Ghost's hands were covered with scars, scrapes, bruises and thick calluses. She turned over the tanned, battered hand and looked at the finger pads. Helen didn't see the familiar loops and whorls of fingerprints. They were callused but smooth.

What did the Gold Ghost do for a living—besides steal? Was she a professional boxer? Did she break rocks? Rocks! What was it about rocks and no prints? Helen searched her brain. Wait, it wasn't rocks. It was bricks.

Bricklayers and construction workers lost their fingerprints because they handled rough materials in their jobs.

Was the Gold Ghost a bricklayer? Why not? The job paid good money. Helen pushed up the sleeve of the woman's black knit turtleneck and saw her tanned forearm was corded with muscle. She certainly seemed strong enough for the job.

Her chest was oddly flat for a woman. Helen didn't have the nerve to pull up her shirt, but she did check her neck. Men had jutting Adam's apples, unless they'd had thyroid cartilage reduction for feminization surgery.

This person's neck was smooth and nut brown. Yep, definitely a woman's neck, Helen decided, with no surgery scars.

Who was the Gold Ghost? Despite the turquoise lipstick, Helen thought her face looked familiar. It was heart-shaped, with a small, neat nose and a generous mouth.

I swear I've seen her before, and when I did, the Gold Ghost's mouth was smiling. Innocently smiling. And she was wearing black gloves on a sunny summer day. But who wears gloves in Florida?

Where have I seen you? Helen thought, as she rummaged through the unconscious woman's pockets. No ID. No money.

Maybe the Gold Ghost has some identification stashed in her backpack by the balcony, she thought. But I'm not leaving her alone. Not this killer.

Helen looked over at Markos. He'd stopped moaning and was sitting up, leaning against that monstrous gold Egyptian coffee table. His face had a greenish tinge, his eyes were closed, and he was sweating. He looked like he was still in pain but being brave.

Helen hoped Phil and the police would get here soon. They would need to call the paramedics.

"Ooooo-unhhhh." The Gold Ghost gave a low moan, as if she

were trapped in a tomb. Helen felt the hair rise on the back of her neck. The Ghost was coming to life.

Helen saw the overturned small table, the heavy mahogany chair on its side, and the bloody ashtray left behind from the fierce struggle. The balcony slider was still propped against the other slider. The Gold Ghost had lifted the heavy glass door as if it were made of foam.

No, you don't, Helen thought. I'm not fighting you again, killer.

The Ghost's eyes fluttered open and took in Helen, then Markos. She seemed confused, but Helen knew it wouldn't be long before she figured out where she was. Helen remembered the rocklike muscle in this woman's arm and saw the chaos she'd created.

I'll be outmatched in a fight with the Gold Ghost, she thought. And I have to protect Markos, who's out of commission for now.

When the Gold Ghost started to sit up, Helen tensed. In a few seconds, she'd remember where she was and attack again.

No! Helen thought. I've had enough.

She grabbed the pepper spray and shot the Gold Ghost in the face. The killer shrieked and clawed her skin, smearing her turquoise lipstick across her face.

Helen watched the screaming woman thrash and roll around, pawing her eyes and flinging blood drops from her head wound.

She couldn't feel any pity for the heartless killer. "Pepper spray won't hurt so much if you don't rub your eyes," Helen told her.

"It hurts! It hurts!" the woman wailed. "My eyes! I'll go blind!"

"I don't think so," Helen said. "But keep crying. Tears help wash away the pepper oil. The police and paramedics will be here soon."

Despite Helen's advice, the Gold Ghost kept rubbing her face, pushing the pepper oil deeper into her sensitive eyes. Now they were bloodred and nearly swollen shut.

"How can you do this to me?" the Gold Ghost howled.

"How could you kill Alex Woodiwiss?" Helen said.

"You mean the old dude?" the Gold Ghost said. "He was, like, ancient. He was gonna die anyway."

"Not right away," Helen said. "And not like that. Alex Woodiwiss was a decorated World War II veteran. You wouldn't be here today if it wasn't for people like him. You deserve to burn—your whole body, not just your eyes."

Ding! Helen heard the bell, as if a fight round had ended.

A wild-eyed Phil rushed into the room and gathered her into his arms. "Helen!" he cried. "Oh, thank God! I heard the howls when the doors opened. I was afraid you'd been hurt. Tell me you're safe. I've been so worried."

Helen held him tight, afraid to let go of the lover she'd feared was dead. He smelled like sweat and machine oil. "You're safe, too," she said, kissing him back. "I was so afraid the Gold Ghost attacked you and left you bleeding on the lobby floor. What took you so long?"

"The elevator went out," Phil said. "There was no warning. I didn't find out until I got your 911 text. Took me forever to start the generator, but now I'm here. The cops were just pulling into the drive. The valet's sending them up. I didn't wait."

He rocked Helen in his arms, then pulled back and checked her face, feeling her soft skin with his fingers to reassure himself. "He didn't hurt you, did he? The Gold Ghost? If he so much as touched a—"

"Phil!" Helen said. "He's a she."

"Huh?" Phil said. Helen noticed his hair had escaped his ponytail and she tried to smooth it down. His silver mane stood out like he'd stuck his finger in a light socket.

Helen shouted over the shrieks, "The Gold Ghost is a woman. That's her on the floor with the smeared turquoise lipstick. I pepper-sprayed her and she got hit in the head."

"You're sure that's a woman?" Phil said. "Just because someone wears lipstick doesn't mean that person is a female."

"I'm pretty sure she's a woman," Helen said. "She kicked Markos in the groin. Hard."

The ear-slicing screams were giving Helen a headache. She resisted a mean urge to kick the Gold Ghost into silence.

"Help is on the way," Phil yelled. "Police and paramedics."

"I wish they'd hurry," she said.

Phil finally noticed Markos. The muscular hunk stood up on colt-shaky legs and then doubled over and ran for the closest bathroom. Helen could hear him throwing up, even over the Ghost's howls.

"Is that a normal reaction?" she asked. "Should Markos be nauseated?"

"When a guy gets kicked that hard?" Phil asked. "You bet."

Markos returned, walking as if the floor were lunging under him, and wiping away tears. He looked embarrassed.

"You okay, buddy?" Phil asked.

"I'm fine," he said. Helen knew he was lying.

"No, you're not. Lie down flat," Phil said. "That will get the blood flowing to your brain and help get rid of that pounding headache."

"How did you know I have a headache?" Markos asked, his voice weak. Helen could barely hear him, and she once more fought her impulse to kick the screeching Ghost.

"Learned it at the school of hard knocks. I bet you cried, too."

Markos looked mortified and nodded, then stopped and held his head.

"No reason to be ashamed," Phil said. "I did, too. Nothing you can do about it. When you get kicked in the groin, signals zing to your brain at two hundred and sixty-five miles an hour, and your body goes crazy. Lie down. You need fluids."

"I'll get him some cold water," Helen said. "How did you know how fast pain signals travel to the brain?"

"The doc told me," Phil said. "What do we do about her?" He pointed at the howling, bedraggled Gold Ghost.

"Let her stay there till the paramedics arrive," Helen said. "Make sure she doesn't get up."

She ran to the kitchen on thick, rubbery legs, found a bottle of water in the fridge, and brought it back to Markos. "Thanks," he said, his voice a pained gasp. "I'm sorry I failed."

"Failed?" Helen said. "You succeeded. You stopped the Gold Ghost so I could bash her in the head—how's that for poetic justice? She's going away for a long time. You did everything right."

"I should have stopped her," he said.

"You did," Helen said.

"No, stopped her totally. You had to—"

Ding!

Police poured into the room, and Helen was grateful. Markos would not forgive himself for what he saw as a failure, and she knew she couldn't convince him otherwise.

Another officer rushed toward the shrieking Ghost, but she kept screaming. Ignoring the noise, Helen explained what had happened to a clean-cut uniform wearing the name tag BAILEY. She told Officer Bailey a disjointed story while she showed him the slider off its tracks, the backpack, the overturned furniture, and the injured Markos on the couch.

"She kicked him good and hard," Helen said, "but despite his injuries, our operative still captured the Gold Ghost."

The police officer turned to the bloody, shrieking creature thrashing around on the floor. "She's not doing anything but screaming," said the African American officer with the shaved head.

"What's your name, ma'am?" Officer Bailey asked.

"I want a lawyer," she yelled.

Bailey got down on his haunches and spoke slowly. "I said, 'Do you have a name?'"

"I want a lawyer," she screamed. *"Get me a lawyer."*

Then she didn't say another word.

CHAPTER 29

"So you don't know her name?" Detective Louisa Longright asked Helen. The Blue Heron Crescent crimes against property detective showed up shortly after the uniforms and claimed her case. They were sitting in the massive penthouse kitchen, the most comfortable room in that vast condo.

"The Gold Ghost didn't tell me her name," Helen said, "and I couldn't find any ID on her."

Detective Longright was thirtysomething and dressed for police success in a dark pinstripe pantsuit and black lace-up shoes. Her unruly brown hair was short and her brown eyes were sharp. Her intelligence made her unconventional face interesting.

Helen wasn't used to working with police detectives she could respect. Most either dismissed her or patronized her or told her they were professional investigators and she was a stupid amateur.

Helen had another plus on this case. Victor Trelford, Coronado client and Silver Glade general manager, gave her and Phil permission to discuss the case with the police. Victor had suited up in the middle of the night and showed up ten minutes after Phil called him.

Helen thought the spiky-haired Victor looked ten years younger when he stepped into the penthouse.

Victor was thrilled that the Gold Ghost had been caught thanks to "his" plan. Phil didn't mind that Victor took the credit for his idea. He was glad this was his last graveyard shift.

At three in the morning, a crime scene team was crawling over the penthouse living room and balcony. The Gold Ghost had been packed off to the hospital, accompanied by two uniforms. Her screams were reduced to whimpers. Helen reveled in the quiet.

Detective Longright took a quick statement from Markos, and the ex-prince promised to stop by police headquarters and sign a formal statement later. Then he was loaded into an ambulance, protesting that he didn't need to go to the hospital.

"Don't worry about the money," Phil had said. "We'll take care of your medical bills. We have to make sure our most important operative is in full working order."

"I'm still an operative?" Markos had asked, brightening slightly.

"Only if you follow orders," Phil told him. "And getting checked at the hospital is a direct order."

Detective Longright had stashed Victor and Phil in separate bedrooms to question later. For now, she was interviewing a tired Helen in the kitchen. The private eye's professionally applied call-girl makeup was smeared and she'd lost a false eyelash. Her hair was limp and her manicure chipped.

"The evidence appears to support your story, Ms. Hawthorne," Detective Longright said. "You were smart to ditch the hooker heels and tight dress."

"You checked my purse?" Helen said.

"We check everything," Longright said. "Your account dovetails with what Mr. Martinez told us."

"Did you find any identification in the Gold Ghost's backpack?" Helen asked.

"Nothing," the detective said. "No house keys, car keys, not even a bus pass. We have no idea where she lives or how she got here. The suspect is still refusing to talk or give her name."

"But you can still arrest her?" Helen said.

"You bet," Longright said. "And Florida is a bad state to be a burglar." Helen wished the Gold Ghost could have seen the detective's scary smile.

"The suspect is looking at a first-degree felony for this job," Longright said.

"Why first degree?" Helen asked. "She didn't take anything."

"She intended to," the detective said. "And under the law, that's what counts. You and your partner, Phil Sagemont, presented Mr. Martinez as a gold collector living in this penthouse during a television interview. The suspect removed a balcony door to this twentieth-floor apartment, so there's no way she can say she pressed the wrong elevator floor by accident.

"Popping the slider out of the track and entering the condo constitutes a home invasion. She also assaulted Mr. Martinez and caused property damage of more than a thousand dollars."

"That much money?" Helen said.

"You had any sliders replaced recently, Ms. Hawthorne? That huge Oriental carpet will have to be cleaned, too, and one of the side tables was broken.

"The suspect is looking at thirty years in prison and a ten-thousand-dollar fine for this job alone. If we can connect her to the other break-ins and the murder of Mr. Woodiwiss, she could get the death penalty. He was a beloved figure in this community, and the people who live here will be out for blood—her blood. Mr. Woodiwiss had powerful and influential friends. The suspect will be lucky if she gets life in prison without parole.

"Did she say anything at all, Ms. Hawthorne, before the police arrived?"

"The Gold Ghost never gave me her name," Helen said. "But she admitted that she'd killed Alexander Woodiwiss."

"She did?" The detective looked surprised. "I find that hard to believe, considering she lawyered up as soon as the uniforms got here."

"Well, she didn't exactly confess, but close enough," Helen said.

"'Close enough' doesn't cut it in court, Ms. Hawthorne. Tell me what she said. Exactly."

Helen tried to think back to earlier this morning and relive the time when the Gold Ghost had invaded the penthouse. She felt her own fear while she and Markos watched the burglar's incredible feat of removing the balcony slider. Helen's neck still ached from the tension. She remembered hovering helplessly while Markos fought to subdue the burglar, and her frustration when she realized the burglar wore a balaclava with a letter-box eye slit and Helen couldn't get close enough to use her pepper spray. Then there was that final, awful moment when Helen slugged her in the head with the ashtray.

She was surprised that didn't feel satisfying at all. Helen felt sick when the glass ashtray connected with the burglar's head.

Now she heard Markos's moans while the Ghost was unconscious. She saw the intruder's blood leaking onto the carpet, and the chaos and confusion in the living room. Then the Ghost started to wake up, and Helen felt the surge of rage when she'd shot the burglar in the face with the pepper spray. That's when the screaming—and the talking—started.

Helen replayed the scene in her memory.

The Gold Ghost was howling, *How can you do this to me?*

How could you kill Alex Woodiwiss? Helen had said.

You mean the old dude? the Gold Ghost had said. *He was, like, ancient. He was gonna die anyway.*

She edited out her own harsh words to the Ghost: *You deserve to burn—your whole body, not just your eyes.*

"That's pretty much all the Ghost told me," Helen said, and those words had the ring of truth.

"And you'll give me a sworn statement," Detective Longright said.

"Yes," Helen said.

"Knowing it can be subpoenaed by the defense for a deposition?"

"Absolutely," Helen said. "I'll also testify at the burglar's trial. How long will it take you to ID her?"

"At least twenty-four hours," the detective said. "And that's if we're lucky. It's a complicated process. First, we'll have to locate the nearby properties with surveillance equipment. Fortunately, Blue Heron Crescent has CCTV cameras everywhere, and they've been upgraded recently.

"Once these burglaries started, the condo managers made sure all their security cameras were working. So did the local businesses. Nobody in this neighborhood would dare use cheap tricks like dummy cameras or rerun the same tired tapes that show nothing but gray blurs and scratches. The condos and businesses promised to keep the recordings for thirty days."

"And you're well within the safe time period," Helen said.

"The death of Mr. Woodiwiss united everyone," Longright said. "The residents of Blue Heron demand nothing but the best—and this time they got it."

"So why the ID delay?" Helen asked.

"We'll have to find someone at each place who has the authority to say it's okay for us to review the footage. Then we'll need someone who knows how to operate the equipment—most condo and store managers don't. Then they'll have to get a copy for us. Even if everyone is cooperative, it will take time."

"Why not give the Ghost's booking photo to the media and post it online?" Helen said. "Someone is sure to recognize her."

"Because we don't know if she's working alone, Ms. Hawthorne. We want to catch all her associates, and if she's fencing the gold, we want to know who has it and get it back. And that means I don't want you and your husband to tip off your reporter friend, Valerie Cannata. I'm giving you a friendly warning. I don't want to arrest either of you for obstruction of justice.

"Do I have your word on that, Ms. Hawthorne?"

"We can keep it quiet until this afternoon," Helen said, "but half of Silver Glade was in the lobby tonight—I mean this morning—when the Gold Ghost left in an ambulance with the police. How fast do you think this news will get out? You owe us that much."

"Okay, I'll accept that," Longright said.

"We do have some ways to nail down her identity. We can get DNA, though that takes time. If the glove is handled right, prints can be developed on the inside of its fingers."

"But the Gold Ghost doesn't have prints," Helen said.

"She probably has *some* prints," the detective said. "While her fingers may not have the standard loops, whorls and arches, they can still be unique in their own way."

"The Gold Ghost seems familiar," Helen said, "but I don't know why. I think I've seen her somewhere—and wearing black gloves. In the summer. But who wears gloves in the South Florida heat?"

"Lots of people, if they're into sports," Longright said. "She could be a golfer, cyclist, rock climber, or weight lifter. She could wear them for driving a car or riding a motorcycle."

Helen felt something stir in the recesses of her tired brain. Longright's words sparked some memory. What was it?

"She was involved in some kind of sport," Helen said slowly. "She had a helmet."

"That could be anything from biking to kickboxing. Do you watch sports?" the detective asked.

"Not really," Helen said. "But I'll keep trying to remember."

"You do that. You can work on your statement in the study. There's a desk in there. Here's my card. Call me if you think of anything."

Helen studied Detective Longright's title. "You handle crimes against property *and* persons?" she said. "I thought most small departments contract out their homicides to the Broward County Sheriff's Office."

"We're not 'most small departments,' Ms. Hawthorne. Blue Heron Crescent has enough money to get what it wants—and it wants their own detectives to handle their murders and burglaries.

"Keep thinking about where you saw the suspect. Because I get what I want—and I want that woman's name."

CHAPTER 30

Helen slept like she was drugged on a bed that belonged in a bordello. The round red velvet confection had a fantabulous gold rococo headboard and a cloud-soft mattress.

She felt the bed slowly rotate and stirred, then opened her eyes and saw her smiling spouse. "Phil?" she said, lifting her head from the red velvet pillow. "What are you doing here? Why is the bed moving?"

"I was watching you sleep," Phil said. "You look gorgeous in all that red. The bed's moving because it has a remote. I can rotate it so you can see the ocean."

"What ocean?" Helen said. She'd been so deeply asleep, she wasn't sure where she was.

"Watch! This remote opens the curtains." He pressed a button on a small white clicker and the red velvet curtains whooshed open, filling the room with glaring sunlight.

Helen pulled the pillow over her face. "Ow!" she said. "All that light hurts. Where are we?"

"In the penthouse at Silver Glade. You caught the Gold Ghost this morning, remember?"

"Oh, right. And Markos got sent to the hospital. How is Markos?"

"He called me as soon as he was released," Phil said. "No serious damage. In fact he has a date with Valerie tonight."

"Oh, good," Helen said. "I was worried. I'm glad he's okay. After he went to the hospital, Detective Longright questioned me for hours and I wrote out a statement and signed it. I was so tired I lay down and took a nap."

She was still wearing her jeans, shirt and shoes. The shirt had more wrinkles than a shar-pei.

"What time is it?" she asked.

"Nine o'clock," he said. "You've been asleep for almost six hours. While you slept, Detective Longright questioned me and Victor. She finished with us about six this morning. Then I went up on the roof."

"What's up on the roof?" Helen said.

"The crime scene team figured out the Gold Ghost rappelled down from the rooftop."

"How did she get up there?" Helen asked.

"That's the big question, isn't it?" he said. "Remember when Victor, the condo manager, said that the security staff at the other condos she'd broken into checked the CCTV footage for twelve hours either side of the break-in?"

"Right," Helen said. "They didn't find anyone who couldn't be accounted for."

"Turns out they didn't look long enough," Phil said. "Now we think the Gold Ghost showed up eighteen or nineteen hours before the burglaries."

"I like that 'we,'" Helen said. "You're working with the police?"

"Detective Longright welcomed my insights," Phil said.

"Seriously?" Helen said. She was sitting up now. The sunlight glared on her face from an odd angle. She looked up and saw the round, gold-framed mirror over the red velvet bed. Who decorated this penthouse?

She could see her face: Her expensive makeup had devolved into a serious case of raccoon eyes.

"Okay, the detective didn't chase me off," Phil said. "And she liked one of my ideas. Also, I know how to work the condo's cranky CCTV system and Victor doesn't. Victor didn't want to go up on the roof—he's afraid of heights—and Detective Longright let me tag along.

"Turns out the Ghost spent all day on the roof. She camped out from eight in the morning until she rappelled down the side to the penthouse just before two a.m."

"She must have been broiled, sitting on that roof all day," Helen said. "It was ninety degrees yesterday."

"No, she was smart, and prepared. We found a small pop-up tent in her backpack that kept the sun off her. She brought bottled water, sandwiches and energy bars. She stowed the trash from her food in the backpack but didn't have room for all the water bottles. She left some of those behind, as well as the water. Well, the water was in a different form, but that got left, too. In a bottle. Several bottles."

Phil stumbled to a stop, his thin, pale face bright pink.

"Good grief, Phil, what did you find that's so embarrassing?"

"Three bottles filled with . . . uh, urine."

"But that's good," Helen said. "The police can get DNA from the bottles. She may have left other bottles on the other condo roofs to connect her to her crimes. And maybe they can pull fingerprints, or smudges, or whatever the burglar has on her hands, and use those."

"Well, that part's good," Phil said, "but are you sure she's a girl? The flat chest, the bottles, the buzzed hair. I still think she's a man."

"I'm as sure as I can be without a strip search that the Gold Ghost is female," Helen said. "Besides, wasn't she taken to the ER? And won't the police search her when she's arrested?"

"Yes, but Longright wouldn't tell me the results. She just laughed when I asked. She wouldn't answer my question, either. She thought that was hilarious."

"What was your hilarious question?" Helen asked.

"The bottles of urine were regular plastic water bottles."

"Yes."

"With narrow openings," he said.

"Right."

"So how do women pee standing up?" Phil said. "Because that's the only way she could fill those bottles."

Helen laughed so hard, she fell back on the bed.

"What?" Phil said. "What's so funny?" He looked hurt.

"You've never been camping with a woman, have you?"

"Camping's not on my list of fun things to do with women," Phil said.

"There's a device some women use when they go camping or if they're in the military or some other place that doesn't have restrooms. It's sort of like a funnel with a tube. It lets women pee standing up. They don't even have to drop their pants, if they buy the right kind."

"Oh," Phil said. "Why didn't the detective just say so? What's so funny?"

"Your face," Helen said. "It's as red as this bed. And will you please turn off the motor? I'm getting dizzy going around in circles."

The bed stopped moving. Helen leaned up against the gold headboard, but a rococo bit stabbed her in the back. She padded it with a velvet pillow and saw what looked like a centipede crawling on the spread. Helen reached down, pulled off her shoe and whacked it.

"What are you doing?" Phil asked.

"I just killed a false eyelash," Helen said. She was glad Phil laughed at that. He still had his sense of humor.

"So we know how the Gold Ghost got down to the penthouse," Helen said, "but how did she get into the building?"

"I figured that one out," Phil said. "All by myself. The answer was in the security footage. This time, we watched them for twenty-four hours before the burglary. If the Ghost brought a tent, food and water, she could stay up on the roof for a long time.

"At eight o'clock the morning of the burglary, seven women from Clean Jean's Housecleaning Service arrived at Silver Glade. They always come at that time on that day. Victor said usually it's six women. The cleaners wear black pants and an ugly pale blue polyester tunic top. The cleaners are mostly foreign, very quiet, and their English is limited. They clean three condos, two women per unit, and they're always signed in by Luz, the crew leader, as 'Clean Jean Crew.'

"The women came in with a lot of baggage. They carried their lunches, buckets, mops, vacuums and cleaning supplies. The condo guards never check anything they carry. The day-shift guard opened the elevator for the seven women. Two cleaners went to the third floor, two to the eighth floor, and two up to the tenth. The seventh woman got off the elevator at another, higher floor."

"The guard didn't notice any activity on the fire stairs?" Helen asked.

"It wouldn't have made any difference if he did," Phil said. "The stairs aren't alarmed during the day and the cleaners sometimes take them rather than wait for the slow elevator. It's faster to walk up a few floors to borrow the furniture polish.

"Three hours later, the six cleaners gathered in the lobby and Luz signed out the crew. The day-shift guard never noticed the seventh woman wasn't there."

"The Gold Ghost," Helen said.

"That's what we think," Phil said. "She took the elevator to another floor, walked up the fire stairs to the roof, and camped out all day. The police are checking the door handles for prints or smudges, or whatever she might have left behind."

"But how did she explain herself to the cleaning crew?" Helen said.

"The police called Clean Jean and the company owner gave them Luz's cell phone number. The cops talked with her before she left for work. Luz said the six cleaners came in her van. The Gold Ghost met them in the parking lot and said she was a new supervisor who was there to learn more about the layout and inner workings of the condo."

"Well, that was true," Helen said. "Although it seems she already knew plenty if she was meeting the cleaning crew."

"This 'new supervisor' told the cleaning crew she'd drive herself home and wouldn't interfere with their work. That was fine with Luz," Phil said.

"What did this fake supervisor look like?"

"Luz called her a gringa," Phil said. "She had brown hair, big sunglasses and weird lipstick."

"Turquoise lipstick?" Helen asked.

"You guessed it. The police found sunglasses and a wig stuffed in the backpack."

"More DNA," Helen said. "And the lipstick was part of her disguise. That offbeat color was all the witnesses would remember about her."

"Exactly. Luz couldn't tell the cops the woman's skin color, height, age or any other useful information."

"What about the fake supervisor's car?" Helen said.

"There was no car," Phil said. "The Ghost walked up the drive. That's on the security cameras. The valet said she never checked a car and he never really noticed anything about her except—"

"The turquoise lipstick," Helen said. "Where did the Ghost get the cleaners' uniform?"

"Anywhere," Phil said. "You can buy a top like that at any big-box store or on the Internet."

"Luz won't lose her job for signing in the fake supervisor, will she?" Helen asked.

"No, Jean seems like a good egg. She told the police that she frequently sends new people along with an experienced team, and Luz heads one of her best. In the future, she will ask Luz to confirm all new arrivals with her. And I think the cleaning crew will have a different check-in procedure at Silver Glade from now on."

"So we know everything about the Gold Ghost except her name," Helen said.

"Right," Phil said. "The Silver Glade security cameras captured her walking from the south, where there are acres of public parking lots and a bus stop. The cops are going to be looking at a lot of security footage in the next few days."

"I know I've seen her before, Phil," Helen said. "I'm sure of it. I wish I could remember where."

"How about if we go home?" he said. "Maybe that will jog your memory."

"I'm ready," she said. "Let me wash my face first."

A disheveled Helen and a weary Phil smiled all the way down to the condo's employee parking lot and climbed into his dusty black Jeep, exhausted but happy. Their work on the Gold Ghost case was almost done, except that Helen knew she recognized the killer. She'd seen her somewhere. The identity buzzed in her brain like a trapped fly. Helen would have no rest until she remembered it.

They drove toward the Coronado in the cool, sunny morning, going in the direction opposite the last of the rush-hour traffic.

"Phil, help me out before I go crazy," Helen said. "Where did I see the Gold Ghost?"

"What do you remember about her?" he asked.

"She was smiling, and it was a nice smile. She was doing something good. She was dressed for a sport—she had black gloves and carried a helmet. But lots of sports have gloves and helmets."

"Was she rappelling?" Phil asked. "Because she wore black gloves and she had a helmet in her backpack."

"Yes!" Helen said. "That's where I saw her. She was rappelling."

"In person? On TV?"

"No, neither one. I don't remember watching any rappelling event, do you?"

Phil shook his head.

"Wait!" Helen said. "I saw her with someone from the Annabel Lee Griffin case. Who was it?"

"Jenny?" Phil said.

"No, and it wasn't Cissy, either." Helen said. "It was a newspaper story. She was with Hugo! That's right. When I was researching Hugo,

I looked up a bunch of newspaper stories about him. He'd been campaigning to be CEO of a big company and hired a publicist, and there were a lot of favorable stories about him.

"One was a feature where Hugo was rappelling down the side of a thirty-story building. He paid the thousand-dollar entry fee for himself and two other women. Let me see if I can find the story."

Helen scrambled through her purse until she found her cell phone and Googled the story with trembling fingers. "Here it is!" she said. "The story and the photos. Here's the Gold Ghost. Look!"

"I can't," Phil said. "I'm driving." He pulled into a parking lot and looked at Helen's phone.

On the screen was a small muscular woman with a determined look on her heart-shaped face and a blond buzz cut. She told the reporter, *I'm a cancer survivor. Nothing scares me anymore, not after chemo and radiation. I came back stronger than ever. Rock climbing is my hobby, and I've been everywhere from Austria to Australia. Rappelling off a thirty-story building is a piece of cake.*

"There's her name," Helen said. "Cady Gummage."

"She's a cancer survivor," Phil said. "That's why she had no breasts. She had a double mastectomy and didn't have reconstructive surgery. And I guess she decided she liked having short hair."

"We've found the Gold Ghost," Helen said. "I'll call Detective Longright with the good news."

"The mystery is solved," Phil said. "It's over."

"Almost," Helen said. "Now I have to find out if Hugo killed Annabel Lee Griffin."

CHAPTER 31

Crackkk!

The lightning flash burst like a bomb in Helen's bedroom. Wind-tossed branches lashed the back window and rain raked the apartment walls.

More lightning lit the room and Helen sat up in bed. Her clock said it was two ten, but it was so dark Helen didn't know if it was two in the morning or two in the afternoon. Phil's side was empty, but he'd slept beside her. She smelled coffee and followed her nose to the kitchen.

Phil was perched on a stool at the breakfast bar that separated the kitchen from the living room, pounding his computer keys. The turquoise Formica counter was cluttered with his half-empty coffee mugs.

He smiled at her and said, "Good afternoon, sleepyhead."

"How long was I asleep?" Helen asked, trying to hide a yawn.

"Since you came home about ten o'clock this morning," he said. "I woke up two hours ago. I've been tying up a couple of loose ends on the Gold Ghost case."

"I thought we were finished when we called Detective Longright and told her who the Gold Ghost was," Helen said. "What's left?" She poured herself a cup of coffee and sat on a stool next to Phil.

"Since Cady Gummage still won't talk," he said, "I found out what she does. She proofreads mortgage documents for a title company."

"Ugh. That has to be soul-sucking boredom," Helen said. "If she hadn't killed Alex Woodiwiss, I might feel sorry for her."

"Even prison may be more interesting than that job," Phil said.

"Oh, I'm sure prison will be interesting," Helen said, "but not in any way she'll enjoy. What's the other loose end?"

"I had to find out how Cady knew which condos to break into," Phil said. "That's a security issue and it affects the whole area. Victor at Silver Glade asked me on behalf of the Blue Heron Crescent Neighborhood Association. The condo managers need to know if their security staff was working with the Gold Ghost. The association chipped in for this final part. We've already e-mailed and signed a contract."

"Good work," Helen said. "At least Victor knows Silver Glade is in the clear. You set a trap for the Ghost using Prince Markos. How did Cady know which condos belonged to gold collectors?"

"I figured it out," Phil said, then took a long sip of coffee.

Helen hated when he made her pry information out of him. He sat there, drinking lukewarm coffee in smug silence, until she finally said, "Okay, I'll bite." Then he jumped up and began pacing Helen's midcentury modern living room while he delivered his lecture. Helen kept her seat at the breakfast bar.

"The Gold Ghost belonged to an online gold coin discussion group," he said. "The Internet has a bunch of forums and discussion groups for all sorts of coin collectors—gold, silver, rare coins. One of the gold coin message boards is called LNYGCC."

Helen looked at him blankly. She was still too sleepy to figure out the initials.

Phil rounded Helen's boomerang-shaped coffee table and said, "That stands for Little New York Gold Coin Collectors. Everyone on the list is a gold coin collector—hoarders, I think Max would call them—and he's right. It's a strange world.

"One thread was devoted to the advantages of gold bullion versus gold coins. Another talked about how to avoid reporting coin buys to the IRS. About a year ago, someone named Goldie26 joined the group and she started a discussion thread about the best way to hide gold coins."

"Could you tell Goldie was a woman?" Helen asked.

"No, she was careful to keep all references to herself gender-neutral. But she knew how to talk to these dudes. Hiding gold coins is a favorite topic for coin collectors."

"And you think Goldie26 is Cady Gummage?" Helen asked.

"I'm almost certain. Twenty-six is her age. Goldie asked a few throwaway questions about the advantages of collecting Krugerrands versus Chinese pandas, but she was mainly interested in the best ways to hide gold coins."

"Nobody suggested a bank safe-deposit box?" Helen said.

"You know what Max said. Collectors jump on anyone who uses that b-word," Phil said.

"Box?" Helen said.

"Bank," Phil said. "I printed out some of the discussion threads." He picked up a stack of printouts on the turquoise Barcalounger. "Look at this answer to the poor guy who suggested a safe-deposit box."

He pointed to a line on a page and Helen read, "'Never forget 1933!'"

"What happened in 'thirty-three?" Helen asked.

"That's when Franklin Roosevelt, 'that traitor to his class'—their words, not mine—'confiscated everyone's gold . . .'"

Helen started reading again: "'. . . and gave us federally printed toilet paper instead. Within a couple of months, the paper dollars these honest, hardworking Americans had received from the government for their gold were already devalued by more than fifty percent. *Fifty percent!*'

"Whoa! These people sound extreme," Helen said. "Here's another over-the-top comment: 'Don't forget what the Turks did to the Armenians.' Didn't the Ottoman Empire slaughter the Armenians in 1915?"

"Yep. Way before 1933," Phil said, "and half a world away from the US. But to a certain type of gold collector, that atrocity was yesterday—and I'm not talking about the murders of innocent people."

"This comment sounds mild in comparison." Helen read, "'If you ask me, the government is a bigger worry than the thieves. It's okay to gun down a thief, but you will not get away with shooting a G-man.' Does anyone say G-man anymore?"

"They do in Little New York," Phil said.

"Here's another swipe at the banks," Helen said. "'Nothing in bank safe-deposit boxes is insured by Uncle Snoops.' I assume that's Uncle Sam?"

"Correct," Phil said. "Many gold collectors hate the federal government, and Goldie26 played them like violins. When the thread about hiding gold would start to die down, she'd whip them up by asking, 'What if the government confiscates our gold again?' Or she'd crank them up with questions like: 'What will we do if the banks close and we can't get our gold out?' 'How do we keep our gold safe when the Feds are printing Monopoly money?' 'How much should we keep on hand if the country goes to hell?'

"She had the poor old collectors scared to death. Goldie26 was a master at starting conversations about how much gold collectors should keep at home. The old boys couldn't resist bragging about the size of their collections.

"You wouldn't believe the devices these collectors used to stash their gold coins."

"Like what?" Helen asked.

"Safes that look like ordinary household items, including fake Barbasol shaving cream cans. An Aquafina bottled water safe. A Dr Pepper soda can safe. A Del Monte fruit cocktail can safe."

"Amazing," Helen said.

"I'm just getting started," Phil said. "Besides brand-name canned goods, soda and water bottles, there are safes disguised as electrical outlets, dictionaries, and working wall clocks. They had safes hidden in their air vents, even hairbrushes."

"Where do you buy stuff like that?" Helen asked.

"At your local spy shop or online. The old dudes couldn't resist talking about how many gold coins they could cram into these things.

"Goldie26 kept these discussions building. Others argued you should make your own safes. Buying one meant other people knew about your gold stash. One man bragged he hid a hundred thousand dollars in gold coins inside hollow curtain rods. Another said he had fifty thousand in gold in pizza boxes in his freezer."

"Talk about cold cash," Helen said.

"A third man hid his Chinese pandas at the bottom of his cat's litter box."

"Ew," Helen said. "I see why the Gold Ghost wore gloves."

"If the gold-hiding thread quieted down, Goldie26 would post the link of the interview with Congressman Ron Paul. He talked about how the American economy was on the verge of collapse."

"Never saw that one," Helen said.

"Survivalists and other conspiracy types love that interview. Congressman Paul says, 'This period is going to be particularly tough on seniors and anyone relying on a fixed income, or money from the government. . . . Trouble is coming—please make sure you, your family and anyone you care about are prepared.'"

"Bet that got the gold hoarders riled up," Helen said.

"It did," Phil said. "They'd start in again, saying their gold was in a dummy PVC pipe under the bathroom sink, or hidden in the fireplace."

"I get the idea," Helen said. "But how did the Gold Ghost know the names of the people who had gold?"

"Because the trusting souls thought their screen names made then anonymous," Phil said. "They didn't realize those names were clues to their identity. The late Alex Woodiwiss—the old man the Gold Ghost bashed in the head—used his initials, the initials of his condo, plus his apartment number: awea1908. It was pretty easy to check the Exeter Arms directory and figure out that Alex Woodiwiss lived in unit 1908. Others used their cars as their screen name ID, like 55tbird. That car was easy to spot. It took me less than an hour to figure out where all the burglary victims lived."

"Did all the coin collectors live on the top two floors?" Helen asked.

"No, they lived in units all over the building. But the Gold Ghost was smart. She knew it was too risky to rappel down to the lower floors because the residents might see her. I've finished typing my report, and as soon as I hit Send, this case is closed."

As Helen cheered that action, Phil's phone rang. "It's Valerie," he said, and put the call on speaker.

"Phil," the Channel 77 reporter said, her voice fast and excited. "I'm sorry I couldn't get back to you sooner. I've been on assignment. Is there a break in the Gold Ghost case?"

"A break?" he said. "The case is broken! Markos caught the killer."

"He did! Was he hurt? Is he safe?"

Helen liked that the ambitious reporter asked first about her lover.

"He's fine," Phil said, and she could hear his smile. "And the killer's arrested. Here's the real scoop—the Gold Ghost is a woman, Cady Gummage."

Phil gave Valerie a quick rundown on the details.

"I'm on my way to the cop shop for confirmation," she said. "This is breaking news. Then I want to interview you and Helen for the six o'clock news. And Markos, too, of course. Especially Markos. Is that okay? I can have a camera crew at your office in two hours."

"We love the publicity—you know that," Phil said. "And we hope you'll give most of the air time to our photogenic operative. Talk with you soon."

"TV publicity is the frosting on the cake," Helen said.

"Really?" Phil said. "I thought it was the gold trim."

CHAPTER 32

The next morning, Helen carried her coffee out by the pool. The new day was flower scented and gilded with sunshine, but Helen felt the black weight of dread.

She waved at Margery, who was hosing down the pool deck and splashing barefoot in the puddles like a kid. Helen's landlady wore purple shorts and a lavender T-shirt, her yard work uniform. Margery grinned when Helen saw her playing in the water. She shut off the hose and joined Helen at an umbrella table.

"How's this for a morning?" Margery asked as she lit a Marlboro and breathed in what Helen guessed was mostly cigarette smoke.

"Okay," Helen said.

"Okay?" Margery said. "You should be popping champagne corks. You and Phil wrapped up the Gold Ghost case and scored ten minutes of TV time. I didn't see your smiling face during Valerie's interview, but I'd rather look at Markos anyway. He's what we used to call a dreamboat."

"He's a hottie, no doubt about it," Helen said.

Her landlady looked at her shrewdly. "Since when did you and Phil get camera shy and let an operative represent your company?"

"Since I'm still undercover for the Annabel Lee Griffin murder," Helen said. "I'm taking that art class to find her killer, remember? I'm due at Bonnet House at ten o'clock."

"Then why the long face? Sorry you weren't on TV?"

"No," Helen said. "Phil and I were happy to let dreamboat Markos get the attention, as long as Valerie mentioned Coronado Investigations."

"Mentioned?" Margery said. "She gave you an infomercial. Why are you moping?"

"I don't want to go to a crematorium today," Helen said.

"I don't want to go to a crematorium any day," Margery said. She waggled her cigarette. "I fire up one day at a time."

"I mean I have to go to a crematorium today and find out if there was anything in Annabel's coffin besides her body."

"This sounds serious," Margery said. "I'll get more coffee and you can tell me about it."

Helen was grateful her shrewd landlady wanted to talk. Laying out the facts helped her see things clearly.

Margery finally returned with a mug of coffee, a plate of warm cinnamon rolls, and a stack of paper napkins. "Thought you wouldn't mind the wait if I nuked these."

There was a respectful silence while Helen pulled apart a fat iced roll and ate the rich, cinnamon-laced coils. Margery seemed pleased to watch Helen eat while she smoked and drank her coffee.

"Did I tell you about Annabel's memorial service?" Helen asked.

"Not really," Margery said. "Last time we talked you were into light hooking and I had to walk you to your cab. Glad you didn't break your ankle with those stilts."

"Any woman who wears those shoes deserves forty thousand a night," Helen said. "Just for standing up."

"Don't tempt me with straight lines," Margery said. "Tell me about Annabel's memorial service. Where was it?"

"At her husband's art studio, a three-million-dollar condo in Silver Glade."

Margery whistled. "Clay's got a condo and a house?"

"And major debt, I think," Helen said. "He uses the condo to give his students 'special instruction.'"

"I bet," Margery said.

"The whole local art scene was at the memorial. The service was catered and a gloomy string quartet sawed away. Robert Horton was there."

"Who's he?" Margery asked.

"Owns an art gallery on Las Olas. He sold Annabel's work until she got too expensive for his customers. My painting class showed up, including my teacher, Yulia, and my client, Jenny."

"Jenny's the real estate agent with the red Tesla?" Margery asked.

"That's her," Helen said. "She insists that Annabel was poisoned by her ex-husband, Hugo."

"Do you think he did it?" Margery asked.

"Annabel ruined Hugo's chance to be a CEO of a major company by blabbing to a detective that he knocked up his office manager. There was a nasty lawsuit, and a DNA test said he was the daddy. That's when Annabel dumped him."

"End of Hugo's hotshot career," Margery said.

"Exactly," Helen said. "The company was still reeling from a sex scandal. But that was years ago. Why would Hugo poison his ex now?"

"Because he's no fool. Killing her right after she crashed his career would be too obvious," Margery said.

"But he is obvious," Helen said. "He's a lout, but I don't think he's a killer."

"Did he come to the memorial?" Margery asked.

"Yes, crass as ever," Helen said, helping herself to another cinnamon roll.

"Why?" Margery asked.

"Hugo didn't kill his ex, but he wanted revenge," Helen said.

"He devoted his life to ruining hers: He made scenes at her major art shows, even took this art class to embarrass her."

"Well, Annabel is beyond embarrassment now," Margery said. "Why go to her memorial: to make sure she was finally dead?"

"Annabel didn't have a viewing," Helen said. "She was cremated, but there were no ashes at the memorial."

Helen stared at the long ash Margery tapped into an ashtray, then continued. "In fact, Annabel was hardly at her own memorial, thanks to the man who organized it, her husband, Clay. He's an artist whose career's going downhill as fast as his wife's was rising. At the memorial, he showed a few of Annabel's early, awkward paintings and photos that were mostly pictures of Clay with his wife in the background."

"So you think he's the killer?" Margery asked.

"Possibly," Helen said. "Clay was unfaithful. He needed money. He resented his talented wife, and he had to neglect his own career to take dull teaching jobs that paid for Annabel's expensive health insurance. He also took out a big life insurance policy on her."

"Then Annabel's sudden death made Clay rich and free," Margery said. "Did she have a life insurance policy on him?"

"No," Helen said. "It looks suspicious, but we need proof."

"Who's *we*?" Margery said. "Are you royalty in exile, or do you have a mouse in your pocket?"

"*We* is myself and Burt Pelham, the Palmetto Hills detective investigating Annabel's murder."

"Right. He came here to talk to us," Margery said. "Bad dye job. New York accent."

"Don't overlook his brains," Helen said.

"Call me shallow, but I couldn't get past his hair."

"Burt and I are both frustrated by this case," Helen said. "I can't talk my client into letting me work with the detective. Jenny wants Hugo to be the killer so badly, I think she'll let the real murderer go free."

"Any other suspects besides the husband?"

"Miranda," Helen said. "She owns a lawn service in Wilton Manors. She's engaged to Lita, the artist who shared Annabel's FAT Village studio. Annabel used to be her lover."

"When?" Margery said.

"Before Annabel married Hugo, she had a fling with Miranda," Helen said. "Miranda says the Annabel affair was no big deal—Lita is the love of her life.

"I suspect Annabel also had a fling with Lita. I know she painted a very sensuous nude of the artist who shared her studio."

"Miranda's fiancée," Margery said.

"Right," Helen said. "I'm pretty sure if Lita and Annabel did hook up, it was a casual fling. But I know Miranda is madly in love with Lita and very jealous."

"How do you know that?" Margery asked.

"I saw Lita confront Clay at the memorial. Lita asked him—in front of everyone—why he'd displayed Annabel's second-rate art. Miranda tried to get Lita to leave, but Lita badgered Clay until he finally admitted that he had put Annabel's works in her casket. Lita shrieked and threw a fit. That's when Miranda dragged her fiancée out of the room and we all pretended nothing had happened."

"So what do you think?" Margery asked.

"That Clay burned his wife's best paintings out of spite. But then I talked to Markos about it in the penthouse, while we waited for the Gold Ghost. Markos said it wouldn't make sense for Clay to burn Annabel's art. He said, *Why would a man hard up for money burn more than fifty thousand dollars? Who sets fire to a stack of cash?*"

"Do you think Clay sold the paintings to that gallery owner, Robert?"

"No," Helen said. "Robert would never get mixed up in a shady art deal. But after class today I'll ask him who would buy them. Then I'll visit the creepy crematorium. I have to know if the paintings really were in Annabel's casket."

"That's the burning question," Margery said, stubbing out her cigarette.

Helen groaned.

"The answer to your case could be in Annabel's coffin. Find out what went up in flames and you'll know who killed her. Get cracking. The sooner you go, the sooner it's over."

Margery gathered up her plate and cup and left. Helen knew her landlady was right. She fed Thumbs and looked in on Phil, who was sleeping late this morning.

Then Helen dug out her art supplies and headed to Bonnet House. Helen took the pea gravel path by the boathouse and stopped to watch an elegant gray-blue heron wading in the mangrove swamp.

It's lovely, she thought.

A fat raccoon perched on a mangrove root, watching her, and a lime green lizard on the path toward class flicked its tail at her.

Helen was the last person to arrive at the loggia. Cissy and Jenny were at their easels—Jenny chic in yellow Armani and Cissy wearing what looked like a crocheted hay bale. Yulia, their teacher, seemed subdued. The atmosphere in the small class was somber and unpleasant.

At least Hugo didn't show up for class. Helen hoped that gasbag was gone for good. She and Jenny couldn't stop staring at Annabel's empty chair, until Yulia said, "This chair is too sad. I will put it away, yes?"

"Please," Helen said. But even after the chair was folded away, Helen and Jenny had trouble concentrating. Jenny dabbed absently at her beach cottage. Helen kept erasing her clumsy sketches.

Only Cissy had the energy to start a new painting. She clipped a photo of the Bonnet House squirrel monkeys to her canvas. Their inquisitive faces stared boldly at the class.

"Oh, you are painting the monkeys," Yulia said. "Their eyes are so expressive. But what happened to your big red flower?"

"I got tired of it," Cissy said.

"So you put it away and you're trying something new?" Yulia

said. "Many artists do that until they are ready to work on a painting again."

"I'm not working on it anymore," Cissy said. "I didn't like the flower. It was too flat, too big and too red."

Why did she sound so defensive? Helen wondered. Who cares?

Yulia did. "It wasn't a bad painting," she told Cissy. "I can show you how to fix it, if you'd like."

Cissy turned on Yulia and hissed, "No! I threw it away, you stupid foreigner. Some things can't be fixed."

CHAPTER 33

Robert Horton himself buzzed Helen into RH Gallery Ltd. The tall, sandy blond gallery owner wore another stylish suit, a silvery gray woven from a cloud. Helen was glad she'd changed into her chic black suit with the short skirt and lace blouse. That outfit made her feel at home in the gallery's luxury.

"Helen, so good to see you," Robert said, his eyes bright with enthusiasm. "Do you have a moment?" he asked.

"Of course," Helen said.

"You have to see the new autumn landscape exhibit." Robert led Helen into the main gallery, its neutral walls ablaze with fiery autumn scenes.

The paintings were traditional, Helen thought, but too alive to be conventional. She admired an oil of red maple leaves against a clear blue sky, then stopped before a painting where the autumn yellow trees had been transformed into a tunnel of gold.

Next she admired a huge horizontal oil: a gray stone tower against red trees. "That one looks like it's on fire," she said.

"It's my favorite, too," Robert said. "This new exhibit will do well. It's June here in Florida, hot and humid, and our fall weather is about the same. Transplanted locals miss fall—the northern fall of their childhoods. They tell me about chilly fall nights and jumping into piles of crunchy leaves."

"And nobody remembers raking those leaves," Helen said.

Robert smiled. "Exactly. Though some clients do miss the smell of burning fall leaves. But you didn't come here to talk about autumn. How may I help you?"

"I want to talk about burning, too," Helen said. "Paintings, not leaves."

Robert raised an eyebrow.

"You remember the scene at Annabel's memorial where Lita screamed at Clay for burning Annabel's paintings?"

"Remember?" Robert said. "It's the talk of the Lauderdale art world. Burning Annabel's art was an atrocity. How dare that"—he stopped, trying to contain his rage—"untalented nobody destroy Annabel's art. It's outrageous. Unforgivable."

"What if Clay didn't?" Helen said.

"Didn't what? Burn Annabel's art?"

"Yes," Helen said.

"Do you know this?" Helen heard the hope in Robert's voice.

"It's a good guess. I'm trying to confirm it."

"I'll do anything to help you. Shall we have coffee in my office?" Robert said. "We can discuss it in privacy."

Helen followed him to his pale, windowless office, dominated by the cobalt blue Robert Wyland painting flanked by two black chairs. Once again, Helen had the odd feeling she was in an aquarium instead of an art gallery.

Robert poured two cups of coffee while Helen sat in a leather chair and admired the massive humpback whales.

A whale of a painting, she thought, then tried to push that phrase out of her mind. She was dressed properly for this interview, but she had to work on her unruly thoughts. This discussion was crucial to her case.

Once Robert was seated and Helen had her coffee, he asked, "Do you think Annabel's work survived?"

"Yes. Clay is supposedly hard up for money," she said.

"I've heard those rumors, too," Robert said. "Their house in Country Club Estates was on the market the day after Annabel's memorial. Listed at two point two million."

"At the memorial, Clay told Hugo his house was for sale," Helen said. "But I didn't think he was serious. He has prospects, but a house that expensive won't sell quickly. The life insurance company won't pay off while there's an active investigation into Annabel's death. If Clay needs money now, it doesn't make sense that he'd burn her work."

"Can you prove he didn't burn her paintings?" Robert was sitting forward in his chair now, alert and interested.

"I'm trying to," she said.

"I hope you're right," Robert said. "What a pathetic excuse for a man! Pretending he burned her paintings. He denied Annabel her last chance for recognition, then turned around and exploited her work."

"How would you hide ten oil paintings in a coffin?" Helen asked.

"Let me think. Annabel still used small canvases for most of her work, mostly sixteen by twenty inches. They could be rolled up in plain two-foot-long cardboard mailing tubes. Two would do, and those would fit easily in a coffin."

"Who would buy those paintings?" Helen asked.

"Not me," Robert said.

Helen thought he looked slightly offended. "Of course not," she said, "or I wouldn't be consulting you."

Robert relaxed and sat back in his chair. "There are a couple of shady dealers in Miami who'd buy them. The art would have no provenance, but if those dealers knew the paintings had been in Annabel's coffin, that would add considerably to the value."

Helen felt sick. "That's horrible."

"They're ghouls," he said. "They don't care where their profits come from."

"How much could Clay get for Annabel's ten coffin paintings?" Helen asked.

"She had talent that was starting to get serious recognition. I'd say they could be worth a hundred thousand. Maybe one fifty or even two hundred thousand."

"Together?" Helen asked.

"Yes. The dealer might sell them individually for more if he broke up the collection. The buyers couldn't show them in public, of course, or lend them to a museum, but that wouldn't deter that kind of collector—they want something no one else has: Annabel's art and a story straight out of Edgar Allan Poe."

"Poor Annabel," Helen said. She wasn't cold, but Robert's words chilled her. She wrapped her hands around her coffee cup for warmth.

"Come to think of it, Clay has been acting like he already has money," Robert said. "He called me yesterday and said he wasn't going to pick up his seascape that didn't sell. He said I could keep it or donate it to charity."

"That's odd," Helen said. "Why would Clay abandon his masterpiece? You'd think he'd try to sell it at the Huffington Gallery. That's the one where he pays to display his paintings, right?"

"Right. Leaving a painting is definitely out of character for him," Robert said. "Well, my dear, I'm afraid I have to cut our meeting short. I have to see a client. Where are you off to next?"

"The crematorium," Helen said.

"You poor thing," Robert said.

"I agree, but it's the only way to find out if Annabel's paintings survived the flames."

"Where was she cremated?" Robert asked.

"Lethe River Crematorium on Powerline Road," Helen said.

"Lethe," Robert repeated. "Curious choice, when there are so many other crematoria here."

"Why?" Helen said.

"In Greek mythology, Lethe is the river of forgetfulness in the underworld," he said. "Clay really wanted to wipe out his wife, didn't he? We mustn't let that happen."

Even a walk through the blazing autumnal scenes couldn't warm Helen after Robert's comment.

It's up to me to save Annabel's legacy, Helen thought. She kept reciting Margery's words: *The sooner you go, the sooner it's over.*

The drive to the Lethe River Crematorium was mercifully short. The building was shoehorned in a small green park next to a factory. Helen saw black smoke belching from the crematorium chimney and parked the Igloo on the other side of the lot. She definitely didn't want those ashes on her white car.

The front of the crematorium was classic American funereal: white prefab Tara columns, black double doors, and somber shrubs. Helen checked the plants' leaves—no ashes.

She was relieved the heavy doors didn't creak when she entered the building. The lobby was papered in pale pink damask and the two brocade couches looked hard and slippery. Torch lamps shone with a pink light.

Helen remembered that butchers used pink lights in their cases to make meat look pinker and wished she hadn't dredged up that fact.

No one sat at the reception desk.

"Hello?" Helen called.

No answer. Helen's high heels made no sound on the thick rose carpet.

"Hello?" she called again and started down a long hall.

Still no answer.

No one was in the cluttered business office. The vast, empty reception room had the charm of an airplane hangar. Helen heard a roaring sound and guessed it was the cremation oven.

"Hello?" she shouted. Her voice echoed. She went back down the hall. The only door left was marked STAFF ONLY.

Helen pushed it open. "Anybody here?" she called.

She was in a warehouse with dingy cinder-block walls and a concrete floor. At the far end, Helen could see the huge steel oven door and hear its subdued roar. A cremation was in progress. Helen's stomach lurched. A real person was being burned, right now.

She repeated Margery's words like a mantra: *The sooner you go, the sooner it's over.* This ordeal was almost over, as soon as she found a staffer.

Six long brown cardboard boxes were stacked along the walls, each big enough to hold a body. From the way the boxes listed, Helen was sure they did. The ends of the boxes were taped with ordinary clear packing tape.

But she still didn't see a live person. Someone has to be here, she thought. That oven wouldn't be untended. Her heels clicked past the stacked boxes and she saw a grimy gray door.

Helen knocked on it. No answer. She tried the handle and it swung open into an office. A twentysomething man with short dark hair was sitting with his feet propped on a cluttered desk, drinking Mountain Dew and reading *Guns & Ammo.* He slopped his drink on the floor when Helen fell into the office.

"Jesus!" he said. "Why don't you knock instead of scaring a dude?"

He didn't look as creepy as Helen expected. He had a pleasant, ordinary face, camo pants and an olive drab T-shirt.

"I did knock," Helen said. "I've been calling for someone ever since I entered the building. Sorry I startled you." She pulled a wad of tissues out of her purse and kneeled down to wipe up the sticky spilled soda.

He watched her without moving from his chair, paying particular attention to her bottom when she bent down to clean the floor. She dropped the sodden tissues in a trash can overflowing with fast-food containers and said, "My name's Helen."

"I'm Ray," he said. Helen was relieved he didn't offer his hand. "How did you get back here? Wasn't the gal out front? Or Shelley in the office?"

"There was no one at the reception desk or anywhere else," Helen said.

"Musta gone out for barbecue," he said. "Hope they bring me some. I'm stuck here doing coupon specials."

Florida had coupons for everything, even funerals. "I've seen coupons for no-frills cremations," Helen said.

"We're the leader," Ray said. "Fifty bucks cheaper than any crematorium from Palm Beach to Miami. You saw those boxes stacked outside?"

Helen nodded.

"All coupon specials." Helen's stomach twisted again.

"Got an old lady in the oven who should be done in about an hour. She's skinny—weighs about seventy-five pounds. We can do her in about an hour and fifty minutes, but she'll get the full two hours. You've got a little more meat on you. I'd say you'd need a good two hours and fifteen minutes at eighteen hundred degrees."

"Uh, right," Helen said. She didn't know if it was worse that he'd checked out her body or sized her up for a cremation. "I have a question, Ray."

"I'm busy."

"I see that," Helen said. "That's a March issue. Maybe you need to buy a new magazine."

She put a twenty-dollar bill on the desk.

"That's a start," Ray said, pocketing the cash. "But magazines are expensive."

Helen put down a second twenty.

"You're getting warmer," Ray said. "But in my business, I know the difference between warm and hot."

Helen held out a third twenty. "It's yours, if you start talking now and tell me something interesting. Otherwise, I leave. I don't have all day."

"So what do you want to know?" he asked.

"A Fort Lauderdale woman, Annabel Lee Griffin, was cremated here recently."

"The artist," he said. "Too bad. She was a babe. Nice hair."

"How did you know she was an artist?" Helen asked.

"Her husband, a prize jerk, brought in two cardboard mailing tubes. He said there were paintings in them and he wanted them burned with his wife."

"And did you?" Helen asked.

"Sure. People burn mementos all the time."

Helen felt sick. Her search was over. She would finish her routine questions and go. "Did the husband attend the cremation?"

"No, just left instructions that the ashes should be shipped to her aunt in Connecticut. No one was here for the cremation. That's not unusual. She had one visitor, though. Her sister."

"Annabel's sister?" Helen said. Annabel has no sister, she thought, or any living relatives except her elderly aunt in Connecticut. Now Helen felt a glow of hope.

"Right," Ray said. "The sister came in that afternoon and wanted to spend a few minutes alone with her."

"Do you remember the sister's name?" Helen asked.

"Didn't ask. Didn't care. The dead girl got all the looks in that family."

"What did her sister look like?" Helen asked.

"Lots of curly hair. Dressed kinda hippie-like. Had one of them big purses with fringe all over."

"And you left her alone with the body?"

"The husband didn't leave any orders not to let anyone see her," Ray said.

Helen wondered how much Cissy had bribed this creep.

"I didn't have to untape anything. The woman was in our cremation casket—her husband complained to Shelley about the price of that. I opened the casket and went back in here. The sister stayed with the body about fifteen minutes, then came and got me when she was done."

"Was the sister carrying anything when she left?" Helen asked.

"Nope."

Just the purse, Helen thought. Which would be big enough for two mailing tubes. Yes! Helen was elated. She'd gambled and guessed right. Annabel's paintings had survived.

"Hey, don't look at me like that," Ray said. "I checked the dead lady before I closed the casket. Even made sure the mailing tubes were still in with her."

"Were the paintings still inside them?" Helen asked.

"Yeah, I opened one. Had a big red flower on it."

CHAPTER 34

Helen calmly shut the door to Ray's office, then rushed out of the crematorium as if the dead had broken out of their cardboard coffins and were chasing her. This time, she didn't notice the black smoke pouring from the chimney. She saw only sunshine and blue sky. This grim trip was worth it: Annabel's paintings had survived.

Helen was also stunned by what she'd learned. Cissy had taken the paintings. Swiped them right out of Annabel's coffin.

Helen pointed the faithful Igloo toward home. She wanted out of her hot suit. Her high heels pinched. While she drove, Helen ruthlessly examined her mistakes.

I've treated Cissy as a complete ditz, she thought. As a silly, harmless woman. Some judge of character I am. Those clacking beads and ragbag clothes hid a treacherous woman. Cissy's colder than an ice cave. She had not only robbed her dead friend's coffin, she'd boldly switched Annabel's valuable paintings with her own worthless daubs.

Anyone could have walked in on Cissy while she was swapping Annabel's paintings for hers. That took nerve. Just being in that back room with the creepy coupon cremations took nerve.

Where were Annabel's stolen paintings now? Did Cissy still have them? Or were they in Miami with a twisted art dealer? Robert, the Las Olas art dealer, will tell me the names of those dicey dealers, but I'd rather let the police recover Annabel's stolen art.

When those paintings are found, what will happen to them? Will they go back to Annabel's jealous husband, Clay? Will Cissy face jail time for saving Annabel's paintings? The local art world would give her a medal. But those aren't my problems.

Helen didn't understand why Cissy wanted to derail Annabel's murder investigation by insisting she'd committed suicide. She doesn't want Annabel's killer caught, Helen decided. Was Cissy protecting her lover, Clay?

Helen tried to make the puzzle pieces fit: How did Cissy know Annabel's paintings would be in her coffin? Did Clay tell her? If so, did he tell her about them before or after their breakup? Or were they in it together? Cissy went straight from our lunch to loot her friend's coffin, Helen thought. That's cold. But so is befriending a woman when you're having an affair with her husband.

Helen wasn't sure that Clay had had a real affair with Cissy. Helen remembered when Clay latched onto her at Annabel's memorial. His voice dripped contempt as he steered her away from Cissy. *I met her on the beach once, and ever since, she's been stalking me. She has this crazy idea that we're soul mates.*

Clay tried to convince me that Cissy had *been after me to leave Annabel. I told her I couldn't do that. I loved my wife and I was faithful.* Eventually, Clay admitted, *In my heart, I was always faithful. But Annabel was sick and a healthy man has needs.*

Hah! Helen thought. Faithful in his heart—but not in his studio. All the guards at Silver Glade knew about his affairs. Did Clay "need"—or maybe that was "use"—Cissy? When he had his pick of pretty, easily impressed students, why have an affair with silly Cissy?

Or am I underestimating her again? Maybe those hippie outfits hide a master of Tantric sex.

Helen didn't know.

She'd listened to Clay explain away Cissy's friendship with his wife: *Cissy confessed to Annabel that she'd lost her head over me, but she'd regretted her rashness. Annabel said she understood. She believed her.*

Was Annabel that gullible? Helen wondered. Cissy seemed to take charge in their friendship: She drove Annabel to art class, hauled her painting supplies and helped Annabel in and out of her car. She'd given Annabel a sympathetic ear, then gleefully gossiped about her late friend, branding Annabel as "wild" because she'd had a lesbian affair.

Clay was an unfaithful liar. But was Cissy any better? Was her friendship with Annabel another lie?

Lita, the artist, insisted Annabel wanted to divorce Clay, but Cissy seemed to have no idea the marriage was in trouble. A divorce would have made Cissy's dream marriage possible. Maybe Annabel wasn't as forgiving—or as blind—as Clay thought. Maybe she was using Cissy as a free chauffeur and an aide.

Helen's cell phone rang, but she let it go to voice mail. She was only a block from the Coronado apartments. After she parked the Igloo, Helen found a message from Jenny. "Please call right away," her client said. "I need to talk to you."

Jenny sounded scared, or worried. When Helen returned her call, Jenny's words poured out in a rush: "That detective Burt Pelham came to see me," she said. "I can't talk about it on the phone. Can you meet me? I'm at the beach."

"Which beach?" Helen asked.

"Lauderdale by the Sea," Jenny said. "I'm at the lot on A1A. Don't worry about the parking fee. I'll pay it. We can walk along the ocean and talk."

"I'll be there in half an hour," Helen said, "as soon as I change into shorts and sandals."

Twenty minutes later, Helen crossed the Commercial Boulevard drawbridge and spotted the colorful fish and sea turtle sculptures that marked the entrance to Lauderdale by the Sea. LBTS was a rare

South Florida beach town smart enough to resist the siren song of the developers. It remained small-scale, colorful and charming, preserving its midcentury modern apartments and buildings.

Jenny's red Tesla was easy to see in the parking lot. Helen pulled the Igloo into a nearby spot. While the meter ate Jenny's money, Helen stretched and breathed in the soft, salty air. She could hear the soothing, primeval sound of the waves and see acres of pink tourists broiling on the beige sand. The water was a pearly turquoise gradually turning a deep blue.

Jenny seemed smaller without her towering heels, and younger without her makeup. Her brown hair blew freely in the soft breeze. The two women slipped off their sandals as soon as they reached the sand.

"When's the last time you were at the beach?" Jenny asked.

"I don't know," Helen said. "Isn't that sad? When I first moved to Fort Lauderdale, I came to the beach all the time. I loved watching the ocean. Now I can't remember the last time I was here. I've become a real Floridian. The wrong kind."

"That's too bad," Jenny said. "I'm the same way. I've let the beach become the place where the tourists go. All this beauty is on my doorstep and I ignore it."

Helen wiggled her toes in the warm, damp sand and felt the sun-warm water rush over her feet. A seagull swooped down and swiped a french fry out of a trash can. A pretty brunette in a red bikini lounged on a blue striped beach towel while a young man rubbed coconut sunscreen on her back.

The couple looked so comfortable together, Helen wished she was here with Phil.

When Helen and Jenny had walked up the beach away from the crowds, Helen said, "Tell me about your conversation with Detective Pelham."

"He showed up at my place this morning," Jenny said. "You know how I feel about that man. Last time, I tried to tell him that Hugo killed Annabel and he ignored me. He even said poison was a woman's weapon."

"When I talked to him, I thought he was smarter than that," Helen said.

"Well, he's changed his tune."

"Now he thinks Hugo is the killer?" Helen asked.

"No," Jenny said. "This time he asked a lot of questions about Clay."

"What kind?" Helen asked. "Tell me exactly what he said."

"There were so many," Jenny said. "But he asked me if Annabel got along with Clay and if she was afraid of him or wanted a divorce."

"What did you tell him?"

"I said Annabel wasn't afraid of her husband. He kept that big expensive house so she could paint the plants and wildlife in the yard. So far as I know, she and Clay got along fine."

"Lita said Annabel was unhappy with Clay and thinking of leaving him," Helen said.

"Who's Lita?"

"The artist who shared a FAT Village studio with Annabel," Helen said.

"Oh, right. Annabel never told me that," Jenny said, and skittered away from the subject. Was she annoyed that Annabel had kept her in the dark? Or was Lita lying?

"The detective asked more questions," Jenny said. "He asked if I knew that Clay vaped or if Annabel knew that nicotine was poisonous."

"Did you?" Helen said. "Did she?"

"Annabel mentioned that Clay had switched to vaping and she was glad there were no more smelly ashtrays all over the house, but that's all. We never discussed its dangers.

"From the way that detective asked these questions, I think he's going to make an arrest."

Helen was so startled she stumbled in the sand. Had Detective Pelham found the proof that would send Clay to jail? What was it?

"Are you okay?" Jenny asked.

"I'm fine," Helen said. "Just took a little trip." Jenny ignored her lame attempt at a joke.

"That's good if Pelham is ready to arrest Clay," Helen said.

"No, it's not," Jenny said. "He's going to arrest the wrong person. I *know* Hugo killed Annabel." She'd stopped walking in the sand and faced Helen to plead her case.

"Annabel was going off in a new direction with her art," Jenny said. "She was becoming more confident and assured. Hugo's taunts didn't seem to bother her anymore. Hugo had access to nicotine through his mother's nicotine patches. He had a good reason to kill Annabel."

"Jenny, you're the client," Helen said. "But you're paying for my expertise. And I believe the detective is right: Clay killed Annabel."

Unless the killer was Cissy. A woman cold enough to steal paintings out of her friend's coffin. But Helen didn't think her client would accept that news.

"Well, I don't! Like you said, I'm the client. I want you to go talk to Hugo again."

Helen almost expected Jenny to stamp her foot. "I will," Helen said, hiding her anger. "But this time, if I don't find any leads that Hugo is the killer, I want your permission to talk to Detective Pelham. I need this, Jenny. Trust me. Please."

Jenny hesitated, watching the endless ocean. Helen let her stare at its pearly blue vastness. Far out on the horizon, they saw a giant container ship, reduced to toy size. The view seemed to give their problem perspective.

"All right," Jenny said. "You've got it. But promise you'll see Hugo first."

CHAPTER 35

Hugo Hythe and his widowed mother, Linda, lived in sprawling seventies luxury at the Landings, a boating community that clung like a barnacle to its even more prestigious neighbor, Bay Colony.

The Landings was on Bayview Drive, a twisting street lined with impressive homes in northeast Fort Lauderdale. In the section that wound through the Landings, Bayview was prettied up with landscaped center medians and policed by car-crunching speed bumps. Extra-wide, with faded white warning stripes, the treacherous speed bumps waited to take out a car's front end.

Helen hit the brakes just in time, before the Igloo slalomed over a speed bump that could have torn out the undercarriage, then turned onto Hugo's street. Like many houses in the Landings, Hugo's home was a long, low rambler with big windows and a wide lawn. Most of the backyards faced a canal. Prehistoric green iguanas sunned themselves on the concrete docks, reminding residents that even in six-figure neighborhoods, nature owned the land.

Helen cruised Hugo's street. She knew that treacherous Cissy lived four doors down. She spotted Cissy's home immediately: a freshly painted pinkish beige house with a manicured lawn. No hint of the hippie outside her dwelling.

I'll have a talk with Cissy about Annabel's paintings after I leave Hugo's, Helen thought.

She had a double reason for visiting Hugo's house. Helen wanted to talk to him and his mother, Linda. She parked by the three-tiered fountain in the Hythes' circular drive and mentally reviewed her pretext for being there.

Helen wasn't sure Hugo would be home during the day, but at least she could talk to his mother without his snarling presence. Linda might let valuable information slip when Hugo wasn't around.

There were no other cars in the drive, but Helen knew someone was home. She heard a TV inside the house.

She crossed the pink paver walkway and rang the doorbell. After a long wait, a woman using a four-legged cane opened the front door and peered out the screen door. She was big, but not fat, with a pleasant, fleshy face and well-cut gray hair. Though her head had a slight tremor, she gave the impression of strength.

Hugo's mother, Helen guessed.

"May I help you?" the woman asked. Like many people in privileged neighborhoods, she seemed to have no fear of strangers, or at least well-groomed white women.

"May I speak to Hugo, please?" Helen asked. "We take an art class together, along with your neighbor, Cissy."

"Hugo's at work now," the woman said. "And then he has to run an errand for me. He won't be back until after six."

Trusting, Helen thought. Linda's just told me she's home alone.

"Oh, that's too bad," Helen said. Another delay, she thought, but at least I'll get one interview. "Are you Mrs. Hythe, his mother?"

The woman smiled. "Yes. But call me Linda. Hugo is my son, and I couldn't ask for a better boy."

"Cissy told me how good he is to you," Helen said. "She said he shops, handles the home maintenance, even brings you your nicotine patches."

"That's right," Linda said. "I couldn't keep this big place without his help. I have early-onset Parkinson's. I'm a Parkie, though not everyone with Parkinson's likes that term. Personally, I don't like saying I have Parkinson's *disease.* It's not contagious, you know."

Maybe not, but Helen thought Linda's smile was infectious. How did this charming woman produce such a rude son?

"Today's not a good day for this Parkie," Linda said. "My balance is a little off and I'm using this." She held up the cane.

What is Linda doing, Helen wondered, showing a stranger her weakness? She wanted to give this trusting woman a "don't talk to strangers" lecture.

"I ran out of nicotine patches almost two weeks ago," Linda said.

Before Annabel died, Helen thought. Of nicotine poisoning.

"I have a confession to make," Helen said. "I also came here to see you, as well as to talk to your son. One of my friends was just diagnosed with early-onset Parkinson's. She's still reeling from the news. Your neighbor Cissy said the nicotine patches work for you. Could I ask you more about them? Maybe I can tell my friend about them. They might help her."

"Of course, dear," Linda said. "Let's go around the back and talk on the patio, where it's shady."

At least Linda is smart enough not to ask a stranger into her home, Helen thought. She and Linda followed the paver walkway to the vast green backyard, where a pleasant patio was nestled under a huge poinciana tree. A gleaming white Hatteras cabin cruiser, tied to the dock, bobbed in the water. Three green lizards sunned themselves on the warm concrete.

"Wonderful view," Helen said. "Is that your yacht?"

"I wish," Linda said, as she and Helen sat at a yellow umbrella table. "We sold our boat after my husband died. We let a friend dock here. There's always a nice breeze and I love watching the water. I even like the lizards. Living dinosaurs are lounging on my dock."

Helen felt bad about lying to this sweet woman. At least these lies won't hurt her, she thought. Unless she tells me something that proves her son, Hugo, killed Annabel.

"I wish Hugo could spend more time here, relaxing," Linda said. "He's been so busy lately."

"I understand his ex-wife died," Helen said.

Linda's anger flared like a skyrocket. "Don't mention that conniving woman," she said, her eyes narrowing. The trembling in her head was more pronounced and suddenly her face didn't seem so pleasant. "She divorced my son and then tried to smear him. Made up a bunch of lies about how he was unfaithful and had a child out of wedlock. Lies!"

DNA doesn't lie, Helen thought, but she said nothing. Hugo evidently didn't tell his mom about the paternity test results.

"Fortunately, Hugo's employer was thrilled to keep him. My son is better off without that mean, bitter woman. I wasn't surprised that she committed suicide."

"The police think Annabel was murdered," Helen said.

"Well, they're wrong. That detective came here to interview Hugo. Got my boy so upset, I didn't have the heart to ask him to go to the store for my nicotine patches. I thought I could do without them.

"Well, I couldn't. My symptoms have returned. This morning, I broke down and asked my boy to pick up some patches for me."

"You don't need a prescription for nicotine patches?" Helen asked.

"Not the kind I use," Linda said. "You can buy them at any pharmacy. Now, tell me about your friend."

"My friend Peggy is sixty-three," Helen said, aging Peggy by more than twenty years. "She was just diagnosed with Parkinson's and she's completely lost."

"We all are at first," Linda said. "Does she go to the Parkinson's center at Nova University or at Broward Health?"

"Uh, not sure," Helen said, feeling even worse.

"Does Peggy smoke?"

"No," Helen said.

"That's too bad," Linda said. "I smoked in high school—teenage rebellion, I guess, but I quit in college. Now I wonder what would have happened if I'd kept on smoking. Maybe I wouldn't be a Parkie. Well, hindsight is twenty-twenty."

"And you might have died of cancer instead of getting Parkinson's," Helen said, then mentally kicked herself for that dumb comment.

"True," Linda said.

"I don't get the connection between smoking and Parkinson's," Helen said.

"There is one," Linda said. "We know smoking is bad for your health, but it may be good for your Parkinson's. Smoking may lower your chance of getting Parkinson's by as much as sixty percent, or so I've heard. They say the nicotine in cigarettes can be therapeutic."

"Amazing," Helen said.

"It is, isn't it? Nicotine got a bad rap thanks to cigarettes—and deserves it. But there are some serious tests going on to see if nicotine patches help with Parkinson's. I think the Michael J. Fox Foundation is doing one. He's the actor, you know. I watch him on *The Good Wife*. Michael is brilliant, and I like that he plays an unsympathetic character on that TV show. Where was I?"

"Talking about serious tests for nicotine patches," Helen said.

"Right. My Hugo tried to get me into one and couldn't. But he did find a sympathetic doctor who suggested that I try the patches. The doctor monitors my use, of course, and the patches have definitely helped me."

"Are the patches dangerous?" Helen asked.

"Well, nicotine is a poison," Linda said. "I could overdose if I chewed nicotine gum and used the patches. Also if I smoked when I wore a patch. But I don't.

"You know what's funny? Nicotine patches are supposed to improve mild memory loss, especially if you're getting Alzheimer's. I don't have anything like that, thank goodness.

"But the patches sure don't help my memory," Linda said. "I thought I had enough patches to last to the end of the month. I know I counted them. I must have counted wrong. I couldn't find my last box. I tore the house apart looking for it. Even Hugo helped me search. We couldn't find those patches anywhere.

"I'd swear I had a whole extra box."

CHAPTER 36

Linda walked Helen out to her car. Hugo's mother moved slowly, carefully placing her four-legged cane on the uneven pavement and pausing after a few steps. Helen wanted to help this brave woman, but she was afraid her offer would seem condescending. Linda struggled along the walkway, her pleasant face determined, her head jittering a little more.

"Tell your friend Peggy to call me if she wants to talk," she said. "Also, there are some very good support groups she can join. I can recommend some."

"You're very kind," Helen said, swallowing her self-disgust as she climbed into the Igloo. Linda waved good-bye from the doorstep.

Helen pulled away from the well-kept house with the soothing fountain, dragging her shame along with her, like tin cans tied to her back bumper. *I've tricked a good woman into betraying her son*, she thought. *I didn't need to walk to my car. I could have slithered to the dock and hung out with the lizards.*

Helen tried to convince herself that she'd done the right thing. *My interview with Linda went better than expected*, she thought.

That missing box of nicotine patches points an accusing finger at Hugo. My client, Jenny, will be thrilled. This confirms her belief that Hugo killed Annabel.

I'll come back after six tonight, see Hugo, prove Jenny is right. And break Linda's heart.

Meanwhile, I need to talk to Cissy about Annabel's paintings.

But Helen couldn't stomach the deceitful Cissy, not after her own perfidious performance. She deliberately turned the Igloo in the opposite direction, driving away from Cissy's home. Helen wandered aimlessly through the Landings. Built mostly in the sixties and seventies, the neighborhood was old for Fort Lauderdale.

Helen drove past the carefully landscaped and perfectly painted homes and envied their appearance of order.

This case was messy, and Helen couldn't fit Cissy into it. When she stole Annabel's art out of her coffin, was Cissy working on her own? Or did she and Clay plot to steal the paintings together, with Clay pretending his lover was an unwanted stalker?

Based on Cissy's lovesick conversation, Helen was sure she adored Clay. Cissy sounded like a bad romance novel. She'd told Helen: *One look, and I knew he was my soul mate.* And: *He's so protective. It's sweet. He even persuaded me to stop smoking and switch to vaping.*

Helen winced when she thought of Cissy's sappy conversation, laced with sighs. *He's an artist. That's why I'm taking this class, so I'll be able to communicate with the man I love. And taking it at Bonnet House is so inspiring. I want to live like Evelyn Bartlett.*

Except Clay and Cissy had neither the talent nor the originality to imitate the exotic, artistic lives of Frederic and Evelyn Bartlett.

Helen's Igloo thunked over a speed bump and jolted her out of her reverie. She slowed down and drove carefully, listening for scraping sounds. She checked the rearview mirror: no trail of fluids leaking from the car. Whew!

Cissy and Clay are in it together, Helen decided. Cissy stole

Annabel's art for Clay. She'll sell it in Miami and they'll share the profits. Clay's scene at the memorial, when he'd told me that Cissy was a stalker, was a drama staged for an audience of one—me.

I'm an idiot. I've let myself be duped by those two. Enough! She felt hot, clean anger surge through her, washing away her shame. She was ready to confront Cissy. She would recover Annabel's art and save her legacy.

And this time, I won't underestimate Cissy. Helen rummaged in her purse for her pepper spray canister and stashed it in her shirt pocket. What if I need backup? Helen felt around in her purse until she found her cell phone, and slipped that into her other pocket.

Two more turns and Helen was back on Hugo's street. As she passed the Hythe home, she could see activity four houses down at Cissy's place. The front yard was landscaped with small, compact plants. Instead of a fountain, Cissy had a black wrought-iron table and chairs in a little garden area. Planted next to them was a FOR SALE sign.

Huh? Cissy never mentioned she was selling her house.

Helen glanced at the street and this time saw the approaching speed bump. She slowed down, rolled over it at a stately pace, stopped the car and watched. Now she could see Cissy's home clearly.

Cissy's garage door was open and her blue Prius was parked in the drive, its trunk open. It was stuffed with suitcases and cloth bags in bright Aztec prints. Cissy was trying to force a bulky duffel into the overloaded trunk. She was a blur of color in her sheer orange Indian print skirt and a tie-dyed dashiki as she moved back and forth, adjusting, pulling, tugging.

Finally, Cissy shoved the big bag into the trunk and slammed the lid. She disappeared inside, then returned moments later lugging her art supplies.

Helen watched Cissy open the Prius's back door. More bright Aztec bags cascaded out. Cissy caught them and crammed them back into the crowded backseat, then wedged in her art supplies. She relaxed a moment, then tried to close the door. It wouldn't budge.

Cissy looked frustrated and exhausted. The bags weren't cooperating. She rearranged them and had almost slammed the door when an avalanche of luggage poured out. Along with the bags and boxes, two brown cardboard mailing tubes tumbled out, then slowly rolled down the long driveway.

Annabel's art? Helen wondered. Time to find out.

An impatient silver Lexus blasted its horn and Helen realized she'd stopped the Igloo in the middle of the street.

"Sorry," she mouthed, but the driver gave her a single-digit salute and roared around Helen's car, hitting the speed bump hard. She heard an ugly scraping sound as the car's brake lights flashed. The expensive Lexus rumbled like a bootlegger's getaway as it lurched down the street.

Yep, you're number one, buddy, Helen thought, and your tantrum cost you a new exhaust system.

She saw Cissy racing down the drive after the runaway mailing tubes, skirts flaring, corkscrew curls flying. Helen blocked the end of the drive, ran out and scooped up both mailing tubes.

"Helen!" Cissy said, leaning breathlessly against the Igloo. Her voice was a wheeze, and her dashikied chest was heaving. "Thank you for saving those. I was on the way to the post office." She stepped forward to claim them.

Helen stepped back. "Really?" she said. "But there's no address on these mailing tubes. No tape, either. If I was mailing something this valuable, I'd tape the ends. And buy plenty of insurance. In fact, I might spring for FedEx."

Helen set one tube on top of the Igloo and popped the white plastic cap off the other.

"Hey! Give me that!" Cissy screamed. "It's not yours!"

But Helen was bigger and quicker than Cissy. She blocked the little woman with her hip, then pulled out the pepper spray.

"Don't shoot," Cissy said, her voice shaking.

"No need to," Helen said. "Just stay right there and don't move."

Helen pulled a rolled-up canvas out of the tube. Several, in fact. Oil paintings. Four. No, five.

"Mind if I vape?" Cissy asked. "It's right here."

Helen saw the e-cigarette and a small bottle on the wrought-iron table. "Help yourself."

Cissy reached for her e-cigarette with trembling hands, poured in more vape juice and began puffing. The vape smelled like raspberry pie fresh from the oven. Cissy relaxed as she breathed deeply. Then the automatic sprinkler system popped on in the garden, drenching her skirt. She squealed and moved closer to Helen, away from the water.

"Careful," Helen said. "Don't come nearer or I'll toss your art in the flower bed."

Cissy stayed. "Don't hurt them," she said, taking another hit on her e-cigarette. Helen's stomach growled. The warm raspberry scent made her hungry. Concentrate, she told herself.

Helen spread the paintings out on the Igloo's roof and examined the first one—a bold study of a black bird and a yellow star fruit against a background of brilliant green tropical leaves. The painting was dramatic, colorful and ironic. The bird had a mocking eye, and the star fruit was bursting with tropical life.

"My, your technique has definitely improved," Helen said. "You've changed your name, too. This painting's signed 'Annabel Lee Griffin.' You're a grave robber, Cissy. No, you break into coffins. How low can you go, stealing from your dead friend?"

Cissy showed no surprise that Helen knew her secret. "Do you think it was easy for me, going into that horrible place?" Cissy said. "I wasn't stealing. I was preserving Annabel's best work. She didn't have any children." Cissy was vaping like crazy, blowing clouds of raspberry-scented smoke. "Clay was going to burn her masterpieces."

"And what are you going to do with them?" Helen asked.

"Protect them," Cissy said.

"By hauling them around?"

"I couldn't leave her paintings in the house. I'm going on vacation."

"With a carful of luggage and your art supplies?"

Cissy shrugged. "I don't pack light," she said, and took another puff on her e-cigarette. The driveway smelled like a bakery. Helen saw the bottle of vape juice—nicotine—was the same color as tea.

Annabel's raspberry tea.

"That's how you got rid of Annabel," Helen said. "You poisoned her with raspberry-flavored vape juice. You poured it in her raspberry tea. You told me Annabel added lots of honey to her iced tea, but the day she died, she complained it tasted bitter."

"No!" Cissy said.

"Yes!" Helen said. "You poisoned Annabel! You planned her murder and stole her paintings. Now you're going to sell them and run."

"No!" Cissy said. "I didn't hurt her. She was my friend!"

"Married to the man you loved," Helen said. "Annabel had everything—talent, a career, and Clay, your soul mate."

"She didn't appreciate him," Cissy said. "He sacrificed everything for her. Everything! He was a true artist but he had to hold down two jobs for her health insurance. He couldn't concentrate on his own work. And did that selfish witch appreciate what he did for her—trudging off to a nowhere school to teach brainless beach bunnies? No! Not even a thank-you. All she thought about was herself."

Helen fished her phone out of her pocket. "You can tell that to Detective Pelham. I'm calling him now."

"No! Wait! Let me explain," Cissy said.

Suddenly she dodged past Helen and tried to make a break for her car, but she slipped on the sprinkler-wet grass. Helen grabbed the wrought-iron chair and trapped her inside its legs.

"Don't move," Helen said. "Or I'll shoot you in the face."

"I didn't kill her," Cissy said. "Clay did. I can prove it."

Helen moved the chair onto the drive, then said, "Get up. Sit. And start talking."

CHAPTER 37

A bedraggled Cissy sat on the wrought-iron chair in her driveway, sniffling like a toddler in time-out—a little girl who'd been playing in the mud. Her thin Indian-print skirt and colorful shirt were soaked and dirt smeared. Even Cissy's springy curly blond hair was subdued.

Helen stood over her captive, pepper spray pointed at her face. Cissy's eyes were so red, they already looked pepper sprayed.

Helen glanced uneasily down the quiet street, expecting the police to come roaring into Cissy's driveway. But no one interfered with her interrogation.

Helen switched on her cell phone's recorder. Helen knew this two-party recording wasn't legal in a Florida court, but she hoped it would help Detective Pelham.

I'm betting the success of my case on these next questions, Helen decided. Cissy claims she has proof that Clay killed Annabel, and I'm going to get it. I'll keep my questions soft and my voice sympathetic. We can have a "we girls" talk while I hold Cissy hostage in her driveway.

"You love Clay, don't you?" Helen said. "Even after everything he's done."

Cissy nodded. "Clay is my soul mate," she said. "He loves me because I understand and admire his work."

"Loves," Helen noted. Not "loved." And she bet "admire" was the operative word in that relationship. Annabel had ceased to admire Clay's work. She'd outgrown him and Clay needed admiration.

"Clay had a major career in New York," Helen said, as if that was an undeniable fact.

"He did," Cissy said, and her tear-stained face glowed with pride. "When I first met Clay, I had stars in my eyes. I'd never met a real New York artist. He was so charming and handsome, not at all affected by his success. I thought he was too good to be true. But then I got to know him—really know him."

"You went to his Silver Glade art studio," Helen said. "For special lessons."

She was proud she'd managed to say that with a straight face.

"Yes," Cissy said. Her voice dropped to a whisper, and Helen had to strain to hear her. "You've been there."

"Only for Annabel's memorial," Helen said.

"But you know what it looks like. You've seen that fantastic view. The first time I was there with Clay was on a stormy afternoon. Lightning lit the sky and the ocean was like a wild animal, roaring and tearing at the beach. Clay's studio, with those huge windows, was like being in the center of the storm. The lightning flashes almost blinded me.

"At first I was frightened. But Clay held me and told me not to be afraid of the force of nature—it was more powerful than both of us. I felt so safe in his arms. He kissed me, and suddenly, we were overcome with passion."

Give me a break, Helen thought, but she made what she hoped was a sympathetic noise, and Cissy kept talking.

"It was wrong. I knew it was wrong," Cissy said, "but our love was greater than the words Clay had spoken to the judge when he married Annabel. Now I wanted to love, honor and obey Clay, all the days of my life. I wanted to be with him in sickness and in health, for richer or poorer."

"Till death parted you?" Helen asked, finishing the rest of the timeless vow.

"Oh, no," Cissy said. "Our love will last forever—beyond the grave, beyond eternity."

Cissy's tear-stricken eyes were shining, and Helen almost felt sorry for her. She really believes this claptrap, she thought.

"Clay said he wished that he was free to marry me."

Right, Helen thought. I bet he said that to all the girls.

"He couldn't abandon his sick wife. She needed him. But she understood that he had needs she couldn't fulfill."

That old, sad story, Helen thought. As the ex-wife of an unfaithful husband, I wonder if I'm the right person to listen to Cissy. I feel like pepper spraying this nitwit and then driving over her.

Cissy must have seen Helen's expression. "Well, he did!" she said. "You've never been in love or you wouldn't look at me like that."

Wrong, Helen thought. I am in love—deeply, passionately in love with a man who is my equal. Phil would never use those tired old lines to lure a gullible woman into bed.

But Helen gritted her teeth and said, "So you decided to stand by him."

"Clay was suffering," Cissy said. "Working a soul-sucking teaching job to get her health insurance to pay for her doctor visits. She was draining his creativity. He was spending his prime artistic years at a sweatshop. I knew if he was free of her, he could start his career again and assume his rightful position in the art world."

Her, Helen thought. Cissy never used Annabel's name. Annabel wasn't a friend or an artist—she wasn't even a person for Cissy.

"At first, Clay and I thought she didn't have much time left. She was sickly and depressed. Some days she couldn't get out of bed. I told you that. She told me she wasn't sure how much longer she could go on like this."

"When did you become friends with Annabel?" Helen asked.

"Clay introduced us and I saw how lonely she was. She needed someone to talk to, to confide in."

Helen wondered when Annabel had found out that Cissy was her husband's mistress. What a blow that must have been.

"I talked her into getting a life insurance policy," Cissy said. "Her career was taking off—at the expense of Clay's. I knew there were life insurance policies for people with chronic fatigue syndrome. Clay took out a million-dollar policy on her. It was expensive, but he said it would be worth it. Once he collected the money . . ."

After Annabel died, Helen translated.

". . . we could live in Britain and he would paint the sea."

"Britain?" Helen said. "Why would you want to live in that cold, rainy climate after Florida's sunshine?"

"Clay wanted a different view of the sea: deeper, wilder, more romantic. Like us."

"But you couldn't marry," Helen prompted, "because Annabel clung to life."

"We waited and waited," Cissy said. "I wanted children—I'm thirty-three—and time was running out.

"And she wasn't happy. Then the doctors thought she might have myasthenia gravis, and she talked about suicide. I felt she needed to look at the facts. I told her that Aristotle Onassis had spent his final days with his eyelids taped open and an attendant who sprayed his dry eyes because he couldn't blink."

Helen felt her skin crawl. What a sweet friend, she thought. I bet you tried to talk Annabel into killing herself.

"But she researched the subject and told me that people could live with it for years. She said she'd learned to live with chronic fatigue syndrome, so she'd live with this, too.

"Finally, Clay realized he would never be free. He'd have even more medical debt. She was seeing specialists from here to Miami. The co-pays alone were killing him. We would never realize our dream."

But they weren't together anymore, Helen thought. Why did Clay and Cissy split? Helen tried a bold guess.

"Clay started seeing other women, didn't he?" Helen said. "It was the strain, wasn't it?"

Cissy blinked in surprise, then nodded. "He was surrounded by temptation." She wiped her streaming eyes.

"Great men make great mistakes," Helen managed to say without gagging.

"He was an artist," Cissy said. "They shouldn't be tied down by petty rules. The other women were just flings. I knew he loved me."

"So you made the ultimate sacrifice for that love," Helen said.

"I helped him," Cissy said. She couldn't look at Helen. "Clay said he had a plan that would be painless. He would pour some e-cigarette liquid into her raspberry iced tea. I smoked flavored vapes—at the time I was using hazelnut coffee. But I bought a bottle of raspberry e-liquid."

"Where did you buy it?" Helen asked. "I don't vape, so I don't know."

"I went to that shop on Fort Lauderdale Beach, Vic's Vaper Hub. Lots of tourists. No one would remember me.

"Clay and I met that night, and the next morning, he poured it in her tea. But his hands shook when he opened the bottle and he spilled some. He texted me that I might have to add more. So I did. It was a kindness, really. You saw how she was that morning. She walked with a cane and was too tired to carry her art supplies."

But she was still vital and able to paint, Helen thought. She forced herself to stay silent.

"She had the lid off her tea thermos in class," Cissy said. "I waited and waited for her to drink some, but she didn't. I was scared to death."

That her friend wouldn't die, Helen thought. She could picture the scene in her mind: curly-haired Cissy in her floaty scarves, torturing that red hibiscus. Their art teacher, Yulia, telling her, *You keep flattening your flower . . . You're too careful. Be bold! What do you have to lose?*

Time, Cissy had said. *The class is over.*

"When did you add the extra vape juice?" Helen said.

"While I helped her pack. Better safe than sorry."

Now Helen saw Annabel and Cissy walking to the parking lot, and Annabel's false friend reminding her to drink her tea—three or four times—until she did, in the rubble-strewn lot. And complained that her tea tasted bitter.

"So why tell me now?" Helen said.

"After I sacrificed everything for him, Clay didn't want to see me anymore. He said he needed his space. He would go to Britain and get established and then I would join him. We were going to wait until the estate was settled.

"Then you started asking questions and he said he was leaving right away. He wouldn't pick up my calls. Last night he texted me that he was leaving. He said I should leave, too."

"What airline is he flying?"

"He's not flying—he's taking a container ship to England. He wanted to paint the sea, remember? A container ship has a few berths for private passengers, but it's not glitzy, like a cruise ship. There's nothing to do. Clay wanted to paint and be inspired. I was supposed to fly into Gatwick and we'd meet in four months in London. He cared enough to tell me."

Maybe he wanted you out of the country before the cops closed in, Helen thought.

"Why did you steal the paintings out of Annabel's coffin?" Helen asked.

"Because I wanted to save her art."

"Right," Helen said.

Cissy heard her sarcasm. "A Miami art dealer wants to sell them to some special clients. He's promised me thousands of dollars. I thought if I had money, Clay would love me again."

"How do I know you're not just making this up?" Helen asked.

"I have my cell phone with Clay's texts."

"Didn't the detective subpoena his phone?"

"This is a burner phone. We both used them." She pulled out an ancient flip phone. "This is mine."

"You texted on that?"

"I got used to it," she said. "I know where he hides his phone, too. It's in his studio."

"Give me the flip phone." Helen held the pepper spray at Cissy's eye level.

Cissy handed over the phone and Helen dropped it in her shirt pocket that had held the pepper spray.

"Is Clay at his studio?" Helen asked.

"No, I called the reception desk," Cissy said. "The guard said Clay hasn't been in since yesterday."

"Why would the guard tell you?" Helen asked.

"Because I tip well," Cissy said. "Also, I called Clay myself. He didn't answer his condo line. It went into voice mail. Someone did pick up the phone at his home, though. I said his name and he hung up. He hasn't left yet for Miami."

"Where is his house?"

"In Coral Ridge Country Club Estates, the subdivision on Bayview."

"Get in my car and direct me," Helen said, holding her cell phone. "Or I'll call the cops."

Helen kept the pepper spray in one hand while she opened the passenger door. She pushed 911 and put her phone in her lap.

"All I have to do is press Send and you go to jail," she said.

CHAPTER 38

"Fasten your seat belt," Helen said.

Cissy sat stubbornly in her seat, refusing to buckle up. Helen pointed her cell phone at her. "Now!" she said. "Or I'll call 911. This is a death-penalty state and you'll be sitting on death row for Annabel's murder. I hear Florida gets its lethal injection drugs from Oklahoma and they don't always work too well. You'll die screaming."

Cissy glared at Helen but snapped on her seat belt.

"Which way to Clay's home?" Helen asked.

"Head south on Bayview, and then cross Commercial," Cissy said, her voice sullen with self-pity.

Once again Helen drove past the sun-splashed medians on Bayview. The Igloo flew over a wide speed bump and landed with a teeth-jarring *whump!*

"Careful!" Cissy shrieked.

Damn, Helen thought. I forgot there was one last bump before we cross the canal and get out of here.

She prayed her beloved white PT Cruiser had escaped injury. Helen drove over the small humped bridge that marked the southern entrance to the Landings, listening carefully for signs of damage: no telltale grind of metal rubbing against metal. No raw, full-throated roar of a ruined exhaust system. No wobble in the suspension.

The sturdy Igloo sped smoothly forward across Commercial Boulevard. True to its name, the wide street was lined with banks, bars, bistros and bakeries.

The Igloo passed the pointed pale green obelisks marking the entrance to the Coral Ridge Country Club Estates.

These houses were twice the size of most homes in the Landings. Many were single-story homes with massive trees, tall hedges and manicured lawns. Yachts bobbed at their deepwater docks.

There were no speed bumps on this section of Bayview, but the blacktop road was unusually twisty. Helen careened along Bayview's curves while Cissy hugged the door handle and whimpered in fear. Helen blew through a church speed zone at fifty miles an hour, praying there were no police. Not yet. Not till they spotted Clay.

"Where's Clay's house?" Helen said. "Before or after the Coral Ridge Country Club?"

"Before. It's close," Cissy said.

"How close?" Helen said.

"There!" Cissy said. "That's his house. The white one on the left."

She screamed as Helen made an abrupt left turn and the Igloo was nearly creamed by a delivery truck. Helen screeched into another circular drive in front of a huge low-slung house with a white tile roof and a sporty black Mercedes S550.

The low, sleek car's trunk was open and crammed with suitcases.

Debt on wheels, Helen thought. That car's at least a hundred thousand dollars and the house is almost two million.

"Clay's still here!" Cissy said.

And looking darn good for a murderer on the run, Helen thought. The artist was the portrait of cool in a blue chambray shirt rolled at the elbows and designer jeans. Clay effortlessly stowed another suitcase in the car trunk, then slammed the lid shut. He hiked an expensive black leather travel bag on his broad shoulder and started to climb in on the driver's side.

Helen could make out his chiseled jawline, but his fringe of bangs hid his eyes.

Cissy powered down her window and shouted, "Clay!"

He ignored her.

"Clay! It's me, Cissy!" She was half hanging out the Igloo's window.

Her lover looked back and brushed his hair out of his eyes, revealing narrow, mean slits.

"Clay," Cissy shouted. "I'm here."

He locked eyes with Cissy. Her eyes were soft and pleading, like a kicked puppy begging not to be hurt again. His were as remote and hard as the surface of the moon. Clay's look of contempt should have stripped the paint off the Igloo. He turned his back on them and shut his car door.

"Clay!" Now Cissy's cry was filled with pain and abandonment.

He ignored her and roared out of his driveway toward the Landings.

"Why is he going that way?" Cissy asked. She clung to the door handle as Helen hurled the Igloo in front of a lawn service truck, narrowly missing its front bumper, and followed Clay north on Bayview.

"Maybe he wants to lose us in the traffic on Commercial," Helen said. "He can catch I-95 off that road and head for Miami."

But Clay's Mercedes blasted across Commercial Boulevard as the light turned yellow. Helen followed, accompanied by a chorus of car horns and upraised middle digits.

"You went through a red light!" Cissy shrieked.

"That's right," Helen said. She decided the risk was worth it. The Mercedes was still in sight, but this wasn't a fair race. Helen knew her trusty Igloo was seriously underpowered. Clay's sports car had twice as many horses as the PT Cruiser.

Clay floored the Mercedes and it flew over the little bridge into the

Landings. The Igloo tried its best to keep up, but its workhorse engine was no match for Clay's powerful sports car. Still, Helen floored the gas pedal.

And saw the speeding Mercedes slam on its brakes.

The speed bumps! Suddenly this pursuit was almost fair. The Mercedes raced forward again, then slammed on its brakes for a bump. Race and brake. Race and brake.

The odd stop-and-sprint chase continued for four speed bumps, with Helen's intrepid Igloo managing to keep pace.

"Hurry, Helen!" Cissy cried.

"Shut up!" Helen said through gritted teeth as she struggled to push her car on the straightaway and spot the speed bumps in time to brake. The cars lurched through the Landings.

After the fourth speed bump, Clay powered through a four-way stop to the angry blare of horns. Helen made a full stop.

"Hurry, he's getting away," Cissy screamed.

"If I get hit by a car, he'll get away for sure," Helen said.

She waited her turn for two cars, then crossed the intersection and floored the Igloo again. Her finger pressed SEND for 911. I should have called the police sooner, she thought. I can't let Clay escape.

"He's turning left at the next block," Cissy shouted. "There are no speed bumps on that street. It borders a canal. We're going to lose him."

Not if the police get here first, Helen thought. She could hear the 911 operator saying, "Nine-one-one. What's your emergency? Nine-one-one . . ."

"Help!" Helen shouted into her cell phone. "I'm pursuing a killer in the Landings. I'm almost at Fifty-sixth. Get the police here. I can't talk."

Helen slammed the brakes again, and the Igloo jounced over the speed bump. Her cell phone clattered to the floor. Helen could hear the 911 operator and hoped the woman believed her plea for help.

Up ahead, she saw Clay make a screeching turn on two wheels.

Now he was heading straight for a yellow moving van parked in the street, its ramp down to unload. Clay swerved to avoid it and nearly hit a ponytailed woman walking her fluffy white Shih Tzu.

Clay swerved again, narrowly missing the woman and her little dog.

The accident seemed to happen in slow motion.

Clay lost control of his black Mercedes on the small humped canal bridge. His car sailed over the bridge railing and crashed into a white yacht tied up at a backyard dock. The front end of the Mercedes smashed through the yacht's pristine white hull. The car's back end was on the dock, sliding toward the water.

A screeching, cracking sound split the air as several million dollars collided. Six sleepy iguanas who'd been sunning themselves on the dock froze in place.

Helen saw Clay power down his window as his car slowly filled with water. Then he slid down in the seat. Helen couldn't see him. Did he pass out? Was he injured?

"Clay!" Cissy's cry was anguished. "I'll save you, honey! Hang on!"

Before Helen could stop her, Cissy ripped off her seat belt, flung open her door and darted into the street toward the bridge.

"Clay!" Cissy cried as she ran toward him. "Get out of the car!"

Clay didn't answer. The Mercedes was gradually sliding into the canal.

Helen scrabbled around the floor of her Cruiser and found her cell phone. The 911 operator was still on the line. Helen talked right over the woman's questions.

"Nine-one-one, are you still there?" Helen said. "We have an accident. A black Mercedes drove into the canal and hit a boat. A white cabin cruiser."

"How many people are in the car?" the operator asked, firmly taking control of the conversation.

"One," Helen said.

"How many in the boat?"

"Nobody, I think," Helen said. "It was docked. We need police and water rescue equipment."

"What is the address, ma'am?"

Helen checked the street signs and recited their names. "Hurry!" she said. "A woman is trying to rescue the driver. He may be unconscious. They could both drown. I'm going to help."

Helen abandoned her cell phone on the seat and left the Igloo in the street.

Cissy had climbed over the low barrier leading up to the bridge. Her flowing Indian-print skirt caught on something, and Cissy ripped it off with swift, sure movements, then stripped off her top. She was braless and wearing granny panties.

The Mercedes was slowly sinking into the canal, trunk first. Helen couldn't see Clay behind the wheel, but the driver's window was rolled down. Water poured into the car. Helen could still see the steering wheel, dashboard, and seats, but the interior was filling fast now.

"Clay!" Cissy screamed. "Hang on, baby. I'm coming. I'll save you."

The Mercedes and the yacht, locked in a deadly union, made cracking, rending screeches. The car's engine hissed and died. Helen saw no sign of life inside.

"Clay, darling, stay alive!" wailed the half-naked Cissy.

She plunged into the water and swam toward the sinking car with strong strokes, a woman determined to save the man she loved.

Then Helen heard the sound she'd been hoping for: the scream of the sirens.

Help was here.

The iguanas on the dock scattered as if they were being raided.

CHAPTER 39

The nearly sideswiped Shih Tzu barked at the invaders on the street, his little body shaking with outrage. His blond, ponytailed owner gathered up her dog and held him close while she watched Clay's rescue. Neighbors gawked and gathered in gossiping groups near the bridge. Even the movers, the cause of this debacle, stopped hauling furniture to see the spectacle.

The street was littered with police cars and rescue vehicles, parked haphazardly. Helen lost count at ten. Light bars disco danced and uniformed officers poured out of their cars and ran down to the dock to help.

Helen saw Cissy holding Clay's head out of the rising water by his blond hair, a half-naked Salome with her trophy.

Clay's face was a rictus of pain, and Helen hoped he hurt like hell. Cissy's surprisingly strong arms strained to keep his head above water. She crooned words into his wet ear that Helen couldn't understand.

At last, enough rescuers arrived and dragged Clay out of the sinking Mercedes. A wet, white-faced Cissy was wrapped in blankets and helped to a waiting ambulance.

"What the hell is going on, Ms. Hawthorne?"

Detective Burt Pelham was at her side. He looked tired and Helen noticed his dyed blond hair showed a quarter inch of steel gray roots, but he was carefully dressed in a navy sports jacket and well-tailored pants.

"I nailed Annabel's killer," she said. "Clay and Cissy were in on it together."

"Both of them?" he said. "I knew he did it."

"I thought he did, too," Helen said. "But I was surprised to find she was in on it, and I have proof. Maybe enough to arrest them both."

"Let's go to my office on wheels," he said.

He opened the door on his unmarked Dodge Charger and moved his iPad, piles of papers and a handheld Motorola radio into the back. Helen slid into the passenger seat.

Pelham said, "How do you know both of them killed Annabel Lee Griffin?"

"Cissy and Clay were lovers," Helen said. "He fed Cissy the old line about how he couldn't leave his sick wife. They both expected Annabel wouldn't last long. But she turned out to be a fighter."

"And they got antsy," he said.

"Exactly," Helen said. "Cissy talked Annabel into buying that fat life insurance policy and Clay and his girlfriend couldn't wait for Annabel to die. But she wouldn't. So Clay poisoned her thermos of raspberry iced tea with raspberry-flavored vape juice."

"I know that," the detective said.

"But he spilled some, and texted Cissy. She topped it off with another shot of poison during Annabel's art class.

"Except Annabel didn't drink the poisoned tea at Bonnet House. Cissy followed her out to the makeshift parking lot across the street, urging her to drink her tea."

"And you know this because . . . ?" the detective asked.

"Cissy told me," Helen said. "We had a cozy chat."

In her driveway, she thought, with pepper spray pointed at her face.

"I thought you were at the painting class."

"I was, but I didn't see her pour anything into Annabel's tea. No one did. They were busy with other things.

"But Cissy told me and I'd switched on my cell phone recorder. I got the whole conversation," Helen said, "but I'm not sure you can use it."

"Glad you recognized that your recording is questionable as far as being admissible in court," Detective Pelham said. "But it sure adds to the probable cause for arrest. Let the lawyers argue the admissibility later. I just hope you don't face charges."

"Me?" Helen said. "Why?"

"You made an illegal recording," he said. "And you knew it was illegal."

He looked her in the eye. "Or maybe you didn't," he said. "Maybe you didn't know how to properly work your cell phone. Is it new?"

"No," Helen said.

"Then I think you must have forgotten to turn it off."

"Right," Helen said. "I'm very forgetful."

"Exactly what I figured happened," he said. "The Constitution refers to what the government cannot do. Not the public. Of course, that doesn't give the public carte blanche to do as they please. They can be charged or sued, but more and more we see these kinds of recordings being used in court."

"Good," Helen said.

"Now, I could play the recording during the interrogation to help elicit a confession," he said, "and then I probably wouldn't have to use it in court."

"Even better," Helen said.

"Why did you get the sudden urge to visit Cissy?" he asked. "Are you friends?"

"Not really," Helen said. "She was in my art class and we had lunch twice. But I found out Cissy stole Annabel's artwork out of her coffin."

He raised an eyebrow. "Her coffin. Care to explain?"

"She was cremated," Helen said. "You were at the memorial when Lita, the artist who shared a studio with Annabel, demanded to know what Clay did with Annabel's art."

"That little lady made quite a scene," Pelham said. "The husband said he burned her paintings. Made up some bull about it being more romantic. I figured he must have really resented his wife's success."

"He did," Helen said. "But Cissy knew those paintings were worth major money. After she helped Clay kill his wife, Clay dropped her for younger, cuter women."

"Happens all the time," the detective said. "Some men never learn."

"Some women never learn, either," Helen said. "Cissy thought if she sold the paintings to a crooked Miami art dealer, she could give the money to Clay and he would love her again."

"How did Clay put the paintings in his wife's coffin?" he asked. "Weren't there a bunch of them? Was there room to stick them on top of her body?"

"There were ten oil paintings," Helen said. "Clay rolled them up and stashed them in two mailing tubes. They were an easy fit."

"So Narcissa Bellanca," Detective Pelham said, "went to the crematorium and stole the art out of the dead woman's coffin? Worse than stealing the pennies off a dead man's eyes. She had nerve."

"I caught her as she was on her way to give the paintings to the Miami dealer," Helen said. "I have Annabel's art in my car."

"Good," he said.

"After Cissy dropped off the paintings, she planned to flee the country. Clay was leaving, too."

"So I should find passports and plane tickets?" he asked.

"A plane ticket to Gatwick for Cissy. A boat ticket for Clay. He was going to take a container ship to Britain. You can use those for evidence."

"It's a start."

"There's more," Helen said. "Cissy had a burner phone with her texts to Clay planning Annabel's murder and their escape. She kept her cell phone. I have it right here."

Pelham's face lit up when Helen fished the phone out of her shirt pocket and handed it to him.

He powered it up, skimmed the texts and gave a shark smile. "These are killer evidence," he said. "Pun intended."

"I also know the vape shop where Cissy bought the raspberry-flavored juice," Helen said.

"That's not a smoking gun," he said, "but it doesn't hurt. Let the defense argue it at trial."

Helen could see the rescue scene out the detective's car windshield. The area was boiling with cops and ambulances. Paramedics were lifting a sodden Clay onto a stretcher. He seemed to be talking.

"I can't have everything wrapped up in a neat bow," Detective Pelham said, "but it would be nice to have that thermos. Lab tests of the residual contents would confirm what Ms. Bellanca said and really add to the credibility of her statement to you."

"Plus you'd have fingerprints," Helen said.

"The husband's prints wouldn't do much, but hers would. Any idea where that thermos might be?"

Helen saw the paramedics rolling Clay into the ambulance, and her mind flashed back to Annabel's hopeless trip to the hospital. Helen was back in the illegal, debris-ridden parking lot with Margery. Jenny and Cissy were telling the paramedics about Annabel's mysterious attack.

But someone else was there, too. An older woman, maybe older than Margery. She had a spindly Chihuahua, gaudy flowered clothes and a red visor. What was her name? Grace? Gretel? Gretchen! Gretchen might know what happened to that thermos.

"I think I have a lead on where it might be," Helen said. "It may take some time."

"It will help," he said, "but we have enough for an arrest right now."

"Wonderful. Can you answer a question for me?" Helen said.

"I'll try."

"Clay wanted to run away to Britain. Why would he go there? The weather is lousy."

"That's easy," he said. "Clay committed murder one—that's the death penalty here in Florida. The British don't like to extradite someone for a death-penalty case.

"And now, if you'll excuse me, I'm going to give the loving couple a matching set of bracelets."

CHAPTER 40

Helen was a cat person, but she knew this much about dog lovers: They traveled in packs.

Bonnet House, that oasis of unchanging Florida beauty, was surrounded by condos, and most local cliff dwellers walked their dogs in the morning, in the late afternoon and again at night.

While the dogs answered nature's call, their owners socialized, exchanging bits of condo news and asking after one another's health. The dog owners all knew one another, and since many in this area were retired, they kept track of their neighbors. The widow in 618 could be trapped in the bath after a fall and that's why she wasn't walking Little Bit today.

Someone would know where to find Gretchen, who dressed in bright clothes and had a cute Chihuahua.

Helen pulled onto Birch Road, the street that ran alongside Bonnet House, at four twenty-six that afternoon. The lot that had been a rubble-strewn wasteland the day of Annabel's murder was now a busy building site.

Two older women were walking tiny dogs. A fluffy brown Yorkie with a perky blue bow belonged to a distinguished-looking woman with glossy white hair. A bright-eyed Pomeranian with a feathery black coat had a fit seventysomething owner with a brown wedge cut. The two dogs sprinkled patches of grass while the women held their leashes and chatted.

Helen parked her car and strolled over to the women.

"Hi," she said. "Do either of you know Gretchen? She's about that high"—Helen held her hand at chest level—"wears bright colors and has a cute little brown Chihuahua."

"We know her," said Ms. Pomeranian, her voice cautious. Good, Helen thought. She didn't say, *Gretchen who?* I'm at the right place. She looked at the concrete canyon surrounding her. I could search those condos for a week and not find Gretchen.

"I'm trying to reach her," Helen said.

"Why?" Ms. Yorkie asked.

Might as well tell the truth, Helen decided. "Several days ago, a woman collapsed in that lot there." She pointed at the construction site.

"We heard about it," Ms. Pomeranian said. "She died, poor thing."

"Yes, she did," Helen said. "Her name was Annabel Lee Griffin. She was an artist and a good one. She was murdered."

Ms. Yorkie gasped. Ms. Pom shook her head.

"Gretchen was walking her dog that morning," Helen said. "She stopped by and asked if she could help.

"I'm a private detective hired by her friend. I believe Gretchen might have seen something that could help us. I'd like to talk to her."

"We can't give you her address," Ms. Yorkie said.

I have to convince these women that it's safe for Gretchen to talk to me.

"The killer is in police custody," Helen said. "He was arrested this afternoon. We want to make sure he stays in jail. Gretchen is a memorable person. I don't want him to be released. He might think Gretchen saw something and track her down."

Clay was nowhere near here when Annabel took sick, Helen thought. But if I mention there are two killers, these women will clam up.

"Well," Ms. Pom said. Helen could almost see the wheels turning in her well-groomed head. Her little Pom sniffed Helen's shoes. She bent down and scratched his ears.

"I could meet her in a public place," Helen said. "The Galleria is nearby. We could have coffee or a glass of wine in one of the restaurants."

"Better make it a margarita," Ms. Pom said.

"Kathleen!" Ms. Yorkie said.

"Well, it's true," Ms. Pom said.

"How about if I write her a note on my business card?" Helen asked. "I'll also put the arresting detective's name and number on it. Would you give it to Gretchen when you see her? Then she can decide if she wants to contact me."

She pulled out a Coronado Investigations card and began writing on the blank side. She'd jotted down Pelham's number when the little Pom said, *Woof!* and began dancing at his owner's feet. The Yorkie's feathery tail was wagging.

"Hi, ladies. I got hung up on a phone call," said a cheerful woman walking a bug-eyed Chihuahua. It was Gretchen, a bright beacon in a sunshine yellow pantsuit and red cartwheel straw hat.

"I know you," she said to Helen. "You were here the day that poor girl took sick in the lot. I was sorry to hear that she died."

"Me, too," Helen said. "Annabel was murdered and her killer is in custody. We want to make sure he stays there."

"Damn right," she said. "I didn't know how to get in touch with you. I'm Gretchen Cezima. I still have that poor lady's thermos."

"You do?" Helen couldn't believe her luck.

"It got left behind when everyone left, and I picked it up. It's a nice one, too. I didn't know if her family would want it or not."

"The police want it," Helen said. "It may help their case. Where is it?"

"On my hall table. It's sort of a junk table. I've been meaning to clean it off, but I never got around to it."

"So you didn't wash the thermos?" Helen asked and held her breath.

"Nope, it's just sitting there, gathering dust. I can clean it up now."

"No!" Helen said. "Don't touch it. This is wonderful, Mrs. Cezima."

"Gretchen," she corrected.

"I'll call the detective in charge, Gretchen." Helen speed-dialed Burt Pelham's cell phone.

"I have good news," she told him.

"I can use some," he said. "Both suspects have lawyered up. Ms. Bellanca says you forced that confession out of her by threatening her with pepper spray. Did you do that, Ms. Hawthorne?"

"I don't have any pepper spray," Helen said, truthfully. She had no idea what had happened to her canister while she was chasing Clay.

"Did she have any pepper spray on her face or body?" Helen asked.

"None," Detective Pelham said.

"I thought so," Helen said.

"Before Mr. Griffin said the magic words—I want a lawyer—he denied having an affair with Ms. Bellanca," Pelham said.

"But you have those text messages," Helen said.

"Yes, we do," he said. "And I'm damn glad. I hope some smart lawyer doesn't try to twist their words."

"If you need visual evidence, check the elevator cameras at Silver Glade Condominiums," Helen said. "The guards knew Cissy and Clay were having an affair, thanks to those cameras. Clay liked shagging women in the elevator and never realized his performance was recorded."

"Good to know," he said.

"I've found Annabel's thermos," Helen said. "Mrs. Gretchen Cezima has it. She took it home and left it untouched on her hall table."

"Ms. Hawthorne, you've made my day. I want to talk to Mrs. Cezima myself. CSI can meet me at her home and take her prints and the thermos and I'll get her statement. What's her address?"

"I'll let Gretchen tell you," Helen said, and handed the phone to her. Gretchen's dog-walking friends moved closer to listen.

"Of course you can come," Gretchen said into the phone. "And you're bringing a CSI team? Like on television? I'll go back and tidy up."

There was a pause, then Gretchen said, "Okay, I won't tidy up. First time I ever had a police order *not* to clean my condo. How about coffee? And doughnuts? Do cops like homemade doughnuts, or is that politically incorrect?"

Another short pause. "Coffee and doughnuts it is. I live just off Birch Road."

Gretchen gave the detective her address, then handed Helen her phone.

"Hoo-boy," she said. "I gotta make coffee. You joining me, Helen?"

"As soon as I make two calls," Helen said.

"You can park in the visitors' lot. Tell the guard you're seeing me." Gretchen waved good-bye to her friends, picked up her little dog, and hurried to her building.

"Thank you, ladies," Helen said, and climbed into the Igloo. There she called Phil and updated him on the case.

"I'm so proud of you," he said. "When do I get to see my smart, successful wife?"

"Between six and six thirty," she said.

"We'll celebrate when you get home," he said.

Helen called Jenny next and told her that Cissy and Clay had been arrested. The news was met with a long silence.

"Hello?" Helen said. "Are you still there, Jenny?"

"Yes," her client said, her voice shaking. "I'm stunned. So you caught two killers."

"For the price of one," Helen said.

"What about Hugo?" Jenny asked. "Was he involved?"

"No way," Helen said. "I wish he had been, but he's only guilty of being a world-class jerk. And he is good to his mother."

Helen heard Jenny sniffling.

"Jenny, I'm sorry I couldn't tie him into the murder plot," she said. "But he really didn't have anything to do with Annabel's murder."

"I'm not crying about that," Jenny said. "I'm just glad that you caught the creeps who killed Annabel. Thank you."

"Oh, wait, I forgot to give you the good news," Helen said. "I found Annabel's paintings. They weren't burned after all."

"How?" Jenny said. "When?"

By the time Helen finished telling her, Jenny was weeping loudly. Even over the phone, Helen could tell those were happy tears.

Helen parked the Igloo at Gretchen's condo. The CSI van had arrived, with Detective Pelham following. The detective introduced Helen to the crime-scene tech, Evie, a short, fit brunette, and the three went up in the elevator together.

Gretchen met them at the seventh floor, which was painted bright orange. "This is so exciting," she said. "I wish I'd cleaned the place." She chattered all the way to her condo, a cluttered one-bedroom with a view of the Bonnet House grounds. Helen heard the dog yapping in the bedroom.

"I'm keeping Buddy out of your way," Gretchen said. "That's the thermos on the hall table. Help yourself to doughnuts and coffee by the couch."

Helen had a cup of coffee and a doughnut while she watched Evie take Gretchen's prints, then work on the metal thermos. By the time Gretchen gave her statement, Evie announced, "We have a match for the suspect's prints."

"On the outside of the thermos?" Pelham asked.

"Yes," Evie said.

Cissy had helped Annabel pack up, Helen thought. Those prints aren't much good. Pelham was tense and silent.

"And there's a clear thumb and forefinger print around the thermos mouth," Evie said, "under the cup. Also a thumbprint inside the cup."

"Good," Detective Pelham said, and stood up.

"Have I helped?" Gretchen asked.

"Immensely," Pelham said, shaking her hand.

Helen was home by six fifteen. Phil met her at the back gate. Margery, Peggy and Daniel, Markos and Valerie cheered as he kissed her. Pete and Patience, the Quaker parrots, said, *Hello! Hello!* in their cage by the pool.

It was a festive group: Markos looked beyond handsome in a fitted black shirt with rolled sleeves. Valerie, in a smart coral sundress, was almost drooling. Daniel and Peggy were dressed for dinner and holding hands. Margery wore a purple caftan and her favorite amethyst necklace.

"We delayed the sunset salute until you returned," Markos said. "I thought it was only right that we celebrate the end of this case with Evelyn Bartlett's Rangpur lime cocktails."

"Perfect," Helen said.

"I made a healthy appetizer, too," Markos said. "Brussels sprouts chips."

Phil eyed the dish on the umbrella table warily.

"But I made some of Evelyn's favorite appetizers," he said. "Blue cheese crisps and that caramelized bacon Phil liked so much."

Phil brightened considerably and reached for a bacon strip, while Markos filled their glasses from a sweating cocktail pitcher.

Phil raised his glass and said, "To Helen, the smartest, hottest shamus in South Florida."

They clinked glasses and drank.

Helen put her arm around Phil's waist and raised her glass. "To another happy couple: Evelyn and Frederic Bartlett. They mastered the art of living."

EPILOGUE

Cissy and Clay both had smart lawyers, but Detective Burt Pelham didn't have to worry about his case. The two attorneys looked at the evidence against their clients and came to the same conclusion: plead guilty and avoid a trial. Cissy's lawyer also suggested she make a deal. So did Clay's attorney, but Cissy's lawyer was faster. Her plea bargain was accepted. She sold out the love of her life and was sentenced to ten years in prison.

Clay now has plenty of time to paint. He was sentenced to life without the possibility of parole. One of his seascapes won third place at an inmates' art show.

Cissy sold her house and car to pay her lawyer, then invested the remainder of the proceeds. She lost most of her savings in a stock market crash. After her release from prison a decade later, she worked as a greeter at the Bargain Art Barn and self-published romance novels. She wrote several letters to Clay in prison, but they were never opened.

. . .

Detective Burt Pelham told Helen that Cissy stuck the X-Acto knife in Helen's tire after Annabel's memorial. "She said you were coming on to Clay at Annabel's memorial."

"What!" Helen said. "She thought I was after that slimewad? He grabbed my arm because he wanted to get away from *her*. She oughta be—"

"Locked up?" Pelham said.

Cady Gummage, the Gold Ghost, wanted a trial, even though she faced the death penalty for the murder of ninety-two-year-old Alexander Woodiwiss. Worse, she insisted on testifying, against the advice of her attorney.

She was sure the jury would understand. "I had an awful job proofreading mortgages," she said. "I started trolling the Internet and found out about gold collectors. It was fun stringing along those old guys, listening to them rant about the government.

"I'd taken up rappelling after I recovered from cancer surgery. I rappelled down one building for charity, and as I went down the side, I could see into the offices. People are so trusting. Valuable things were just sitting there."

That's when Cady decided to liberate the gold stashed in the upper floors of the Little New York condos. "They weren't doing anything with the money, and I was drowning in medical debt. I didn't mean to kill Alex, but he didn't have that long to live anyway."

Her lawyer stared in horror as she added, "I was bored to death and that gold was my ticket to freedom."

The jury, whose average age was seventy-five, gave Cady the chance to discover true boredom. She got seventy years in prison. She will be older than Mr. Woodiwiss when she's released.

Detective Burton Pelham and Louisa Longright, the Gold Ghost detective, received raises and commendations for their work.

. . .

Valerie was nominated for four Emmy Awards. She won an Emmy for her coverage of the Gold Ghost and another for Annabel Lee Griffin's story. This year, Valerie did not go to the Emmy Awards alone. She was escorted by Markos. No one recognized the adoring Cuban American hottie as the fake sheik in her award-winning story.

Ruth McCormick Orton, Annabel's aunt, insisted on paying Helen's fee, even though Jenny Carter had promptly paid her bill. Jenny refused to let Helen refund her payment. "Keep it as a bonus," she said.

Lita sold Annabel's nude portrait of herself to an out-of-state collector shortly before her wedding to Miranda. She invested the money in Miranda's lawn service and now paints full-time. Lita is a happily married up-and-coming Florida artist.

In her will, Annabel left everything, including her art, to Clay, but her "beloved husband" could not inherit it or collect her life insurance. Convicted killers cannot profit from their crimes. Annabel's seventeen oil paintings and numerous sketches went to her closest relative, Aunt Ruth in Connecticut.

Ruth Orton kept two paintings. She gave one to Jenny. "My niece's killers wouldn't have been caught if you hadn't insisted on an investigation," Ruth told Jenny. Helen thought Detective Pelham would have nabbed them, but she kept quiet.

Ruth kept the other painting and admired it daily until she died at age ninety-seven. Then it was donated to a museum in the town where Annabel grew up. The painting and its romantic story are a popular exhibit.

Ruth asked gallery owner Robert Horton to sell Annabel's fifteen other paintings. She wanted the proceeds to fund an art scholarship in Annabel's name.

Helen asked Robert if he was going to hold an auction.

"No chance," Robert said. "It's hard to sell the work of a young artist at an auction since she had no real history of sales, which most auction houses want. But I can make a list of potential buyers and sell her work through an exhibition. The fact that there will be no more paintings by this artist should raise the prices."

It did. The story of the beautiful, talented young artist, her jealous husband and her faithless friend went viral. A media storm of publicity followed, and collectors came from as far away as New York, London and California to the opening. Helen and Phil had coveted invitations to the black-tie opening party.

The night of the exhibition party, Helen wore her amazing Herve Leger bandage dress and the sexy Jimmy Choos.

Phil whistled when Helen appeared at his apartment door. "Are you my escort for the evening?" he asked her. "You're a knockout."

"So are you," she said, adjusting his bow tie and kissing his nose.

"Do we have to go?" he asked.

"Afraid so," Helen said.

There was barely room to move at the party, and nearly every painting had a red dot on it. Thanks to Jenny's generous bonus, Helen could afford to buy one of Annabel's early works, the wild parrot in a lemon tree.

She admired her purchase while she sipped champagne. "This is all because of you," Phil told her, surveying the crowd.

"I wish we could have saved Annabel," Helen said.

"You did the next best thing. You saved her art. If you hadn't braved that horrible crematorium and confronted Cissy, she might have sold Annabel's paintings. Annabel's work will go to art lovers and she'll be remembered with a generous scholarship. Artists live through their work and in our memories, and . . ."

"And what?" Helen said.

"I can't think about anything but you and that hot dress and those shoes," Phil said, and kissed her so hard Helen spilled champagne down his tux. Neither one cared. Both were breathless.

"Let's go home and I'll show you my etchings," Phil said.